THE FUNOLOGIST

BLAIR BRYAN

TEAL BUTTERFLY PRESS

ONE

No self-respecting forty-year-old man wants to be living in his mother's basement, so it's a good thing I'm more of the self-deprecating type. Your mom's basement is the place you land temporarily when life kicks you in the teeth or serves you up a nice big shit sandwich. It's to be used as a fail-safe, a backup plan, the only thing that stands between you and homelessness. Boomeranging is supposed to be a tail-tucking, soul-sucking, short period of time where you gather your resources and rebuild. Unfortunately, my return was four years ago. A shit sandwich in the form of my second forced vacation to the psych ward still left a bitter aftertaste in my mouth. Even after all the vodka I used to wash it down, it lingered and lingered.

I cradled my pounding head in my hands and sat up on the secondhand lifeless mattress shoved up against the damp corner on the floor. Morning light peeked in from a cracked dirty window and dappled against the concrete walls kissed with mildew. The wrinkled sheets were stained with the takeout Sesame Chicken I had eaten the night before. As I combed through my hit-and-miss memories from the prior evening, devouring the soggy chicken was the last thing I remembered. I struggled to piece events together, putting on my detective hat, sifting and sorting for clues, scrolling through my phone for pictures and evidence.

How the hell did I get back here?

I stumbled to the mirror with my head on fire and pinching from the habitual half a bottle of vodka I'd consumed. Vodka is the closet alkie's first choice when imbibing because we think it is undetectable, but it really isn't. We like to lie to ourselves like that. It's easier to lie, and so we find ourselves lying about everything. Did you drink today? No. Did you swipe that twenty from my nightstand? Of course not, Ma. Don't be silly.

I didn't identify as an alcoholic; I just developed a habit of leaning on vodka to take the edge off, to help me sleep, to calm the constant rush hour of overlapping screeching voices in my mind. What started as an attempt to self-medicate a real problem stuck around like bad decisions seem to do. I ran and ran, but I could never seem to outrun the pain and worthlessness that plagued me. So, I added it to the stack of bad choices I made that started when the first voices began when I was fifteen.

Almost three decades later, I could pinpoint the why; I just couldn't figure out a compelling enough reason to stop. When you take a journey into darkness, it doesn't happen instantaneously. It is taken one single step after the next. One day, months or years later, you wake up and find yourself so far from center you can't even fathom what you need to do to get back on track. And so you don't. You continue. You hide and if you have a conscience at all, you try to hurt the fewest people possible as you descend deeper into hell.

I felt the wall up like a sixteen-year-old boy with a girl in the backseat of his car on prom night, and finally connected with the light switch that blasted fluorescent light onto my face. I leaned in and looked at myself in the mirror for the first time in a long time. My hair was graying and thinning, forming a crop circle-type band around my emerging bald head, my blue eyes were red-rimmed and bloodshot, and my skin was pockmarked and graying from the lack of eating anything with nutritional value. Not appreciating the view at all, I continued my inventory down and pinched the little bit of extra flab on my tummy, the natural result of eating Chinese takeout three nights a week and zero ab crunches. On the hotness scale of one to ten, I was a negative thirteen.

In this world, if you aren't pretty, you have to have a good personality, but more importantly, a great sense of humor. Funny is the great equalizer, transforming the ugly to mildly attractive since the dawn of time. Making people laugh was my superpower, so I channeled all my energy onto the stage. When I was on fire and the crowd was rolling, I felt like a god, like I could do anything. And when they were silent and bored, or worse, heckling me, I felt like sucking on the end of the loaded shotgun that sat in the corner of my closet. Hidden away from the watchful and nervous eyes of my mother. A reminder that I always had a choice, and at any second, I could make a different one.

"Freddie, breakfast is ready." My sweet mother, Dottie called down from her perch at the top of the stairs, the morning sun making her shadow slant down the wall. Her arthritis made it hard for her to navigate the stairs, so thankfully, she didn't get to see or experience the current level of squalor I was living in.

I stumbled up toward her voice and rubbed my prickly jawline, opening the door with a small forced smile that felt tight on my cheeks.

"Good morning, my beautiful boy," she called out, using

the familiar greeting she had used every day since before I could answer her back. Dressed in a baby blue house dress and worn slippers, her thinning gray hair was cropped close to her head. Her pale eyes looked into mine behind glasses that sat on the bridge of her nose as she engaged in her most important daily task—analyzing my current mental state. She seemed to exist in a perpetual state of exhaustion, and I felt the guilt rear up every time I acknowledged it. I was the source of her weariness. Years of psychiatrists and doctor visits, calls to the school for disciplinary problems, and job losses had left their mark on her face. Deep, dark circles and a roadmap of wrinkles had taken up permanent residence there, yet she never complained.

"Good morning, Mama," I said back as I kissed her soft cheek, and she tipped the ancient Mr. Coffee carafe filled with decaf toward my mug. Caffeine was "bad" for someone in my condition. It was on the handwritten list of "Foods Freddie Must Avoid" held up by a faded piglet magnet on her ancient, sweating refrigerator.

Words were important. Words define you. They made up the jokes that I told. They were used to classify my behaviors and identify my afflictions on the quest to define the sixty-four thousand dollar question. What was wrong with Freddie?

The biggest problem with words is, when you exhibit signs of mental illness as a teenager, doctors aren't exactly forthcoming with them. There is a lot of speculation. A lot of, "We think you might be…" or, "You exhibit signs of…" but not a lot of definitive answers. It's not like you have a physical disease. Symptoms themselves can't be used to narrow down a diagnosis conclusively. A disease of the mind is much harder to define, with overlapping characteristics and fuzzier lines.

Words were tossed around—manic depressive, borderline

personality disorder, obsessive-compulsive disorder, bipolar. From the all-you-can-eat smorgasbord of insanity, I dabbled in nearly everything. What started as quirkiness and anxiety as a child, grew into eccentric risk-taking behavior as a teenager, and culminated in my first hospital committal in my early twenties. It was a wild ride there, but I finally had a diagnosis. Bipolar disorder with occasional hallucinations and OCD. Some experts say bipolar and OCD are linked. Apparently, there's a twenty percent chance of having them both, so I guess I hit the mental illness jackpot. A real twofer.

Sounds like a good time, am I right? It wasn't. Finally getting a diagnosis *was* a relief at first. There was a concrete reason that explained why my brain worked differently than other people I knew. Being able to blame a real quantifiable disorder was gratifying initially, but then the anger settled in and stayed. The mania, though, that sweet dark genius! She was someone I enjoyed as my tango partner. She never disappointed!

I used to be jealous of other people who floated through life unencumbered by the weight of mental illness on their shoulders. They got up, put on their clothes, kissed their wives, and headed to the office. On the weekends, they might cut a little loose, enjoy a six-pack, or take in a movie. It was a predictable, easy-to-navigate existence that I thought I wanted. But if I'm really honest, mania can unleash creativity in such unfathomable greatness, I welcomed my demons. I always knew a crash would inevitably come, but before that, I had incredible breakthroughs. Glimpses of grandeur, where I was able to use more of my magnificent brain to reach highs the normies couldn't even comprehend. It was my blessing and my curse.

Russell Brand, Mel Gibson, Kurt Cobain—from where I stood, I was in awesome company. Okay, maybe not Mel

Gibson so much, but even Old Blue Eyes himself, Frank Sinatra was blessed with this difference. Their manic Mondays created some of the best comedy and musical gold ever produced. I felt oddly blessed to be part of this brotherhood. I could never tell Ma that. It would crush her.

"Don't forget to take your pills," Ma reminded sweetly. "I set them out with your oatmeal."

I hated the pills. They made me feel empty, dense, heavy, and numbed out to everything. Taking anti-psychotics was like walking through mud up to my waist. I dutifully put them in my mouth anyway, their bitterness stabbing my tongue, and tried to swallow, but I couldn't. They were stuck to the roof of my dry mouth, their acidic burn souring my stomach. When she turned around to wash the dishes, I spit them into my hand and tucked them into the half of a white paper towel that was folded in a triangle neatly next to my bowl then cursed myself for letting her down again.

She believed the meds would save me. The problem was that I didn't want to be saved. It was a song and dance where we each played our assigned roles. She put out the medication thinking it was best for me, and I pretended to take it thinking that was best for her.

A tinkling sound rang out as she dumped oat bran into a bowl and joined me at the table.

"You got in late last night," she observed.

"Yeah, we went out after the show." I knew Ma wanted to hear I was spending time with friends instead of isolating. Little white lies I habitually told so she wouldn't worry.

"That's good." She slurped at the milk on her spoon. "What are you doing today, dear?"

"The usual. Going to get some writing done." It was what I always said, whether or not it was the truth. For Christmas last year, Ma gave me a thick leather notebook; it was my most prized possession. The book was bound with a thick strap that held it closed, and inside, scribbled in my illegible handwriting were punch lines and set-ups. Jokes I wanted to try on stage.

"Someday, I'm gonna see your name up in lights," she said and winked at me. "My Freddie is destined for great things."

"Thanks, Mama." She was always my biggest fan, and I lived to make her proud, or at the very least, a little less disappointed.

Her voice got somber for a minute. "Just remember, when you make it big, money is the root of all evil."

The Christian Broadcast Network blared behind us, as they were engaged in their annual fundraising event. The salt and pepper-haired hosts begged for pledges to help them complete God's most important mission on earth. My brow crinkled at the obvious hypocrisy that was harder to swallow than the oatmeal currently lodged in my throat. "What?" she asked defensively, putting the puzzle together, pinching her lips together to prevent a grin. Mom loved Jesus but wasn't so far up his ass that she couldn't see anything else.

"The irony, Ma. It's the irony. It gets me every time."

"Oh, you." She smiled, waving her finger at me with an exasperated grin. "You've been making people laugh since you were in kindergarten. Remember that?" She looked into the mist of her memories fondly, and a small smile tugged at the corners of her mouth. "That reporter came to your school and asked what you would do if you were the principal. Remember what you said?" She pushed my arm playfully.

"I told him I'd quit and get a new job I'd enjoy," I repeated on rote. It was a memory she walked me through at least once a month, and I always indulged her many strolls down memory lane.

"You killed." She smiled wide, spots of chewed-up oat bran speckled brown on her pink tongue.

"I did," I agreed. "I just hope my comedy prowess didn't peak in elementary school."

"What are you talking about, Freddie? You have your whole life ahead of you. You are just getting started."

I grimaced and tried to buy into her Positive Patty spin on my future. I was halfway done already with a string of personal and professional failures a mile wide. But the wide-eyed admiration of my mother never waned. She never gave up on me, and for the life of me, I could never understand why.

I scooped a spoonful of oatmeal into my mouth, tasteless gooey slop that I gulped down obediently. I forced myself to eat the pear she had lovingly cut into slices, but that just felt bland and mushy in my mouth.

Dutifully, I put my dishes in the dishwasher. "Thanks, Ma," I said and then disappeared into the basement again. My days were mundane and hum-drum for the most part—a complete and total snooze fest. The only bright flashes were on stage, where I didn't have to be the guy who lived in his mom's basement. On stage, I could be anyone and say anything. I could create an entirely new existence and live out any fantasy I wanted to live. Maybe that's why I loved it so much. When your real life was as dull as mine, escaping was the ultimate fantasy.

TWO

The stage was my home, the only place I felt capable, powerful, and normal. Usually, I held down a stool in the corner of the bar waiting to go on, reading through my notebook. Whenever I got an idea for a joke or a punchline or a situation that was funny, I wrote it down in the book with my crooked penmanship that wasn't winning any awards.

The Punch Line was a beer-soaked, nicotine-stained dive in the basement of a jazz club in downtown Kansas City. The building has been in Paulie's family for decades, and it looked like it. Mint green walls, a faux brick backdrop, and spotlights so red hot it was like they turned into magnifying glasses and you were the ant on stage. It always felt like you were just one bright concentration of sunlight away from bursting into flames. The Punch Line was a dump, but a lovable dump. I was a comedy bottom feeder, hustling to get my time on stage, showing up early to pass out flyers for the shows on the sidewalks to earn my time. Comedy was an old school institution and you had to pay your dues.

Paulie could be kind of a jerk. He still held a grudge from my first performance, when I threw him and his precious club under the bus. Nervous on stage for the first time, I said, "I love to tell people I work at The Punch Line."

A smattering of whoops and hollers came from the regulars as I continued, "They'd always ask, 'Well, what's The Punch Line?'"

"The fact that they advertise this place as a 'fine dining dinner club and entertainment establishment.'" I giggled with finger quotes and waited as the crowd roared. At the end of my set, I walked down the steps, heading into the backroom for an after-set celebratory drink that often turned into seven, when a red-faced Paulie jumped in front of my face.

"Never use that joke again. Don't you know you're not supposed to bite the hand that feeds you?"

"Come on, Paulie, it was a joke and it landed. And let's be real, the only food this place is providing for me is stale popcorn." I pointed over to the greasy popcorn machine, circa 1982 that was lodged in the corner of the bar, cranking out enough kernels every night to feed a small village.

He walked away in a huff, and I brushed it off, not knowing it would stick in his craw for as long as it did. He got over it eventually, and since for the most part I was mildly successful, I was allowed to continue to entertain the crowds for tips as long as I removed that joke from the set.

It was Friday night and Cora came by and offered me a screwdriver. Cora was too skinny, flat-chested, and petite, but crammed into that puny physique was a fierceness and strength that was missing in most men.

She knew my drink by heart and smiled as she slid it next to me, knowing I didn't like to be disturbed when I was writing in my notebook. I heard a few random laughs in the background and the magical sound of ice tinkling in glasses. Then Paulie blasted through the pre-set quiet, "And now, a man among men, a bitter disappointment in the sack, and the kind of guy you bring home to drive your daddy crazy—our resident Funologist is in the building—Freddie… An…gel." He dragged it out like I was a boxer in a televised fight.

The applause lifted me from my barstool, and I floated onto the stage. I smiled wide and waved the audience to quiet down, laughing at myself.

"Disappointed, aren't ya?" I leered into the microphone while I sensually rubbed my soft belly. "It's okay to admit it. With a name like Freddie Angel, you expected more. Am I right?" The audience snickered. "Yeah, that name was the first of many, many shortcomings in my life. My mama set me up for failure from the get-go. It's my real name. No joke. After the show, I can show you my ID in the lobby." I waggled my eyebrows. "And by ID, I mean my *I… D*," pointing to my dick when saying the last letter. "And by you, I mean…" I pointed to two of the hottest chicks in the audience, "you and you," Then at an older man, "But not you, sir." The audience cut up and I was able to take my first full breath. The adrenaline surged high and hot but cleared when the first joke landed, and then I could get into my rhythm.

"Being a comedian is hard," I whined and waited. "If you don't make people laugh, suddenly the club loses your number. Sometimes I think I should have aimed a little lower when choosing a career. You know there are some jobs where you can literally screw it *all the way up* and still be employed? Case in point… weatherman." I pretended to use my hands to indicate the direction of the jet stream. "'Today, it is going to be sunny and 70s. Enjoy the sunshine. Back to you, Bob,'" I said in my best broadcasting voice, cupping the microphone with my hand. "Then a storm pops up and an F4 tornado flattens everything." I pressed my knees together and put my hand on my mouth, embarrassed. "'Oopsie, my bad.'" The audience giggled. "Or a road construction worker." I shifted my hand to my chin and looked down into the audience. "Keep digging, Jorge. You got this, my man. Carl, Joe, and I are going to sit here and watch your form and supervise while I sext my latest tinder whore. Good job outta you, Jorge."

"Where are my momma's boys at?" I shouted into the microphone and was rewarded with a couple of whoops and scattered applause. "Okay. Okay, there are definitely a few of us out there." I shook my head. "Fifteen… it was brutal to grow up with a single mother. Taking the long showers." I used my fingers to make quotes in the air when I said the word showers. "Jizzing into socks." I changed my voice to mimic my mom. "'Freddie, you go through so much lotion. I just don't understand it.'" The audience laughed. "'I am going to make an appointment with Dr. Berstein right away. Maybe you have eczema or a thyroid condition. We need to get to the bottom of this.'"

"'No, Ma!' I'd shout up the basement stairs while I was wanking it to a dogeared Playboy." I grabbed the mic stand and waited. "My mom is so gullible. God, I love that woman. When I was a kid, every weekend she'd go to Blockbuster Video. Show of hands, how many know what Blockbuster was?" I waited, seeing that over half of them did not. "Let me enlighten you," I pantomimed like I was riding a horse while the old people in the audience laughed. "Back in olden times, groups of people would venture out into the wild in our covered wagons to procure video tapes from a fine institution called Blockbuster Video. This was many, many moons before the internet existed." I waited to let it sink in. "Before the internet, you say?" I bit my lip, letting the words linger. "Yes, it was a simpler time." I stood quietly waiting; comedy is all about the pause. "Anyway, my mom is a sweet and innocent lady. Every weekend, she'd drive her horse and buggy to Blockbuster and bring home a fat stack of video-tapes. One day, in the middle of the pile was a film entitled *Spanking the Monkey*." I froze, my body feigning shock, making my eyes huge as I blinked slowly and glanced from side to side without moving my head while the audience giggled awkwardly. It was the perfect setup. "I vividly remember eating a peanut butter sandwich while I rifled through them, and that title stopped me dead in my tracks," I paused and tapped my index finger to my cheek as I made my expression inquisitive. Half the job of telling a good joke is the delivery. It requires you to twist and contort your face into playful expressions. "Well, well, well. What do we have here?"

I switched over to my 'mom' voice. "'Freddie, we have seen nearly everything in the store. The clerk said it got four stars and he highly recommended it.'"

"'Did he now?' I asked her. 'Color me *intrigued*.'" I paused again for effect and tapped my index finger on my lips like I was carefully considering the clerk's recommendation. "So, what did I do? You bet your ass I ran downstairs and popped that tape right into the VCR, pressed play, but to my dismay the credits scrolled." I huffed my frustration into the microphone. "Looks like someone never heard of 'be kind, rewind,'" I paused again shaking my head in disgust. "Sinners." The audience laughed again. "So, I pushed rewind and waited. You know, children today will never know how agonizingly long it takes to rewind a VHS tape. We have spoiled them and created an instant gratification generation." I surmised pausing again for laughs, then exaggerated, "Finally, *twenty-five minutes later*, it was ready for my viewing pleasure. I pushed the button, settled back into the sofa with my popcorn, and discovered that *Spanking the Monkey* was a trail blazing, coming of age film about..." I paused and looked around the audience, "Spanking… the… monkey." Laughter erupted in the room and I soaked it up. You had to savor those moments of joy and know when to pause so the audience didn't miss your next joke. When it died down again, I asked sweetly, "Mom?"

"'Yes, dear?'"

"Do you know what spanking the monkey means?"

"'What do you mean, honey?'"

"It's slang for choking the chicken. Waxing the pole, having a party with Rosie Palmer and her five friends."

"'What?' My mom turned all shades of red and marched down the stairs, yanking the tape out of the VCR. I have never seen the woman move as fast as she did that day. I heard her mumbling how she was going to go back to *that store* and give *that clerk* a piece of her mind. The next day, to my horror and amazement, she strode into Blockbuster, dragging me, waving that smut tape in her hand, demanding the pimply-faced clerk lock it up and put it in the adult section.

"'This video has corrupted my innocent son.'"

I grimaced. "Yeah, Ma, we'll go with that. *That's* what corrupted me."

The audience snorted and clapped.

The rest of my set moved quickly, and at the end of it, they loved me. "Thanks for listening. You all have been amazing. I'm Freddie Angel and remember to give your bartenders…" I paused and held the microphone out to the audience, "…just… the… tip!" The crowd chanted back at me. I was becoming a pretty big fish in a very small pond, and my catchphrase had caught on. It wasn't my best work, but it wasn't my worst either. There was no greater high than having a good set. Making people laugh was like breathing oxygen for me. I couldn't live without it. I walked back to the bar and took a seat at a stool, wiping the sweat from my forehead with the back of my hand.

"From your biggest fan," Cora said as she slid a vodka cranberry over.

I lifted my glass in salute in the direction that Cora pointed at. "It's nice to have a fan that is so concerned about my urinary tract."

Cora snorted when she laughed, a quirk I found magical the first time I'd heard it, and when I told her so, she turned twelve thousand adorable shades of red.

I sipped the drink, and in a few minutes, it softened my razor-sharp edges. Fortified by the vodka, I watched Cora work. I'd had a crush on her since Paulie brought her in to sling the weak drinks the club served a few months ago. An hour later, the club was starting to clear out. She wiped down the sticky countertop and then tucked a straw behind her ear like it was a pencil. She rocked a red pixie cut that made her blue eyes electric, and her golden hoops winked when they caught the spotlight. But it was her mouth I couldn't stop fixating on. You know that little half-moon shape on the top of a woman's lips? I think they call it a cupid's bow or some shit? It made me weak in the knees. I wanted to press the pad of my thumb across it. I was certain that her lips felt like satin, and I found myself wondering what they would feel like on mine. Noticing my eyes on her, she flashed me a wink and a quick smile. To her, I was just Freddie. To me, she was the sun.

THREE

O n the way home from the club, I stumbled into the little gas station a block from my house. Ma lived in a tiny fifties bungalow that was on the seedier side of town less than a mile from the club. Not having the typical earthly trappings of success like owning an automobile, I usually had to hoof it to the club or catch a bus. Once a week, on Friday's, I bought a scratch ticket, a fifth of Popov, and a roller dog.

The same guy was always behind the counter. Steve. I tested my new material on him, and if his normally expressionless face cracked a smile, I knew I had a hit.

"What do you call a useless piece of skin on a penis?" I asked him.

"What?" he asked drily from behind his thick Coke bottle glasses. I tried not to notice the white flakes that sat on the shoulders of his black uniform polo shirt.

"A man."

That earned me a slight up twinge on the corners of his lips and a *humph* noise. "Good one," he said robotically. "The usual?" Steve asked, then turned and reached up to pull down one of the scratch tickets. While his back was turned, I tugged the hot dog in the white paper boat away from him, worried the white flecks on his shoulders would rain down, rendering my wiener inedible.

"Ha! Maybe that is your problem with women," a voice said. *"Your wiener is inedible*!" I heard loud laughter.

"Shut up!" I hissed, and Steve jumped and looked around uncomfortably. "Sorry," I mumbled and abruptly turned back to him with a flourish. "Yes, my good sir. Dealer's choice." I threw down my tip money on the counter, then tucked the ticket into my pocket and bit into the roller dog. It tasted like it had started spinning at four am this morning. Wrinkled, tan, and shriveled, it was oddly reminiscent of my own male member.

"Samesies!" a hysterical woman screeched into my ear. I shook my head to clear it, stepped out into the cold air, and walked the rest of the way home. Mom was asleep when I got there, but a note next to a loaf of banana bread made me smile. I cut myself a thick slice, and then after looking it over carefully, had to throw it in the garbage. Cooked bananas and walnuts always ended up looking like spider legs to me. Black and wiggly, they turned my stomach. I buried it deep in the trash can, underneath a church bulletin so it wouldn't hurt her feelings.

The phone rang in my pocket, and I pulled it out, the lottery ticket slipping out with it.

"Fritz!" A voice I loathed but was related to and thusly required to speak to leered into the phone. His delivery was deep and booming and almost like a radio personality. Tommy was all about appearances and projecting success.

"Tommy," I confirmed.

"How's Mom?"

"The same. You know how she is."

"She's a saint," Tommy admitted. "The fact that she puts up with you alone makes her worthy of being canonized."

"Did you need something?"

"Yeah, I was wondering when exactly you think you might be back on your feet."

I exhaled deeply. This was a tiresome, recycled conversation that we had at least once a month.

"You living there was supposed to be a temporary thing. You know she wanted to sell her house and move to a retirement community. And now is the best time to put it on the market."

"I don't know. I ain't exactly living the dream," I answered. "Things didn't work out the way I was hoping. It's taking longer than I thought it would."

"Hoping? Jesus, Freddie! You aren't a teenage prom queen hoping the captain of the football team asks you to the big dance. Hoping doesn't get shit accomplished. What steps are you taking *exactly* to get your shit together?" he demanded. "Do you even have a job?"

"I work at the comedy club."

He laughed into the phone. "You mean that dive that pays you in screwdrivers, under the table handies, and tips? Come on, I'm talking about a real job."

"It *is* a real job."

"It's unfair for Mom to live out her golden years having to take care of a forty-year-old man."

The anger was bubbling up in my belly. Interactions with Tommy were always aggravating. "Are we done?" I started picking at the ticket with my fingernail. The gold residue gathered under my thumbnail and made it appear dirty.

"You're a leech, a bottom feeder, living off Mom's retirement fund. She's taken care of you for long enough."

A prickle of rage started up my spine, and I grabbed the

bottle of Popov, unscrewed the cap, and took two long gulps. The burn hitting the back of my throat made this conversation a little more bearable.

"You're a loser. You are never going to be anything. It's time to get a job and get out."

I ended the call and threw the phone across the room. The screen was already a cracked mess anyway. I scratched the ticket absentmindedly, and a chest of coins appeared with the dot matrix print screaming $50,000 winner in a pixelated font. I took another long gulp from the bottle of vodka and scratched off the next square, revealing an identical chest of coins. I'd bought one ticket a week since I was eighteen. Just one. In my mind, if the universe, or God, or whatever deity you believe in wanted you to win, you only needed one. I scratched the next square, and a third chest appeared. My heart started to pound. I pulled the card closer to read the fine print. Match all four and win the $50,000 jackpot. I scratched the last one and there it was. Stunned, I blinked to clear my eyes and study the symbols that were beginning to swim from the vodka. Reading the game's rules again to myself out loud confirmed what I already knew. I just won fifty thousand dollars on a freaking scratch-off lottery ticket.

Fifty thousand dollars!

My hand was shaking, so I poured a shot into a dirty glass to celebrate. I tipped it up and toward the phone that I'd launched across the room just minutes earlier. "Hey, Tommy, looks like you were wrong about me after all. I *am* a winner!" I tucked the ticket into my shirt pocket and heard, "Money is the root of all evil." Mom's voice distorted and then turned into a sick laugh from a distance. I poured another shot to stop it from echoing in my brain. An hour and three shots later, the room was spinning and my stomach was roiling. I tripped down the stairs to my bed and stripped my pants off, falling back onto the bed in my stained tightie whities and a t-shirt.

"*Train wreck*," I heard someone sneer, loud and hateful, and then disappear into a sea of aggravated whispering. "*You're a mess. Go get that shotgun and suck on it. Pull the trigger, you waste of space. Tommy is right. You will never amount to anything.*"

If I could have found my feet, I might have crossed the room and done just that. I was miserable, my skin itchy and inflamed, so I clawed at my face. Then the vision of my dear sweet mother swam over me, floating from the darkness, her face distorted and liquefied. "You're my beautiful boy," she said with a smile. Her voice echoed from one wall to the other. The idea of her finding me later, likely missing all or part of my jaw in a crimson pool, would crush her. My heart raced and tears gathered at the corner of my eyes.

"*She'd be better off with you.*" Tommy's face flashed in my mind.

"On that, we agree," I answered.

"*You need to show them who you are dealing with. You grab that gun and you put it in Tommy's face. It doesn't even matter if he's your brother or not. You show him that when he disrespects you, there are consequences.*" So many voices in the room were spinning and talking on top of each other, but I was alone.

I closed my eyes as nausea welled up into my throat, and I swallowed the gathering saliva hard. I turned on my side and retched into a cardboard box, unable to make it to the toilet. Later. I would deal with it later when I was feeling better.

"*You're never going to feel better. You're a piece of shit, and you'll always be a piece of shit.*"

"*End it all. End it now.*" More demonic whispering filled the room, ushering in the paranoia.

I pressed my hands to my ears to stop the muffled screaming and thump of my heartbeat that throbbed in my ears.

"*Cora is a slut. All women are whores who use you.*" A bitter shrew of a woman leered into the void, and when spittle hit my face, I cringed.

I hit my ears to stop the assault on Cora. "She is not! You take that back."

"*You are unlovable. A woman like Cora would never waste her time with someone like you.*"

"*Kill yourself.*"

"*Yeah, Freddie, go kill yourself!*" The voices got louder and chorused together in a sick display of hate surging through me. They started to chant, "*Kill yourself. Kill yourself.*" Three syllables spit out with venom chanted on repeat in my head, and the volume tripled until it was all I could hear. It blocked out every other ambient sound.

"No!" I screamed and fought them. "Stop it!" Right now!" I reached out for a bottle of pills and pressed down with my hands while the screaming continued, getting more and more frustrated as I worked to open the child-proof container. The voices got louder, screeches building into a deafening crescendo that relentlessly pounded in time to the pounding in my head. Finally, the top flew off the bottle and landed with a thud on the floor, sending tiny blue pills bursting from the mouth of the container onto the ground below. I scooped up two and washed them down with vodka then rocked myself in the bed. Finally, blessed darkness came. The voices stopped and I got a reprieve.

FOUR

My eyes opened, and my brain felt like Dr. Lecter himself was digging around my temporal lobes with an ice pick. The stabbing pain throbbed and throbbed, and I tried to rub my temples with my thumbs to dispel some of the tension, but it was lodged there and not going anywhere.

I always slept like a baby. Up every two hours, fussy and inconsolable, followed by several hours of tossing and turning. Insomnia had settled in for the duration in my early twenties, and I was lucky if I got more than four hours of sleep each night. I wiped at my eyes with my fingers and surveyed the mess around me. The angsty whispers had quieted down. I sat up and put my head in my hands, grateful for the break in the action. I tried to gather my thoughts together, but it was like herding cats. Something big happened last night, but as usual, significant chunks were missing from the night before. Tommy. Vodka. Ticket. Small memory snippets unraveled and opened and shifted together in a jumbled storyboard timeline.

Oh, shit! The ticket!

"Freddie! I made your favorite," Ma's voice called from the top of the stairs.

"Gimme a sec!" I shouted up, scanning the room for the least dirty pair of crumpled jeans on the floor. I pulled them to my nose, inhaled, and grimaced. Completely unmotivated, I had put off laundry as long as physically possible, but I was going to have to face the music and soon. I scrambled to find the shirt from last night and squeezed the fabric, relief flooding in when I felt thick card stock. Reaching inside the pocket, I fished out the ticket.

Holy shit, it wasn't a dream.

This two-inch by three-inch card in my hand was worth $50,000. I flopped back down on the bed as thrilling bursts built in my belly, skyrocketing my mood higher and higher and pulling the tension tight. Overwhelm flooded into me next. There was suddenly so much to do, and I didn't know where to start.

"Freddie!" Mom called down again louder, getting frustrated.

"Coming!" I shouted back up. After tucking the ticket back inside, I walked up the stairs with my hand protectively over my heart and the pocket where the ticket was cradled.

Mom's gray hair fit like a helmet close to her head since she had taken to giving herself haircuts to save money after Dad died. The summer of my twelfth year on the planet, to my complete and utter horror and amazement, she brought home a flow-bee.

"Hey, if it's good enough for George Clooney, it's good enough for us!" She enthused when she brought home the ripped box of spare parts, pleased as punch with her purchase that was one step above the dreaded bowl cut. Ma loved to save money, maybe *lived* to save money was more accurate.

When someone would pay her a compliment about the shoes she was wearing, instead of saying thank you, she'd declare proudly, "You won't believe the deal I got! Under five bucks!" As a teenager, I was horrified at her gleeful penny-pinching. Nothing was more embarrassing than Ma's bargain hunting. I wished the ground would open up and swallow me whole when she dragged me to early bird garage sales. Pawing through boxes and tables full of other people's cast-offs didn't get my motor running like it did for Ma.

She sneezed into a napkin and swiped at her watery eyes underneath the huge glasses that she'd owned for almost a decade.

"Bless you," I said and walked over to kiss her cheek.

"I made French toast!" she sang out, slipping three browned slices coated in a glistening pat of butter onto a plate. I sat down at the table and tried to smile. My face felt stiff like clay that had been left out in the sun to cure. "Did you have the night terrors again, sweetie? I thought I heard something last night."

"It was a rough one."

"I thought so." She sat down next to me and reached out to stroke my forearm. "Do you need to see Dr. McGivern again?" she asked quietly. He was my psychiatrist.

"No, Ma." I dismissed her request. "I am fine. Everything is fine." I poured a liberal amount of syrup onto the plate. "Actually, I am *better* than fine," I added as I licked a sticky drop of syrup from my thumb.

"Really?" she asked with hope-filled eyes.

"You are looking at a bonafide lottery winner."

"What?" She was instantly confused.

"I won fifty thou on a scratch-off."

"You didn't!" She smacked my arm with the back of her hand.

"I did!" I said with a real smile and proudly pulled the card out of my pocket and flashed it toward her.

She turned it over and over in her hands, wary of it, suspicious of the power it held. "I don't know. You know the saying—more money, more problems," she cautioned.

"Jesus, Ma. You're the only person I know who wouldn't want her son to win the lottery."

"It's not that, honey…" She tried to explain as I tuned her out and turned back toward the TV that blared across the room. She was addicted to daytime TV. *777 Club* reruns and the chatty talk shows filled her void. A commercial for erectile dysfunction came on. The irony tickled me so pink I giggled.

"Ready to find a place for your passion?" a deep voice asked. "You can love life again… all of it." I was temporarily enthralled by a suggestive wink from a charismatic white-haired man strolling down the beach, hand in hand with his wife. She was a gorgeous former super model with a smile so huge she had to be getting it at least three times a week, thanks to blue boner pills. A smile like that is *not* natural. "Ask your doctor about Viagra." They laughed and danced into the sunset, and then it cut to the money shot of them snuggling in matching claw foot tubs, overlooking mountains and waterfalls somewhere off the coast of Oregon.

"I can't believe that filth is allowed on daytime television. This country is going to pot," Ma mumbled under her breath about the destruction of our modern society. She yanked off her glasses dramatically and opted for a pair of dollar store readers that perched on her nose as she opened her dogeared copy of the King James Bible. She muttered to herself as she turned the pages, looking for something.

"Here it is," she declared. "Galatians 5:19." She cleared her throat and began, "Now the works of the flesh are evident: sexual immorality, impurity, sensuality, idolatry, sorcery, envy, drunkenness, orgies, and things like these. I warn you, as I warned you before, that those who do such things will not inherit the kingdom of God."

I weighed them in my mind. Orgies… Kingdom of God. Orgies… Kingdom of God. Orgies won, hands down, but in my forty circles around the sun, I hadn't had the opportunity to participate in an actual orgy—yet. It was looking like the Kingdom of God was going to win by default, and that revelation crushed my soul.

"Ma, If I gotta pick one, you know it's gonna be orgies," I said, knowing I was pressing my luck, which is exactly why I said it. My default setting when talking to Ma was shock and awe.

She rolled her eyes and waved a hand at me, ignoring the comment. "Okay, funny man." She laughed. "Don't mind me, I'll just be over here praying for your soul."

"It's a lost cause, Mama."

I kissed her cheek and cleared the dishes then loaded the dishwasher. Finally, the pounding in my head had slowed to a painful throb, the mind-numbing edge thankfully gone. In the shower, I scrubbed my skin clean and washed what was left of my thinning hair by swirling my hands around counterclockwise fifty strokes. Then I rinsed for a count of one hundred. Then fifty more counterclockwise strokes and another rinse for a count of one hundred. It's a ritual. I can't help myself. I do it until it feels right, until it feels like it is okay to stop.

Whistling and with an abnormal burst of motivation, I threw a load of dirty laundry in the basket, forgetting about the ticket, and dumped it into the washer. I turned the knob to the hot setting, added detergent, and then water gushed in as it started to fill. I walked into the kitchen and opened my socials, cruising through pet photos and pranks, killing time until the laundry was done.

"Shit! The ticket!" I remembered, and ran back to the washer and yanked open the lid. There was only an inch of water in the bottom of the drum as I prayed fervently to Doug Robinson, the host of the *777 Club* to keep my ticket safe.

"Dear Mr. Robinson, if the ticket is dry, I will donate ten percent for you to buy another gold-plated microphone, and I will never masturbate again."

Panicked and wired, I rifled through the washer drum item by item and finally found the shirt. It was soaked through except for the left-hand side that was resting on a pair of dirty jeans. I pulled the card from the pocket and checked it for damage. Surprisingly, it had remained dry. Holding it victorious in the air, I circled around and around and the whispers started in again.

"*Money is the root of all evil. Money is the root of all evil.*" It began barely imperceptibly and then grew louder, chanting in a chorus in my mind.

I slapped the side of my head hard and they quieted down.

"*Hey, mister, you wanna be famous?*" a little boy in a cowboy hat asked deep inside my psyche. Part of me did. A little piece of my soul craved celebrity, the warm shine of instant acceptance from others, the incredible high of a theater full of people hanging on my every word. Their laughter short-circuiting my flawed brain synapses and coursing adrenaline and dopamine through my system. To be loved and adored like that by perfect strangers would fix everything. It would fix me.

I made a plan.

#1 Put the ticket away for safekeeping.

#2 Go to the Lottery Headquarters on Monday.

I found an envelope and sealed it and then tucked it in the closet, behind the case where the loaded shotgun waited for me to grow some balls. It was the only place I knew no one would ever find it.

FIVE

Having the ticket in my possession was a fast pass to anxiety city. Something could happen to it. What if there was a fire? What if Tommy came to visit unannounced and decided to rifle through my things, trying to convince Ma to put the house on the market? I counted down the hours over the rest of the weekend, and on Monday morning at nine am, I hopped on a bus and walked into the Missouri State Lottery Headquarters. A bored woman with frizzy hair sat behind a desk and looked at me. "Can I help you?"

"Why, yes, you can!" I said too cheerily, tapping into my Freddie Angel persona. There was the guy on stage who reeked of confidence and had the magical ability to make people laugh, and then there was the other Freddie Angel, the insecure disappointment who lived in his mama's basement. To get things done, I learned early on that the stage persona was the way to deal with the public.

She chomped her gum that barely masked the coffee on her breath.

"I'm sure you hear this every day, but I seem to have won some money on a scratch-off ticket, and I am here to fetch it."

I smiled at her with the fake smile, hoping it distracted her from the trembling in my hands.

I should have had a nip to calm my nerves.

"Yeah, dumbass, great idea. Going into a meeting tipsy is always the answer," a woman taunted me from afar, but not so far that I didn't feel the disgust that permeated her insult.

Frizzy hair handed me a stack of documents that included tax forms and told me to fill them out, offering a Bic pen with a bright red carnation taped with green painter's tape at the end of it. A weird office practice I never understood. Pens don't magically bloom, but whatever. I accepted the floral writing instrument, settled in, and filled out all the forms. Pressing hard to push through the carbon, I scrawled my signature like I was someone important on the bottom.

I handed the clipboard to her and held the pen behind my back, then presented it to her with a flourish. Bowing down and trying to curtsy, both my knees cracked. "My lady, I bequeath unto you this sincerest token of my appreciation." I tipped my head up in time to see a small smile dance across her face. "And now, if you can call for the crane, I believe I do not have the ability to return my body into an upright position."

She chuckled, barely perceptibly, but I still counted it as a win. During daily interactions with people, I often kept score, tallying up wins and losses based on facial expressions. Every conversation was a chance to hone my craft, to sprinkle a little humor into the mundane drudgery of life. It was a double-edged sword, though. When I was popping and the interactions were positive, I fed off the energy, but when I bombed, I used these moments as proof of my personal failures and beat myself up with them at night. Like a professional athlete studying tapes for the next game, I walked through my day each night, tallying up my comedic wins and beating myself up for my losses.

I sat back down and waited for them to call my name. A few minutes later, I was whisked into a paneled office where a giant check sat on an easel made out to me. The rush of seeing my name scrawled across it took my breath away as I walked over to it. My hands clamped on either side of my cheeks *Home Alone* style.

"Hello, Mr. Angel." A smart-looking woman walked forward, offering me her hand. "Congratulations on your win! Are you comfortable posing for pictures for the lottery commission to use on social media?"

"Why, yes, I think I *am* ready for my close-up, Mr. DeMille," I said and instantly regretted it. The joke overshot her twenty-something blonde head and never landed.

Loss column. Check.

The office was so silent, I swear I could hear her blink for several painful seconds. "Never mind," I mumbled.

She pulled out her phone, and I held the check with both hands, caressing it like a lover. "Money isn't going to change me," I bragged. "I was an asshole before; now I will just be an asshole with money."

"Fantastic." She dismissed my pitiful attempt at self-deprecating humor, annoyance ringing in her words, and I flushed pink. Terrified, I realized something. She didn't like me.

"Newsflash... no one likes you," a voice hissed, and I looked behind my shoulder at the empty room.

I smiled as best I could. I have always been self-conscious of the gap in my front teeth. Keeping my lips together, I forced the corners of my mouth up.

"Okay. I have what I need," she finally said and held up a cashier's check. "Here, I'll trade you."

"I was wondering… can I keep them both?"

"Uh, sure," she answered as she handed them to me, and I walked out of the building. The real check was tucked deep in the pocket of my jeans. I turned the face of the giant check and hugged it to my chest as I waited for the bus. Finally, with a whoosh of air brakes and screeching metal on metal, the bus pulled up to the stop, sending me into a coughing fit from the exhaust. I walked up the steps, flashed my bus pass to the scanner, and sat down on the nearly full bus. At the next stop, a little old lady climbed the steps, a frail thing that reminded me of Ma. She hesitated, looking around for a place to sit. Her warm eyes met mine with a quick smile, and I stood. "You can sit here," I offered.

"Thank you, dear." She slowly lowered herself into the seat. I wasn't entirely sure she was going to be able to get back up without help. "What do you have there?" she asked innocently.

I turned the check toward her, and it got everyone's attention very quickly. The whole bus quieted down, and their eyes slid over the giant check, greed deepening and darkening them. "I got lucky," I said sheepishly and then turned it back around and hugged it protectively to my chest.

"*Your luck has run out*," was whispered in hushed tones. I poked a finger in my ear and jiggled it to clear it.

"That's incredible. I've never met a lottery winner before," she said with a twinkle in her eyes. "Fifty thousand dollars?"

"More like thirty-eight after taxes, but yes."

"Unfortunately, Uncle Sam always has his hand out first," she commiserated. "But still, that's quite a windfall! What are you going to do with your winnings?"

"Well, I *was* thinking hookers and blow," I deadpanned and the younger guys around me snickered as her eyes widened. "Sorry, ma'am, if that is too vulgar. I can't help myself. I'm a comedian. Vulgar comes with the territory."

"You are?"

"Yes, ma'am."

"Well, that's a first for me, too. What an exciting day today is turning out to be!" she exclaimed, making me fall in love with her immediately.

"I tell you what, come down to The Punch Line this Saturday and I will buy you a drink," I said to her, and then on an overly generous whim, I said more loudly in the bus, "Actually, you're all invited. Come see my set and I'll buy the first round!"

"*A fool and his money soon parted.*" Another hissed platitude filled my brain that I had to work to push away.

Applause filled the bus. Free beer will almost always encourage that kind of response. I fed on their approval, soaking it up like a sponge, always looking for my next hit to avoid drying out completely. It turned down the chatter between my ears, drowning out the judgmental mutterings.

"Oh my!" she said. "I just might!"

"What's your name?"

"Darlene."

"Darlene, I'm Freddie Angel. Pleased to meet you."

SIX

A block past the bus stop, the shiny glass and granite Kansas City Savings and Loan sat. I walked into the bright lobby of the bank with my giant lottery check. Hushed tones and beige walls greeted me, and cubicles filled with women and men dressed in drab-colored clothing sat consumed by documents on desks in front of them. I waited in line, twirling the check like one of those teenagers on the corner who slings signs for hours on end, drawing attention to crappy little eateries in ugly strip malls.

A teller opened up, and I walked to her station and handed her the enormous check, knocking over an entire container of pens that rained down on her counter.

"Sorry, doll," I said with a smile. "Lady Luck has finally smiled on Freddie Angel. I'd like to cash this bad boy."

Her brow furrowed as she studied the check and then stated, "This is a prop they use for photo-ops. I need the official check they gave you at the Lottery Headquarters."

I set the check against the wall and reached into my pocket for the real check, signed the back, and promptly handed it to her.

"Which account can I put this in for you?"

"I'm just looking for cash, sweetheart."

The word sweetheart earned me a glare.

Loss Column. Check. Know your audience, dumbass. Read the room.

"Sorry." I cleared my throat and then continued with less bravado. "I'd just like to cash it."

She looked at me like I had grown an extra head.

"You want almost forty thousand dollars in cash?" she asked, shocked. "I'm going to have to talk to my supervisor."

"About what?"

"This is a sizable amount. I am not sure we can accommodate your request."

"But this is a *bank*," I reasoned. "You only have one job —to magically turn paper checks into cash."

She pursed her lips together, her face pulled tight, matching the taut bun that controlled every strand of her hair. "Please, excuse me." She disappeared into the hallway, and I overheard her speaking in hushed tones to an older gentleman in a brown suit. He appeared in front of me with a curt smile.

"Mr. Angel, Dana has told me you wish to make a sizable cash withdrawal that will deplete our cash resources. I will have to put an order in, and you will need to return for the balance. Right now, I can authorize the release of ten thousand dollars to you if you require cash."

"Are you serious?" I was shocked. "What's locked in the vault then? Epstein's little black book? Colonel Sanders's secret recipe?" I chuckled. "No, I got it, your hairy balls in a red velvet pouch?" I mimed rolling his tiny balls in my hands and then leaned in to whisper, "Those things are so microscopic, there's got to be tons of room leftover to hold the cash." The words rang out before I could censor them. The teller's eyes bugged as she tittered with repressed laughter, and the manager's face flashed with anger.

Win column. Check.

Ever the professional, he pushed through the rage, pointedly ignored the offensive comment, and continued in a brusque business-like tone. "I'm sorry for the inconvenience. I can have the rest of the cash available in forty-eight hours, but I would be remiss if I didn't warn you about the security issue created by having that kind of cash on your person. It is not recommended."

He was a judgmental prick, but I started to realize he might have a point. "How 'bout this, chief? Can you give me five-grand in hundies, and I'll return in a couple of days for the rest?"

He turned to the teller with a brief nod, and she counted out my cash.

"Thank you kindly, ma'am." I pretended to tip an invisible cowboy hat toward her.

I tucked the crisp green bills into my pocket, picked up my gigantic check, and walked out of there with a new money spring in my step. Life was looking up for Freddie Angel.

———

Two days later, I returned to the bank with a briefcase. I stacked it full of twenties and fifties and locked it tight, feeling a little *Agent 007* rush. I changed buses three times on the way home, looking over my shoulder as paranoia surged the entire way, sighing in relief when it was finally safely buried in the back of my closet. Paulie called begging for a last-minute fill-in at The Punch Line, and I was hoping to stay on his good side so I agreed. On Wednesday nights, the club was mostly empty, so I thought I'd try out some new material and see if any of it was good enough to become part of my regular set.

I struggled to get in a groove during my set, and beads of sweat gathered on my forehead in staunch protest of my weak jokes. One bead broke free and trickled down my cheek as the panic began to build deep in my belly. The spotlight was suddenly sweltering, and my self-doubt and self-loathing cued up and started to taunt me in whispers.

My focus was shot, but I forged ahead anyway. Then in stereo, I heard a voice that made my blood boil. "Dick!" A man shouted from the back of the room. "Worthless hack! You suck!"

I covered my eyes, shielding them from the spotlight that was too bright. Searching the crowd for the source of the voice that seemed to be swirling and moving. He stood up, a bulky backlit shape, looking like a gorilla of a man. I didn't need to see his face to recognize who it was.

Tommy.

I tried to focus back on the set and push the insults out of the way. "So… today I went to the bank to withdraw some money. It's literally the only thing they have there, and they were all out." I waited to let that sink in. "All out of money. Eight tellers and no money. Can you believe that shit? What do those tellers count all day without any money? Shocking, I know."

"What's shocking is how much you suck!" Tommy shouted.

I stumbled over my next words. My mouth closed up like the recurring dream I had as a kid, where my lips fused together and the skin morphed and grew over them until my mouth disappeared and left me with incoherent murmuring the only effective means of communication. I wiped my face with my hand, sweaty and wet, the panic embedding in deeper as the need to fill the dead air surged forward. I scrambled to fill it, groping for a remnant of any joke, probing my mind, scraping the bottom of the comedic barrel—Yo Mama jokes.

"Who loves a good Yo Mama joke?" I asked.

The small audience clapped feebly.

"Yo mama so old, she was a waitress at the Last supper," I said in the microphone to placid applause. "Yo momma so ugly, she makes Jabba the Hut look like Brad Pitt."

"Yo mama so stupid, she gave birth to the dumbest kid in America!" Tommy bellowed out from the back of the room. More petrifying silence penetrated the space.

Why was he Mom's favorite again?

The urge to tattle tale on my douchebag of a brother emerged, but I quickly discarded it. I wasn't a seven-year-old kid anymore, and it would just hurt Mom's feelings anyway. She didn't like it when we fought.

I stumbled through the rest of my set and then walked off the stage to weak applause, immediately downing a shot of vodka before Tommy made his presence known.

"Hey, shit-stain," he sneered and knocked back a shot of Jager. He pounded me in the shoulder, the kind of bro-sef bullshit that always turned my stomach.

"Tommy," I said without making eye contact, my eyes fixed on the chalkboard with the specials written in Cora's pretty handwriting. "What are you doing here?"

"I decided to come see my little brother in all his glory." He looked me over. "Gotta say, the whole experience was vastly underwhelming." He looked around the club. "This place is a dump. I mean, I get it. It's the perfect backdrop for your mid-life crisis." He took another shot while I sipped on a merciful beer that Cora set silently next to me.

"Look, we need to talk about putting Mom's house on the market in the spring. I want to get her on the waiting list at Golden Oaks."

"Mom doesn't want to leave her house," I answered. "She told me the only way they are carrying her out of there is in a pine box."

"That's because she knows you will have no place to go."

I sighed a deep, heavy sigh. I was sick to death of having the same conversation over and over with him. "She said she's happy at home and she likes the company."

"What else is she supposed to say? That she's ashamed her youngest has failed to launch? That she's settling in because she's accepted her fate? You know Mom would never do that."

I swung my gaze over to meet his steely eyes. The news of my lottery win was on the tip of my tongue. I wanted to tell him, to wipe that smug look off his face, but I knew he would ruin it like he ruined everything. He was Dad through and through. Rough, mean, and hard to be around. The kind of guy that sucked all of the oxygen out of the room and had a penchant for making you feel tiny in his presence. Insignificant and worthless.

"I have to go," I said, draining the beer and pulling on my jacket as a barrier against the cooler weather that had settled in after Halloween.

"Running away again? Jesus, Fritz, you're pathetic."

"You know I hate it when you call me that," I said through gritted teeth. I balled my hands at my sides to keep myself from punching him. I knew if I did, it would just make him laugh harder and add more fuel to the fire. Tommy was a dedicated cross-fitter. His chest was massive like steel after years of punishing workouts six days a week, and I was more the consistency of flabby rubber. I had to get out of there.

"Tommy's right. You're a wimp," someone hissed in my head. *"A worthless shell of a man. No wonder Dottie lives in a constant state of denial."*

I shook my head to clear it and walked away, catching Cora's concerned eyes on the way out. I shoved my hands in my pockets and hunkered down, walking fast and furious away from the club, as far away as possible from Tommy.

SEVEN

Garages terrify me. I cannot go into one without getting the shakes, my heart rate accelerating, my breathing becoming shallow. I avoid them like the plague. It might be the reason I don't own a car currently, that and the fact until just recently, my current financial obligations made owning one a luxury I couldn't afford.

"Hold it still, boy," Dad demanded. I was seven, dressed in play clothes that I never actually got to play in. Jeans and a t-shirt with tennis shoes that were too tight. Hand-me-downs I was afraid to admit to Mom I had outgrown. I curled my toes tightly inside my shoes, grasping onto a cold metal flashlight, and shakily directing the cone of light to spill onto the car's engine. The car yawned wide, exposing all of its mechanics, the hood propped up by a metal rod. He yanked the light out of my hand, clearly disgusted with me already.

"Go make yourself useful and get me the five-sixteenths crescent wrench."

Obediently, I walked over to his toolbox, opened a drawer, and stared down at the mass of metal, hoping the right tool would reveal itself to me. Praying a shaft of golden light would shine down on it from heaven. Screwdrivers and wrenches sat arranged in perfect rows from smallest to largest in his toolbox. I didn't even know what a crescent wrench was; I just knew that if I didn't find it fast and put it in his hand, there would be hell to pay.

Seconds pulled like taffy into long, drawn-out minutes as I panicked, afraid to make a choice, knowing it would probably be wrong. I walked through the options, looking for something crescent-*shaped*, pulling out each drawer to examine the contents. The metal hinges squealed, betraying my lack of knowledge. I reached out to pick one up, finally committed to a decision, when my head lurched forward from the force of a blow at the back of my skull. Stunned, I fell forward onto the tools, my hands bracing my fall as sharp edges of a saw blade cut into my palms. I cried out.

"Shut up or I'll give you something to cry about," he snarled. "How stupid are you?" He yanked out the wrench and pressed it roughly into the skin of my cheek. The cold steel made me shiver.

Don't say anything. It will only make it worse.

"This one, stupid." He shook it in front of my face. "What a moron you turned out to be, just like your mother."

It was like flipping a switch. He turned to walk back to the open engine, and I lunged at him, his words spurring me on. I was too little, and he just laughed and pushed me away like a rag doll. My shoulder hit the edge of the toolbox, and a jolt of pain shot from my elbow to fingertips.

"So, the little mama's boy thinks he's a big man now?" he taunted as his eyes narrowed at me. "Don't start something you aren't man enough to finish." He pulled out an old dumbbell and handed it to me. "Hold this over your head until I tell you to stop."

I heaved it up, and thirty seconds later, my arms began to

tremble. Then my elbows bowed and my entire body started to shake. Beads of sweat broke out on my face and raced down my cheeks in the dirty tracks already burned by the tears. I shifted my weight from side to side, crawling out of my skin.

"I'm going to make a man out of you yet." He savored my struggle, using a toothpick to clean his teeth, watching me sway and shake with effort. "Higher," he demanded, and I tried, but my arms were already flopping like noodles. They had become burning limbs protesting against the weight. I watched a dandelion seed take flight from my shoe and swirl up into the air and out into the wind, wishing I could join it, ride it like the magic umbrella I dreamt about this morning. I fixated my vision on the cool, clear patch of blue sky, wishing I could teleport like they did on *Star Trek*. I'd give anything to have Scotty beam me up and away right that second.

I began to whimper and bit down the sound, trying to swallow it, but he always sussed it out. He measured and tabulated every infraction from the time I was in nursery school. Leaving the door open too long. Not putting my bowl in the sink. Walking into the house with muddy shoes.

Tommy was the golden boy. In Dad's eyes, he could do no wrong. I was a screw-up and he rode me like a pony. One kid always gets singled out. The other one flies under the radar. Two very different lives lived under the same roof.

Life isn't fair, Freddie.

His parenting style was like that of an evil dictator bordering on mob boss, and I was hyper-aware of his location and proximity at all times. The only chance I got to relax was when he was at work. Weekends were pure torture, an endless series of tasks to complete for his constant critique while Tommy sat in our bedroom reading comic books. If the tasks weren't completed the right way, *his way*, then I was forced to prove my manhood by feats of physical strength. This was his second favorite way—his belt being numero uno.

He bent down to my level, his palms propped up on his thick thighs and his face so close to mine I could smell the stale stench of cigarettes on his breath. He filled the space, intimidating me, making me shrink. "Pain is the ultimate teacher, Freddie. I hold you to a high standard because I love you."

Love?

Even at seven years old, I knew that was not how love was supposed to feel. It's a long process to develop intense hatred toward your father. There's a series of events that scar you. It's the insults slung your way for minor infractions.

"Faggot! Dumbass! Moron!"

Each one of them is a cut. Each one of them builds up your scar tissue. It's the time when he promises to take you for ice cream and then because you can't decide what flavor fast enough, forces you to sit down without any and watch him savor his chocolate-dipped vanilla cone, your mouth watering the entire time as you curse yourself for the hesitation. If you had just made a decision faster, you'd be sitting next to him enjoying a strawberry malt.

It's the day you overhear your parents talking about your future, and your dad laughing at your mom's idea to send you to college. "Freddie? That kid's an idiot. There is no way I am spending a penny of my hard-earned money on his education."

It's the cracks to the back of your head and the stinging slaps to your fingers for touching his things without permission.

It's the accusations of you losing his keys when you clearly put them in the dish on the entry table the night before. A habit that was literally beaten into you. A habit that forces you to check the dish fourteen times before you go to bed to relieve the pit of worry in your stomach that started as a seed and grew into the thick trunk of an unyielding tree, splintering your soft tissues whenever you move.

It's the embarrassment of waking up in a warm puddle of your own urine and seeing the disgust slide into his eyes, taking up space there alongside hatred and contempt. Your older brother mocking you and threatening to tell the kids at school if you don't write his book report.

It's words murmured behind walls, becoming louder and turning into screams and wails. The sound of glass shattering and then pressing a pillow over your ears, trying to block it out while carrying the guilt that you should be doing something to protect your mom.

Some people shouldn't have children. Unfortunately, these are the people that end up with them anyway. You don't need to know a single thing about raising children before you can become a parent, but you need to go to great lengths to prove your worthiness to adopt a shelter dog. It's an unbalanced and unfair world we live in.

I dreamed about him dying. Clutching his chest and having a heart attack from the cigarettes he religiously chain-smoked. I fantasized about it so much it became an obsession, a Quentin Tarantino-esque movie that played out in my head every night. Where I was the hero and Dad met a violent and revenge-worthy death. I'd wake up from those dreams with a huge smile on my face.

And then in a miraculous twist of fate when I was twelve, he had that heart attack. Ma found him out in the garage and summoned an ambulance that came and took him away. When she told me died, I sobbed. Not because I was sad, but because I was *thrilled* he was gone. They were tears of joy. Abusive men never leave on their own and seek out weak partners who make excuses for their bad behavior. I loved Ma, but I knew her limitations. She was a sticker, someone who made a commitment and always followed through, even to her own detriment. She was never going to leave him, and now the decision was taken out of her hands.

After she told me and I hugged her tight, I rode my bike to my secret hiding place, which was a ring of bushes at the park that I could sit in unseen and listen to the other children laughing and playing. There, I could celebrate my emancipation. God had answered my most fervent prayer. Hidden in the thick lilac branches and cloaked in green leaves, I laughed until I sobbed, clutching my stomach in equal parts agony and relief. Once I regained control, I swallowed hard, terrified that Ma would find out I had something to do with it. Did I dream it into existence? Was I that powerful?

Later that night at dinner, Tommy and I sat at the table, quietly eating mashed potatoes like we were any normal family on any normal day. I could finally breathe again, but the scars he left behind remained. Buried deep, they left their mark on my body and my mind.

EIGHT

Humming to myself, I walked into the club a few days later with a new swagger, the folded wad of Benjamins confined to a money clip shoved deep in my pocket, giving me the bulging confidence of ten men. It's funny how quickly a little money in your pocket makes you feel invincible. Sitting at the bar, I heard the new kid bombing, and I strained, trying to listen to his act. He threw out punch line after punch line and never connected. At the end of his set, he walked into the lounge looking like a beaten dog with his head hung low. He sat dejectedly on a stool at the other end of the bar, his skinny leg jiggling up and down, trying to dispel the anxious burn of failure. I knew exactly how he was feeling. That was comedy. The highs shot you into the stratosphere, and the lows turned you into a sad, suicidal clown. There was nothing in-between.

I waved Cora over. "Hey, doll, can you give that poor guy whatever he wants?" I pulled out three twenties and left them on the bar. "Give yourself a nice tip, but keep 'em coming for him. Tell him it's medicinal. It'll help kill the sting."

On stage, my introduction was blaring into the microphone. I got up and rolled my shoulders like I was stepping into a boxing ring and then ran out onto the stage as the sparse crowd clapped.

"Hello, hello, hello!" I barked into the mic. "The doctor… is… in! I'm Freddie Angel, The Punch Line's certified resident Funologist." There were a couple of whoops from the back of the room. "Thank you for that, sir!" I saluted him and settled in for my first joke. "So, if this comedy thing doesn't work out, I've decided it is time for me to start a religion." A few snorts were heard from the crowd. "No, no, no, hear me out." I waved my hands to quiet the objections of the crowd. "It's genius, I promise." I looked into the spotlight that made it hard to see anything else. "What other lifestyle allows you to take four wives, gives you the ability to father dozens of children, and lets you completely avoid paying even a penny of taxes?" People started to giggle. "I'd write my own commandments. Ooh, I got one… 'Thou shalt not start a day without a blow job.'"

The men in attendance burst into applause. "Looks like I have a few Funology disciples in the flock already," I said sarcastically and made a cross in front of myself. "Bacon be with you."

I let it linger and then said, "And you'd be required to answer, '*And also with you.*'"

Laughing, I looked down. "The rules are strict, though. You'd have to really commit. You'd have to leave the conventional material trappings of the world behind and embrace the mandatory Garden of Eden dress code." The men clapped louder. "Let it all hang out, sisters. Adorning your body in more than your birthday suit is sacrilege and goes against the very core fundamental beliefs of Funology."

I paused like I was considering it. "Worst part of that will be the sunburn on your soft spots." I pressed a finger to my lips like I made an important discovery. "The prophet, aka, this guy," I hiked a thumb toward my chest, "requires three virgins to apply sunscreen to his naked body every six hours." More men snickered as I laughed at the idea. "And you'd have a built-in excuse for everything. I'm a Funologist, it's against my religion to work more than ten hours a week."

I looked down and held onto the mic stand loosely, tipping the mic at an angle to my mouth. "Instead of passing around that old dirty chalice of congregational spit, you'd be required to BYOB. Oh, and the bread of life would be covered in cheese. Sky's the limit, people. I'm just spitballing here." The laughter rippled from wall to wall, surging me on.

"Our hymns would be 90s hip hop." I started to chant old school Snoop Dog and Dr. Dre lyrics as the crowd clapped. "It would be a true Nirvana that would probably smell like teen spirit." I chuckled and waited. Comedy was about beats. Giving the audience a chance to process what they heard. Nerves could get the better of you, and that was why pacing was so important. That was why I watched reruns of comedy specials constantly. Picking up a tiny nugget that would improve my performance, getting incrementally better at my craft. I worked hard to earn those laughs, tossing out joke after joke and seeing if they would land. The new and improved Freddie Angel was on fire. I owned that stage, and at the end of my set, walked off it feeling ten feet tall.

———

I climbed onto my perch at the bar as the post-performance adrenaline surged, where I scribbled notes in my book while absentmindedly waiting for a flash of brilliance to shoot through me and onto the page. Jokes are birthed through you. It's the writing process at its most magical, the perfect word summoned from the ether at the perfect time. I have no idea how it happens; it just does. Like we are all walking around with whole stories floating above our heads and then we just pluck one like a ripe pear and eat it.

"You're pretty pleased with yourself." Cora came up behind me and I jumped. She always had me on edge. In the club, I liked to sit at the corner of the bar where I could watch her work. I would sit and study her profile while she poured shots of Jim Beam and refilled beers. Now, she was standing so close I could smell her shampoo—peaches and sunshine. I breathed her in. "You had a great set."

"Thanks," I said as warmth spread to my cheeks. Her sincere praise flushed me with joy.

"No offense, but Funology sounds a little like a cult." She smiled, revealing a white perfect row of top teeth with crooked bottom ones. The imperfection only made her more perfect in my mind.

"But does it sound like a cult you'd like to *join*?" I asked as I forced goofy sexiness into my voice. "Because I might have an opening in my harem."

She rolled her eyes at the thought, and her quick smile crinkled at her eyes. "I'd be disqualified, lost my V card a million years ago."

"The prophet may make an exception," I teased with a smirk.

"Not gonna lie, joining a cult sounds pretty amazing right now. I'm ready to give up full control of my life," she admitted with a frown.

I swiveled my barstool toward her and shut my notebook, asking, "What's up, buttercup? Dr. Freddie is in."

"I'm single and ready to mingle. Starting over again, but I think my picker is broken."

"Darlin' you don't have a pecker," I drawled with a bad southern accent.

"PICK-er," she overemphasized and then gave up, rolling her eyes at me. "I want to have some fun now that I'm single again. My ex was such a buzzkill."

"Is that right?" This was the exact opening I had been praying for since the day she walked into The Punch Line. "You've come to the right place. You know they don't call me the Funologist for nothing." I waggled my eyebrows at her playfully and bobbed my head side to side. Cheesy as hell, but it made her laugh.

"Well, I'm off in an hour," she offered.

"Perfect." I smiled and patted my jacket pocket. "I've got just the thing to get you out of this funk."

The rest of the hour passed quickly, and I drank a lot of water. I wanted to remember every second of this night. I didn't want to numb out and soften the edges until they were obliterated. I wanted to record all the memories in my mind so I could walk through them again and again.

She grabbed her jacket, and we walked out into the cool November night. "So, do I need to bow or kiss your ring or something?" she teased. "And for the record, it's way past morning, so your blow job commandment is off the table." The streetlights backlit her short spiky pixie cut until she glowed.

I laughed a real laugh, a belly laugh, one that I hadn't let myself indulge in for so long it felt foreign. I looked at my watch. "Well, in that case, looks like I only need to stretch this out for another seven and a half hours."

She pushed me playfully, and heat stamped my shoulder where she touched it. There were two abandoned lime green scooters in the next block that caught my eye, and I began to lead us toward them.

"Hmm. Might the lady care to indulge in a little midnight joyride?" I asked with a hoity-toity, offensive British accent.

"Firstly, I am not a lady, and secondly, I've never actually ridden one of those," she admitted.

"Then it's time to change that." I pulled out my phone and logged in to unlock and prepay for the scooter rental, my hands shaking, and I prayed Cora didn't notice. I pulled a flask from my pocket, took a sip to stop the shakes, then handed it to her. She took a nip and handed it back, and I tucked it into my coat pocket. "Your chariot awaits," I gallantly said with a bow as I slid the unlocked scooter to her. She smiled and held the handlebars in her hands, looking at the controls, trying to figure it out, cranking the rubber grip in her hand.

"Care to make this a little more interesting?" she asked playfully.

"What did you have in mind?"

"A little race?" She smiled. "To the taco truck on Everett Parkway?"

"What do I get when I win?" I bragged, slipping easily into my Freddie Angel stage persona that oozed confidence.

She shook her head. "When *I* win," she corrected, "you have to buy me tacos." She jumped on the scooter and cranked it as hard as it would go, and she was off, shooting down the sidewalks at fifteen miles per hour. She looked over her shoulder, laughing at me as I struggled to keep up. I was starting to wonder if the battery on my scooter was as middle-aged as I was as I limped along like a turtle. She shot through an intersection that sidelined me at a red light, and when I caught up with her at the taco truck, she was pink-faced from the cool air and gloating.

"Man, these tacos are going to taste so sweet."

"Sweet?" I asked, confused.

"Sweet like victory!" she exclaimed, punching one tiny fist in the air. It was adorable.

"I would be delighted to buy your victory tacos," I offered as I tipped my scooter to rest on the wall and took care to set hers against mine. We walked to the front of the trailer and ordered at the window. I caught a glimpse of a three-year-old little girl sleeping on a pile of coats in the corner of the food truck.

"Hey, man, is that your daughter?" I asked the cook. He was a short Hispanic man, with a quick smile and a face full of impeccably groomed facial hair.

"Yes, that's Abriella." He leaned in closer, and I caught a glimpse of just how weary his face was. Thick lines and tired eyes.

"She's beautiful." Cora smiled.

"She is," I confirmed, and she stirred then settled in again with a sigh like a kitten.

Three minutes later, four boats filled with Carne Asada and crispy pork tacos appeared steaming in the window, along with two Cokes to wash them down.

A man doesn't drag his three-year-old to work all day and into the night unless there is no other place for her to go, and he sure as hell doesn't lay her on the ground in a greasy food truck unless he has no other options. I pulled the money clip from my pocket and tugged four hundred-dollar bills from it, setting them on the counter.

His eyes widened in shock, and then he burst into tears when he realized I was giving it to him. "Oh, sweet Jesus. I don't know what to say," he cried as tears fell down his cheeks. "This is more money than I make in a week. I didn't know how I was going to buy pull-ups tomorrow. We're eating the leftovers that we can't serve to customers." He clutched my hand tightly, and although it felt awkward, I pushed through it. "You have no idea how much I need this money." He wiped tears away from his eyes and looked around the taco truck in a panic. "Can I give you anything?"

"You've already given us the best tacos on this side of town," I said and picked up two of the boats while a speechless Cora grabbed hers and we walked silently to the picnic table nearby. I sat down and took a long sip of Coke before biting into the first one. The earthy cilantro and sharp red onion slaw were the best part.

"You have nothing to say?" Cora asked, still stunned by my interaction with the man.

"About what?"

"Don't be so humble, Freddie."

"He looked like he needed help, and I was in a position to give it to him so it all worked out."

Cora took a bite of her taco and chewed it slowly and thoughtfully. "I'm starting to think I don't know you at all."

I smiled giddily, gloating that in Cora's eyes I was a man of mystery. Even in my limited experience, I knew that was never a bad thing when it came to the ladies.

"But would you like to?" I asked shyly, afraid to look into her eyes and ruin the magic of the moment.

"I think I might."

NINE

The next morning, my eyes popped open, and I stared at the ceiling for a moment. My usual vodka-induced headache couldn't dull the blissful memory of the night before with Cora. I walked through our date again, hour by hour, the big triumphant smile on her face as she scootered away from me for the win forever etched into my mind. Beautiful.

When things in your life go wrong for so long, and then finally start going right, you have to take a second to marvel at the miracle.

The cook clutching my hand with absolute gratitude on his face and his tears of joy. For once in my life, another man looked at me with utter respect. I didn't realize until that moment how starved I was for it. It was a need so palpable yet neglected, that when I basked in the glow of his approval, it changed me. For one bright, shining moment, I felt whole and worthy.

Then the warm glow in Cora's eyes as I realized the act might have earned me a promotion from the friend zone. A hint of possibility glinted with her now, like a mirror winking in the sun. Hope flooded me. This was the chance I had been waiting for.

Giving the money away to the cook made me feel buoyant and filled with purpose. It was an act I did on a whim. If I'm brutally honest with myself, it *was* a spontaneous gesture, but it was also motivated by my desire to look better in Cora's eyes. But after I did it, man, what a high! I can't accurately describe the peaceful elation that filled me. It was an intense wave of pleasure and pride that I surfed onto a brand new shore. I wanted to feel that rush again. I *had* to.

There is a whole briefcase of money stuffed into the closet.

I have 37,211 more chances to feel that giddiness and joy.

Imagine how light I'll feel when it's empty, when all the loose ends are tied up.

In a life where every day of my first forty years was the same as the last, I finally had a chance to escape the mundane. It gave me something to look forward to. It gave me a purpose.

The Red Hot Chili Peppers started up in my head, a bizarre concert for one of their smash hit *Give it Away*, sung by the voices in my head.

Money is the root of all evil.

You can't take it with you.

Mo' Money Mo' Problems.

When it's gone it's gone.

It was a chorus of whispers and taunts, all building to the crescendo of truth. I had to give it all away. All of it. Every penny. Transferring it from the briefcase into the hands of strangers, people who deserved it more than I did. The idea filled me with effervescent giddiness. I bounced out of bed and swallowed a handful of ibuprofen. It was time to get this party started.

After breakfast with Ma, I strode into The Art Store and More with purpose. It was a second-generation, family-run business with a decent craft department. Short aisles with colorful squares of felt arranged in a tidy rainbow formation, pom poms, and pipe cleaners. Charcoal and oil pastels assembled like army soldiers in neat rows. During my first committal, I was begrudgingly introduced to art therapy. A therapist put a paintbrush in my hand, and since I had nothing to do but wait, I churned out some truly terrible paintings. Hours ticked by as I focused on painting at an easel, and when I was finally released, Ma would bring me here to wander the aisles. Faithfully clipping her in-store coupons to indulge this newfound "healthy" coping mechanism and dragging me to the free days at the Nelson-Atkins Museum of Art.

The anonymous artist Banksy was just hitting the art scene and quickly got my attention. I remember seeing his painting with the rat wearing a peace sign leaning against a picket sign that said, "Because I'm worthless." A hip-hop-style rat of NIMH, brave enough to say the words I couldn't. Seeing his painting was a revelation. I didn't know art could be so raw, so honest. I adored his pithy commentary on the absurd commercial lives we currently live. He's ballsy as hell and I respect that. Banksy doesn't ask for permission, he takes it. Paints what he wants, where he wants, and doesn't give a rip about anyone's feelings on the matter. Banksy is the man.

I wanted to adopt that mentality and incorporate it into my comedy. Less apologizing, more creative risks. I think Ma was relieved when I poured my creativity into comedy because notebooks were much cheaper to come by than canvases and paints. But the store was still one of my favorite places to waste time and people-watch. From the scene kids with bangs perpetually in their eyes, to the primped and perfect little princess girls with pigtails and bows, to the queer kids who expressed themselves fearlessly with rainbows and vibrant color. Quite the gamut of Kansas City's creative humanity could be found wandering the aisles.

Inspired, I loaded one of their red plastic baskets with packages of the largest googly eyes I could find. I cleared the store out, pulling them off the hook by the handful. I was walking down the paint aisle toward the registers when a little blonde waif of no more than twelve caught my eye. I know this sounds silly, but I feel energy from people. Physically feel it. Tommy called me a sap, a pathetic little girly man, but I can go to the funeral of a complete stranger, and the collective despair in the room will make me sob uncontrollably. It is like being tuned into a radio frequency only I can hear, the emotional wavelength of strangers' emotions broadcast through a loud speaker directly into my ear in high def.

Longing. Need. Sadness. Hopelessness.

She was emitting these emotions. They swirled into the air around her like a tornado, then collided with me. I couldn't avoid them if I wanted to. I watched her longingly pick up tube after tube of watercolors and oils, read the labels, her eyes crossing slightly, then sigh and discard them back in the display.

She was wearing jeans that were too short, her pink ankles peeking out under the tattered hems. Her gray, oversized hoodie fell mid-thigh, and dirty Converse tennis shoes were on her feet. I glanced around uncomfortably, looking to see if a parent was hovering close by. She wiped her face and started to bite her nails, as I studied her. She picked up a tube of paint and studied it, then looked around skittishly to see if anyone was watching. Her eyes locked on mine, and she jumped like she'd been burned and dropped the tube of paint on the ground. She dipped to the ground to scoop it up and hastily returned it to its proper place on the shelf, turning pink.

"Hey there." I asked gently, "Are you okay?"

She wiped her face with the back of her hand as she thrust her fingers back up to her mouth, chewing at nail beds that were already red and swollen.

"Are you lost?"

"No," she answered, spitting one of the fingernails from her mouth into the air. "I come here during the day when my mom is at work."

"Why are you so sad?"

"I miss my paints," she said simply as she reached out and dragged a finger across the tubes of pigment in the aisle, one by one, filled with wistful longing. The intensity of which panged my heart. Wistful longing was an emotion I understood intimately.

"What happened to them?"

"I had to leave them behind at my old house. We had to run away in the middle of the night. My mom only had room in the car for the important things, and we drove all night and ended up here. I'm the new kid at school again with no friends. Without painting, I feel lost."

"That sounds terrifying."

"This is my third do-over."

"Do-over?"

"It happens all the time. Mom falls in love, gets married, falls out of love, and we move," she recounted dully as a chunk of greasy blonde hair fell forward on her face. "I'm on my fourth dad," she explained, rubbing her eyes that suddenly seemed so old. The emotional exhaustion was wearing down the fire in her eyes until they were barely a smolder. This was a little girl who had seen some things, who had been dragged from one shitty situation into the next during her short life. She picked up a tube of Chinese red. "This was my favorite color," she offered.

I surveyed the colors until I found the chartreuse and pulled it out for her. "This is mine. Fancy people call it chartreuse, but I like to call it bright ass green."

My joke was rewarded with a quick upturn of the corners of her mouth. I got the feeling she didn't laugh or smile very much, and a shot of pain stabbed my heart.

"My second stepdad bought me a full set of paints and horsehair brushes, but I had to do things to get them."

Instantly, I felt sick. I knew exactly what *things* she was referring to.

"What's your name?" I asked.

"Bailey," she said shyly then looked down. "I'm not supposed to talk to strangers."

"I'm Freddie Angel," I answered then engulfed her tiny hand in my meaty one. "So, there you have it. We aren't strangers anymore." She nodded and looked back down at her shoes. "Well, Bailey, today is your lucky day."

Her eyes darted to mine, trying to decode what that statement meant.

"I'm somewhat of an art connoisseur."

"What's a connoisseur?" she asked, leaning in closer as she twirled a swatch of hair around her finger, around and around, a soothing gesture I recognized.

"Someone who really loves something," I explained and then continued, "I've recently come into some money, and I was thinking I would like to bankroll an aspiring artist. Do you happen to know anyone like that?"

She leaned in but eyed me suspiciously. "What would I need to do?"

"Absolutely nothing. Just pick out your paints and carry them to the cash register."

"Seriously?" she asked with the kind of stalwart wariness that only abused children display.

"Yes. Seriously. Now get started." I handed her a basket from the end cap on the aisle as she chose five of the smallest tubes of paint and a pad of watercolor paper. She showed me the basket shyly. "Is this okay?"

"Of course not," I chided with a crooked smile. "You know, Bailey, you're really bad at this," I teased, then grabbed the basket from her arm and added one tube of every color, a handful of brushes, and four more packages of paper to the basket. Her eyes widened, their pale blue irises dancing in a sea of white, getting swept into a liquid ocean of tears at her lashes as a hand clamped to her mouth. Filling the basket, I marched up to the cash register as she trailed behind me.

Seeing the googly eyes on the counter, she asked, "What do you need all those eyes for?"

I looked around and then whispered conspiratorially, "A very special, top-secret project."

One hundred and twenty-seven dollars and a Snickers bar later, I handed her the bag, and she followed me out of the store.

"Did you need help carrying this home?" I asked. "It's pretty heavy."

She was unsure and hesitated.

"I don't want to get you in trouble," I said, "but I *do* want to make sure you get home safe with all these supplies."

She considered it for a minute, biting on her bottom lip.

"You can trust me—I'm a certified Funologist."

"What's that?" she asked, intrigued.

"Well, it's my job to bring happiness and joy to as many people as I can."

"That's a real job?" She hugged her bag of paints to her chest like a newborn baby as we walked down the sidewalk.

"That sack is as big as you are," I said, watching her struggle with it. "Gimme that." I tucked my wrist into the handles, then ripped open the candy bar and broke it in half, handing her one of the pieces. She devoured it in two bites and then ducked across the street, leading the way. We paused in front of a stop sign, and I pulled out the biggest set of googly eyes from the bag and added them to it as she giggled.

"You see, Bailey, Funologists are tasked with a very important mission." I handed her a pair of eyes and said, "Do you think you can find a place to put these bad boys?"

Her eyes lit up, and she ran to the dumpster and added them to the brown metal box. I high-fived her when she came back to stand beside me, and we surveyed her work.

"You're a natural," I said. "Perfect placement. You are definitely Funologist material."

I pulled out another set and placed them over my eyes, stood next to the dumpster, and blindly pulled out my cell phone, holding it out for her. "Will you do the honors and take a photo for me? Make sure you get the dumpster in the background. Everyone needs to see your handiwork." I felt her pull the phone from my hand and replace it a few minutes later. Then I asked, "Do I have beautiful eyes?" She giggled, and then I peeled them off, along with most of my eyelashes, and handed them to Bailey who ran over to a tree and pressed the adhesive eyes onto the trunk.

I hash-tagged the photo #whoworeitbetter #thefunologist #freddieangelisthefunologist and posted it to all my social media profiles. All the way to her home, we left googly eyes in our wake. On the trunk of a car, on a realtor's face in an advertisement on the dirty back of a bus stop bench. We stopped at a gas station, and I was the lookout man as Bailey placed them on the milk jugs and ancient eggs sitting in cardboard cartons in the cooler. Every pair of eyes Bailey left behind made her laugh even more, and each giggle made her sound more like a child and less like a beaten-down pseudo woman. My heart lightened, and the mumbling in my mind vanished. For once, the voices were blissfully quiet.

She took a left-hand turn toward a set of beaten-up apartments that sunk into the ground. The kind of place where people went to start over in the middle of the night.

"This is it," she said as I handed her back the bag full of paints.

I held out a hand. "It was nice to meet you, Bailey. Now, you go paint something magnificent."

"Oh, I will!" she said. "I'm going to be a Funologist someday, just like you."

She turned toward the door, and at the last moment turned around and waved again at me. "Bye, Freddie Angel," she called out. "Thank you!" She climbed the two broken steps, then I watched her disappear into the dark apartment building.

Speechless, her appreciation stunned me. I was used to incompetence, of people being forced to take care of me. Gratitude coming from strangers was novel, and a foreign warm feeling pulsed through me, making me smile, then laugh, then almost burst into tears. I think it was joy.

TEN

The next morning, still on my high from helping out Bailey, I was at the grocery store standing in line at the checkout. I sat my gallon of milk and bag of waxy chocolate mini donuts on the metal divider to keep them from skidding down the belt and merging into the pile of groceries of the young family in front of me. Crisp-colored newsprint and glossy magazines sat stacked in rows—*People*, *The Star*, and *Us Weekly*.

"Finally, a Baby!" A yellow headline screamed with a photo of a glowing Gwen Stefani and Blake Shelton arm in arm. "After a secret struggle, Blake's lifetime dream is coming true!"

If only it were that easy.

The cynicism cued up, a judge in robes that presided over the pink folds and wiry synapses of my brain.

"Your sloth disgusts me, you dodgy wanker," the Queen condemned me from her post on the front page of the Star. The photograph morphed and swirled, coming to life in front of my clouded eyes. Fascinated, I watched the Queen wag her thick pointy finger tipped with yellowing fingernails at me

while she death-gripped her fat little corgi. *"Someone is a little nutter,"* I heard. Her index finger clocked in small circles outside her ear in the universal sign for crazy.

"Shut up," I mumbled to the Queen of England and smacked the side of my head.

"Stop being a lazy sod, Freddie. It is right time you grew a pair." She stared at me unamused over the top of her glasses.

I snorted. "I didn't realize Your Highness had taken such a shine to my balls," I replied.

"Dead from the neck up, I say!"

I stuck a finger in my ear and jiggled it to muffle the rest of her pithy English insults, closing my eyes to block out the visual stimulation. When visually overwhelmed, the voices always got louder. It's like having a built-in studio audience with an 80s sitcom laugh-track and a mob of mean girls cataloging and measuring each of your personal failures with glee. Whole conversations were always taking place inside me, a full-tilt cinematic experience for one, distracting me from my real life.

When I opened my eyes, a little boy in a puffy navy jacket with dirty mittens clipped to the cuffs was staring at me. His huge blue eyes were rimmed with thick lashes and staring at me unflinchingly. He broke away and focused on the boxes of candy bars deliberately shelved at his height, then eagerly grabbed a Hershey bar. "Mom, can I? Please?" he begged.

His sister was a toddler confined to the cart and being forcibly buckled in to stop her from escaping. "Put it back. We don't have enough money for that," his pretty but worn thin mom responded. When he didn't act immediately, she snapped her fingers at him until he put the bar in her outstretched palm. She shoved it haphazardly with one hand into the row of cardboard boxes before turning back to the cart.

She began to load her groceries onto the conveyor belt, rolling the cart back and forth a few inches with her foot to keep her daughter from fussing. Her anxiety and worry were a dark purple cloud I got sucked into, and my skin stretched tight and began to hum. Faster and faster, my internal world sped up, whirring and spinning.

She paused and turned to me. "I've got coupons and food stamps," she admitted apologetically as her head hung a little lower. "It will probably take a while. You might want to pick another lane."

"It's okay," I tried to reassure her. "I've got nothing *but* time." I pulled the previously discarded Hershey bar off the display and suddenly had the little boy's full attention.

"Sit down, sweetheart," she told her daughter, who had managed to free herself from the cart enough to stand on the seat. Shoving her daughter's thick thighs back into the cart, she worked faster to put things on the conveyor belt with one hand. When she was finished, she drummed her fingers on the edge of the belt, dispelling nervous energy.

In the cart, her dark-haired daughter began to wail. Fresh panic surged as she searched for distractions to placate her and quickly landed on the box of fruit snacks waiting to be scanned. She tore open the box, ripped open a package of fruit snacks, and handed it to the fussy little girl.

"You're not supposed to do that," the male clerk said, irritated. "You can't eat it until you own it. I could call the police."

"Sorry," the mom muttered as she visibly shrank and fixated on the digital screen of the credit card terminal, watching the total accumulating higher and higher. Each swipe made her fingers drum faster and faster. She bit her lip and began to shake as it climbed. Beep…Beep…Beep. Each one made her flinch as if it was physically painful. I could feel invisible fingers pressing on my Adam's apple. The razor-sharp tension passed from her to me, and I began to absorb it. I clawed at my throat; witnessing the transaction made me desperate for more air.

Finally, with the last of her groceries scanned, the balding clerk said, "One hundred and eighty-seven dollars." He pushed his thick glasses up the bridge of his nose with his middle finger, looking at me.

Did he just flip me off? Stop being paranoid, Freddie.

She swiped her benefits card, and it beeped in protest.

"You must have exhausted your benefits. The total is still one hundred and eighty-seven dollars." The clerk scratched his head, leaving red lines where his dirty fingernails trailed.

"It can't be." Her voice strained. "It was supposed to reload today." Flustered, she yanked out a credit card from her crackled leather purse and swiped it.

"It says declined," the clerk said. "Try another card."

"I don't have another card," the mother admitted, her gaze lingering on the milk, cereal, and bread that was on the belt while her daughter's tears transformed into a full-on wail that went unacknowledged. The mom was laser-focused, mentally calculating the cost of the items and ranking them from most to least necessary.

"I know," she said. "Shh, sweetheart." She struggled to pull her daughter free from the cart, yanking up in frustration at the scuffed tennis shoes that refused to untangle from the leg holes of the cart. The cart began to roll as the little girl cried, making her face redden and fat tears spill down her cheeks, her arms and legs flailing in protest, now in full-on meltdown mode.

I reached out to help steady the cart.

"Thanks, mister," the young mother said with a tight smile.

Finally free, she began to sway and jiggle her daughter as only mothers know instinctively how to do. Side to side, she shifted like an ocean wave while humming into her ear, her palm pressed against the baby's dark curls on the back of her soft head.

"I'm hungry," the little boy at her hip said and rubbed his eyes while she ignored him. "Mommy," he said louder and tugged on the bottom of her coat. "I'm so hungry."

Little cracks began to shatter and run across her, a network of hairline fissures disintegrating her patience and dissolving her into chaos. I heard a loud crack and then blinked, envisioning her imploding and dissolving into dust right in front of me.

"You WIC mothers are all the same," the clerk said, clearly annoyed. "Nothing but white trash, getting a hand out from the system." He spat the words at her. "And shut that kid up. This is a place of business, not a playground."

"Excuse me," I said loudly and pushed forward, inserting myself into the clerk's field of view. "I'd like to pay for these groceries, but I have to insist that you stop being a dick and treat this woman with the respect that motherhood deserves." I handed him the candy bar. "And add this to the bill." He scanned it then handed it back rudely, pushing it into my hand.

"Apologize to her," I demanded in a deep, authoritative voice that sounded foreign coming from me.

"C'mon, man. I didn't say anything you weren't already thinking."

"I assure you I was not."

He rolled his eyes again, refusing to give in to my demand.

"Apologize," I growled at him, "or I'm contacting corporate."

"Fine. Sorry," he blurted just to shut me up, then huffed and rolled his eyes.

It was insincere, but still a win, and I decided to drop it. I peeled off two hundred-dollar bills from the stack in my coat and handed them to the clerk as the mother's eyes swept up to meet mine. Hers were large and brimming with tears, mine bloodshot and blue. I passed the chocolate bar to her and then bent down to her son's level. "That's for you, but only after you have dinner." He smiled widely, revealing gaping holes in his mouth where his front teeth should be.

"Uh oh, looks like your mom needs a new boy! You're falling apart already!" Which made him giggle.

"No, I'm not!"

I straightened back up and smiled at her.

"Thank you," she said. "I'm having the worst day. I was up all night with Ella, she's teething and feverish. There's no food in the house. All our laundry is dirty. It's a mess, really." She burst into tears.

"What's your name?" I asked, trying to distract her with questions. I felt dreadfully inadequate when faced with the big emotions of most women.

"Molly," she said, sniffling.

"Well, Molly, being a mother is hard work." I smiled at her. "In my eyes, mothers are saints. I wouldn't be half the man I am today without my Ma."

"*Half the man?*" An ugly voice sneered in my head. "*You think you're actually half?*"

She smiled and wiped at her eyes.

"Actually, you're the one helping me out. I'm conducting a very serious social experiment," I offered in explanation.

"Rescuing single mothers who are about to snap?" She laughed as she threw herself under the bus.

"You'd be surprised how many of us are just barely holding it together." I smiled warmly at her as the whispering began again, and I pushed it further away.

"I'm Freddie Angel—the Funologist," I introduced. "You may have heard of me," I said, biting my tongue self-deprecatingly and jiggling my head from side to side. "I'm sure my reputation has greatly preceded itself." I pretended to toss my hair like I've seen Cher do in interviews, making those weird grunting noises she makes that I picked up from *Saturday Night Live* skits.

She laughed. "To be honest, if you haven't made a guest appearance on *Sesame Street* recently, I probably haven't."

"Can't say that I have, but I wouldn't turn it down. A fan is a fan, and besides, half my fans are shitting themselves already."

She laughed hard.

Win column. Check.

"Pardon my French," I added, indicating her son. "I don't have any kids and always forget there are little ears around. I've been told I'm an acquired taste." I tried to smile and explained, "Well, I won the lottery last week and decided to spread the joy to as many people as I can, and you, my dear, made the cut. Will you take a picture with me so I can post?"

"Sure." She pulled her daughter from the cart, and we both bent down with the kids and smiled as I pointed the camera at us for a selfie. I posted it to social media with the hashtags #thefunologist #freddieangelisthefunologist #singlemomsrock. Then I bagged her groceries for her and stacked them neatly back into the cart.

"Do you need help loading these into your car?" I offered.

Her eyes widened. "I couldn't ask you to do that, too.

You've already done so much." I looked at her daughter, who was falling asleep in her arms, and put my finger to my lips to quiet her.

"Looks like you have your hands full there," I whispered. "I'll just get these into the trunk while you get the kids in their car seats, and you can head home."

Her shoulders dropped and she nodded, relaxing for the first time. Following her out to the car, I pushed the cart and then jumped up on the bar between the front wheels and rode it, rolling down the parking lot with the cold wind slapping my face. The cart began to pick up speed, and I swerved it away as she opened the trunk of a rusted minivan. I circled the parking lot a second time, pumped my legs, and coasted to a stop by her trunk. Then I loaded her trunk full of groceries.

After the kids were settled in their car seats, she returned to me. "What's your name again? I'm sorry, I was so distracted."

"Freddie Angel, resident Funologist at your service," I said, shaking her hand and then bowing deeply. My back twinged, and I let out a little yelp. "Never get old, Molly. It's a bitch! No one tells you that you can hurt yourself just by rolling over in bed."

She laughed. "I'll have to remember that."

I pulled one more bill from my coat pocket and held it out for her. Stunned, she eyed me. After a long minute, she reached up to take it, and I held it tight.

"My only condition is that you spend this on yourself. A mani-pedi, a massage. Hell, buy yourself a dozen roses, woman, but nothing for the kids. You use this to take care of yourself."

She burst into tears as I placed the bill in her hand.

"Promise me," I prompted. "Be selfish for once, take care of Molly."

"I promise," she choked out and then flung her arms around my neck. I awkwardly clapped her on the back, the human contact teasing tears from my own eyes. I didn't realize how much I craved a hug until she planted one on me.

"Thank you, Freddie. You are an angel."

ELEVEN

The next evening, I strode into Krispy Kreme with a plastic grocery bag full of mayo squeeze bottles and marched up to the counter where a pimply-faced teenager with glasses stood wrapped in his beige polo shirt and paper hat. I glanced at his name tag. Kevin. He looked like a Kevin, probably a gamer desperately in need of a haircut and some Clearasil, the kind of guy who plays Dungeon and Dragons on the weekends with fellow dweebs at the comic book store.

My stomach rumbled with delight when the first waft of the sugary grease-laden air hit my nostrils. It was so loud it got weird, and the poor kid's eyes darted from side to side, trying to detect the source of the sound. "Whoa, big fella," I said, squeezing my pudge with my finger and thumb. "Looks like it might be feeding time at the zoo." Kevin's beady eyes crawled over to meet mine, unamused.

Lose column. Check.

There is nothing like an original Krispy Kreme donut, when you take that first bite into the glazed sugar shell, sinking your teeth into soft, pillowy dough. I can eat a dozen by myself, one right after the other, without any regrets.

"Can I help you?" he asked, bored as hell.

"I'd like a dozen original and a chocolate milk." He pulled a box of warm donuts out and set them on the counter as I paid with cash, leaving him a ten-dollar tip, just enough to get his attention.

"Now, Kevin, there could be more where that came from." His gaze rolled back to mine, slightly more interested now. "I was hoping you'd be able to sell me some Bismarcks without the filling."

"We don't have any of those left this late in the day."

I pointed to the neon hot now sign in the window that was lit up.

"That's only for original glazed."

I pulled my money clip out and held it on the counter. "Would Mr. Jackson be able to persuade you to make an exception?" I asked sweetly and licked my index finger before making a dramatic display of pulling a twenty from the stack and standing it on its edge on the glass case that separated us.

"Maybe." He eyed the cash, looking down at it greedily.

"How about his twin brother?" I pulled another twenty out and set it on the counter.

Then another one. "Triplets? Wow, Kevin, you drive a hard bargain."

He finally nodded, then walked to the cooler and then the fryer, where he plopped a dozen doughnuts onto the conveyor belt. In twenty minutes, they had completed the fryer and icing track and were cool enough to box up.

Ordering an Uber was an extravagance I could afford now, so I hopped in when it pulled up to the curb and headed downtown. My driver was an Indian man whose smiling badge printed and taped to the back of the seat identified him as Pradeep Anand. He turned and beamed at me. "I'm going to be your driver." Then he pointed to a small cooler on the floor behind the driver seat. "Help yourself to a bottle of water or fruit juice."

"That's very kind," I said. "Don't mind if I do." I pulled out a bottle of water. "How's the Uber gig?"

"It's good, but you live and die by your ratings." His accent was thick and his voice melodic as it lilted up and down. I had to strain to focus to understand what he was saying. "Anything less than five stars is the kiss of death. Even a four-star rating is not good enough and the app will make the bigger and better fares invisible to you."

"That's a tough gig," I commiserated. "Everyone's a critic and the most vocal ones are always the hardest to please." There was a faded photo of a woman holding a child taped to the dashboard. I leaned forward to study it more clearly. "Who's that?"

"My wife and my son," he said proudly. "I do this so Pranav will have more opportunities."

"What about you, Pradeep?" I asked. "Are you content to surrender your life for your son?"

"I believe you shouldn't bring a child into this world unless you are prepared to sacrifice." He looked at the photo fondly. "Pranav will be an aeronautical engineer someday, bouncing weightlessly at the international space station, and then he will return home to a ticker-tape parade and be wealthy enough to take care of his papa in his golden years." Pradeep recounted dreamily the detailed future he already curated for his young son, then laughed.

"I gotta give it to ya, that's one hell of a retirement plan," I said as guilt set in when I realized I was currently living the exact reverse of that with Ma.

He pulled up in front of The Punch Line. "Could I pay you to wait here while I fill these?"

"Certainly. Take all the time you need, but you must remember the meter is always running."

"Of course," I mumbled, then turned toward the box and ripped the plastic off the first mayo bottle, thrusting the tip into the donut. I squeezed until the Hellman's made the donut plump up pregnant, snickering to myself. I gingerly returned it to the box and continued to fill the donuts, one at a time, as Pradeep eyeballed me from the rear view mirror, befuddled. I left two donuts unfilled, one in each corner, and then shut the lid and fastened it together.

Pulling a twenty out of my money clip, I handed it to Pradeep.

"Thank you, thank you, dear friend." He pressed his palms together in a namaste gesture and bowed his head. I opened the door and stepped out into the cold air. "Make sure you rate me five stars!" he called out and I barely had enough time to shut the door as he drove off to his next fare. Turning, I walked into The Punch Line and set the box down on the sticky oak bar, waiting for Paulie to emerge from his office.

"Ooh! Krispy Kreme—my favorite!" Cora gushed when she landed in front of me. "Can I have one?" I opened the box, pulled one of the good ones out, and handed it to her. The other unfilled one, I was going to snag as a decoy when I saw Paulie striding toward me.

"Krispy Kreme?" Paulie exclaimed, eagerly eyeing the box.

"Correct-amundo, my man. I got your favorite—custard-filled." I waggled my eyebrows at him and proudly held open the box. "Take two, they're small." I carefully angled the box so the good donut was as far away from his reach as possible.

"Don't mind if I do," he said, reaching in and then thrusting the donut into his mouth, devouring half of it in one bite. His face crinkled a second later, his caterpillar eyebrows knit together, and he stopped chewing. Obvious confusion painted his features, but he powered through, continuing to chew, and finally swallowed. Transfixed, I watched his Adam's apple make the long journey from the top of his neck to the bottom, grinding my teeth together to stop myself from busting a gut. To my astonishment, he took another bite.

"So good, right?" I asked, pressing my lips together to stop the smile that threatened at the corners of my mouth. He stopped chewing and ran to the bathroom as I dissolved into a fit of giggles.

"Freddie… What did you do?" Cora asked in a school-marm tone.

"Nothing." But I refused to make eye contact.

"Spill it, mister."

"Okay, okay. There might have been a "special feature flavor" at Krispy Kreme today." I used air quotes with my fingers.

"Mine tasted fine," she said.

"The special was only for Paulie. They call it Mega Mayo."

"Oh, shit. You didn't." She laughed to herself.

Paulie came out of the bathroom finally, looking a little green and wiping his mouth with a bar rag.

"Eat one," he demanded.

"It's a delicacy, Paulie. Krispy Kreme is trying out a new savory doughnut line." I pulled the good one from the corner of the box.

"No. This one." He pulled another one out that was bursting with Hellman's, and my stomach soured.

"Yum!" I said out loud, trying to psych myself up to eat it. I took a big bite and fought through swallowing it because I knew if I was unable to complete this one simple task, my days were numbered at The Punch Line. Mayo squirted out onto my chin, but I swallowed like a trophy wife after a visit to the jewelry store. It took everything in me not to go running to the bathroom. Cora placed a well-timed sympathy orange juice in my hand that I gulped down, anything to kill the greasy aftertaste in my mouth.

"I'm going to reshuffle the order tonight, Freddie. Since you're so funny today, you can start us off."

"Come on, Paulie," I begged. First up was the worst spot in the line-up. It was before the drinks were really flowing and was peppered with hard, uncomfortable silences to fight through. The laughs were harder to come by since the stink of the workday was still clinging to our patrons. People came for happy hour to forget about real life for a while and to avoid going home to their families. It was a tough crowd and one that I thought I had earned my way out of.

"It was just a joke. Can't you take a joke?" I asked. "This is a comedy club, for Christ's sake."

"Then I suggest you get up there and tell some jokes." He strode away onto the stage to announce me.

"Hey there, ladies and gentleman, I'd like to welcome you to the Punch Line. Tonight, we've got three great comedians for you, or I should say two great comedians and a half-wit. You might know him as our resident Funolgist, the man that puts the "un" in fun, Freddie…. Angellllll."

He threw the microphone at me with a glare and stomped away.

"Thank you for that warm, heartfelt introduction, Paulie," I said out of spite to the smattering of applause from three of the four people in the audience.

"So, I may have inadvertently earned a spot in the dog house at work." I started in, hoping to use my stage time to apologize and get back into Paulie's good graces. "I know it's hard to believe, but sometimes when the little angel and the little devil on my shoulders duke it out, the devil wins." I paused. "Today, the little devil told me to head over to Krispy Kreme and fill the donuts with mayonnaise and then offer a couple to my boss."

Small chuckles swept through the sparse audience. "Yeah. Sounded like a great idea at the time, so I pulled the trigger. Then the angel piped in and said, 'Hey, dumbass, that's the guy who writes your checks.'" I let that sink in. "My angel can be a little salty." I paused again. "I thought I was going to get through the experience unscathed. But alas, the devil had other plans. I was also forced to partake in this pastry delicacy." I looked out into the audience. "Are there any doctors in the house? Because it is highly likely that I will have a major cardiac event right here, in the next sixty minutes, after consuming that much grease and mayonnaise. If you listen carefully, you can actually hear my arteries hardening in real-time." I paused and tipped the microphone toward my heart, then cupped it with my closed hand and continued in a serious, documentary tone. "The test subject has displayed a significant decrease in blood volume. Blood is forced to pump through its constipated veins, straining and struggling like it has been ingesting a diet of only cheese." I looked up into the light. "Who thinks Paulie should forgive me?" There was tepid applause. "Come up here, buddy. Let's hug it out."

"No, you dick," he shouted back, a hint of amusement tinging the insult, filling me with relief.

"I see you're going to play hard to get." I sashayed across the stage. "Challenge accepted." The audience snickered.

"Speaking of bad food choices," I pivoted to the next topic. "I love my mom, but she is a terrible cook." A middle-aged woman in the front row let out a whoop. "Oh, I hear someone else may have shared a similar fate as a child. My condolences, ma'am." I paused then continued, "Ma is a black belt penny-pincher. On Sunday mornings when I was a kid, she would scour the Kansas City Star for double coupon opportunities. Ma was a true pioneer. She was extreme couponing before it was a thing." I paused with a smile, thinking about Ma. "The woman would spend hours scouting out the best deals in the metro, then take an hour to arrange her coupon caddy, a thick Velcro wallet that made any cashier shiver in horror when she pulled it out and ripped it open.

"You know what you'll never find a coupon for? Ribeye… Lobster… Caviar." I looked down at my foot with a smile.

"She served me up some questionable meat products over the years. Mostly gristle. You know the toughest cuts of meat that get stuck in your teeth? It's like she went to the meat counter and said to the butcher who was busy cleaning up the discarded fat and gristle from cutting the steaks, chops, and ground beef for their real customers. 'You're not just going to throw that away, are you? It's so wasteful. Scoop it into a pile and I'll give you forty cents a pound,' and if it was a special occasion like my birthday, she might ask him to add a handful of hamburger. 'I can feed that to Freddie, he'll eat anything.'

"It wasn't until I got older that I realized that there were other meat products available. *Delicious* meat products that you could actually chew. With your *teeth*." I paused and heard a faint chuckle. "I was like Aladdin, in a whole new world. I vividly remember sitting at the table at a friend's house, eating roast beef for the first time. It was tender and delicious and it baffled me. I was so used to breaking out the machete required to cut the meat Ma made. Or having to chew each bite ten thousand times like some kind of meat-flavored bubble yum.

"She used to make this culinary delight that I called the Bucket of Fuck," I said to sparse laughter. "It changed constantly but consisted of whatever was leftover in our fridge, plus whatever canned goods she picked up at the dented can sale. Corn, beans, tomatoes, okra. Are you writing this recipe down?" I asked with a grin as I paused. "You're going to want to because it *is* as good as it sounds." I rubbed my soft belly affectionately. "Yummy in my tumbly." The crowd giggled. "I'd pick up a spoon, scoop up a huge bite of it, and say lovingly to the corn, 'This isn't goodbye, old friend… it's see you later.'" The two men in the audience laughed. "Then I'd plug my nose and swallow spoonful after spoonful of it until it was gone." I mimed the act, pinching my nose shut with the hand holding the microphone and then scooping as fast as possible. "I have no idea if that helped kill the taste or not, but it felt like it might. I had to do something. I had to take my power back." I let the silence linger. "I'd love to bring Gordon Ramsey home for dinner. I'd serve him up a nice big bowl of that and then wait." I brought my hands to my face and strummed my fingers across my cheeks.

I shifted my voice to a terrible British accent. "Dottie, you seriously have surprised me," I said as I straightened to a ramrod-straight posture. "Ma would be nearly teary-eyed from the compliment from a chef as accomplished as Ramsey." I switched back to the accent. "…with how truly inedible this is." I spat out in disgust, "This isn't fit for my dog."

I walked two steps across the stage and waited. "I wish I could go through my life like he does, doling out the truth bombs, don't you? It would be so freeing."

"If your girlfriend ever asks, 'Does this outfit make me look fat?' No, your arse does. ."I welcome it, the brutal honesty." I continued on with my set and wrapped up ten minutes later. Then I returned to my perch in the back bar, waiting for Cora to come by with a medicinal screwdriver.

"How's Paulie?" I asked tentatively. "Am I still in the doghouse?"

"He's pretty pissed," she confirmed.

"Agreeably, not my smartest decision, but you have to admit it was hilarious," I stated and hoisted the cold, sweating glass to my lips. "He'll get over it, eventually."

"Pulling pranks on your boss is never a good idea," she offered.

"You're probably right, I just never seem to be able to get out of my own way." I held up the glass wryly in a mock toast to her. "It's a gift." With nothing left to lose, I turned to her and said, "Soooo," drawing out the word, trying to shore up my confidence before I plunged into the question I had been dying to ask her all night, "are you doing anything tomorrow night?"

She pursed her lips together to consider the question, and I focused again on that sexy cupid's bow. I was so sure her lips were forming into a no, that I was stunned speechless when she flipped the script on me and I heard the word "Yes" come out of her mouth.

"Really?" I asked, a smile breaking out across my face and fading my recent disappointing set and missteps with Paulie into oblivion.

"Yeah. I think I'd be up for that. Text me the details." She turned away to serve the line that was quickly forming at the bar as it got busier, and a burst of joy shot through me. Fizzling up like a bottle of pop that was shaken up. My night just got exponentially better.

TWELVE

The next night, I took a shower, swirling the shampoo around my hair counterclockwise fifty strokes. Then I rinsed for a count of one hundred. Then fifty more counterclockwise strokes and another rinse for a count of one hundred. I dried off and then pulled on the last remaining semi-clean clothes I owned and spent the next two hours on laundry. Smelling good was part of the Freddie Angel Deluxe Dating Package.

Mom watched me with a knowing smile.

"Do you have plans this evening?" she asked.

"As a matter of fact, I do," I answered sunnily, flashing her a big smile.

"With a woman?"

"Yeah, Ma, a *real* woman actually agreed to go out with me," I deadpanned.

"That's not what I meant, silly boy," she tried to explain and gave up quickly. "Where are you taking her?"

"Steak and Shake," I answered, my mouth already watering, dreaming of the chili fries and steak burger I would consume before the night was over.

"You should put on some of your father's cologne." She walked into her bedroom and retrieved an ancient bottle of Stetson. She opened it and handed it to me. The strong scent rankled and nauseated my stomach.

"No, Ma, soap is where it's at." I pushed away her hand that held the offensive cologne. Stetson was the scent of fear and domination that permeated every moment of my childhood. I couldn't stand it.

"Don't you want to woo her?"

"I love you, Ma, but I'm pretty sure smelling like a seventy-year-old man isn't going to be quite the panty dropper you think it is."

"Oh, Freddie," she admonished me. "You always love to say things to get my goat, don't you?"

"I've gotten your goat so much, I'm pretty sure you own an Indian Restaurant."

She rolled her eyes and smiled despite herself.

"She's here," I said, looking down at my phone.

"Have a great time, sweetheart. Remember to be a gentleman," she advised as I hugged her and kissed her satiny soft cheek.

"Thanks, Ma." I slipped out the backdoor, gulping in huge breaths of air to clear the scent of Stetson from my lungs. It was lodged so deep I could taste it. I spit onto the sidewalk that lined the side of the house where Cora couldn't see, trying to clear it out. Then I took a little nip of peppermint schnapps that filled the flask in my coat pocket, wiping my mouth with the back of my hand as I turned the corner.

Smiling, I pulled open the groaning door of her ancient burgundy Buick. She kicked the empty burger wrappers on the floor to the side.

"Sorry!" she apologized. "It might look like I live in here because I do." She snorted at her own joke, and I was instantly flooded with warmth. "Where to, Buckaroo?" she sang out with a smile.

"I was thinking Steak and Shake on 11th and Grande?" I offered with a wary smile, praying it was good enough.

"Perfect! A man after my own heart!" she gushed.

You're right. I am after your heart.

She eased us down the pothole encrusted streets, the Buick a smooth, buttery ride. Then she turned on the radio and sang boldly off-key, the worst rendition of *Enter Sandman* I had ever heard in my entire life. Being in the "entertainment industry," I have been fortunate enough to be exposed to many painful karaoke versions of *Enter Sandman*. It was so off-putting and pitchy, I practically heard packs of wild dogs howling in the vicinity.

"Terrible, right?" She winked at me with a grin that just melted me more.

"The worst," I agreed, taking the opportunity to stare at her longer, knowing she was preoccupied with driving as my heart hammered in my chest. My fingers instinctively inched closer, waiting for the right moment to wrap around hers.

"Hey, you gotta be number one at something," she threw back. I studied a silver snake piercing that hugged the top of her ear as she pulled us into a parking space, and then we headed to the door.

"Be a gentleman."

I heard Ma's voice in my ear and rushed in front of her to open the door, almost smacking her in the forehead with it. She ducked her head back with another giggle-snort to avoid the potential concussion.

"Dumb ass," I heard a man say, and I ground down on my teeth.

Inside, Steak and Shake was hopping with only one beleaguered full-figured waitress in sight, running the entire front of the house. A baby was crying and patrons were shoveling spoonfuls of vegetable beef soup into their mouths. I was grateful for the noise to drown out the internal tug of war that was happening.

"Seat yourself!" she yelled over her shoulder at us as she sailed by with a platter laden with fries and burgers that made my mouth water.

I escorted Cora to the only booth left and tried to smile at her.

"*Say something, dummy*," a man's voice hissed deep in my ear. I feverishly scanned my brain for topics that would sound somewhat intelligent and came up empty. Thankfully, before it got too awkward, our waitress landed at the table and flopped down two enormous laminated menus.

"I'm Shelby, I'll be taking care of you," she said as she removed the pen from behind her ear and stood poised with her order pad. A minuscule diamond chip winked from its resting place on her ring finger. "Sorry for the wait. We are slammed today, and two waitresses called in sick, so you're stuck with me." She smiled a weary smile and pulled a grimace as she looked around. "Come to think of it, this *entire* restaurant is stuck with me." Her sentence ended with a single abrupt, "Ha! You poor bastards," she teased with a smirk that revealed one dimple in her cheek.

"Hi, Shelby," I said, trying to put her at ease. "I'll have a chocolate shake to start, extra whip. And for the lady?" I asked Cora, who licked her lips and nodded eagerly, an act that flushed blood to my face. Tongue-tied and taking a full second to recover, I finally added, "Make that two."

"Easy enough," she said and ran away.

"Man, Shelby has got her work cut out for her tonight," Cora admitted, surveying the packed restaurant. The man at the table next to us raised his empty glass in the air and shook it impatiently. The ice rumbled as it slammed back and forth against the polystyrene glass.

"Who do you gotta bang to get a refill around here?" he shouted obnoxiously, making mothers with small children within earshot visibly cringe.

His question was ignored, which just made him shake it more violently.

Cora shook her head in disgust then stood. "Me. You gotta bang me," she answered and strode to his table, yanking his glass out of his outstretched hand, then walked it behind the counter where the fountain drink machine sat. She pressed it against the Coke lever and waited as it filled, walked it over to the man, and plopped it down in front of him.

"There," she shot at him. "Are you happy now?"

"But it was supposed to be rootbeer!" the man said angrily.

"It's wet, isn't it?" Cora asked. "Dude, you get what you get, and you don't throw a fit." It was enough to shut him up, and she returned to our table triumphantly where she punctuated her victory with a small bow.

I laughed at her antics, adding a slow clap. "That was quite a show. You've got some balls."

"Big ones," she interjected.

"Is there any other kind worth having?" I asked.

Shelby came back to the table with our shakes. "Thanks for doing that. I've been running around here like a circus monkey on crack, but there's only one of me and twenty of them." She pulled out her pad again. "Are you ready to order?"

"Two steakburger deluxes with one order of fries and one order of…"

"Onion rings," Cora finished for me. "So we can share."

I grabbed my heart dramatically, getting a little emotional

from her answer. "You complete me," I said, making a cheesy heart shape with my thumb and fingers.

"Well, you had me at hello," she answered with a wink and slurped on her shake.

"Tell me more," I said as I blinked at her beguilingly, batting my pale eyelashes, tucking my chin into my shoulder. My ultra-feminine pose made her laugh—the deep throaty laugh I'd do nearly anything to hear. "I want to know everything there is to know about you."

"I've never met anyone like you," she admitted softly.

"You're gonna have to give me more than that, darlin'," I drawled, trying to deflect the intensity of my desire for a complete explanation. "I can't tell if that is a good thing or a bad thing."

"It's a good thing," she confirmed, and inside me one tight knot untangled and I could breathe more deeply.

Shelby practically skated around the dining room, taking care of customers, and the tables started to clear one by one. Our burgers arrived later than normal, but it didn't matter. Sitting in a booth with Cora's undivided attention was captivating. I would have willingly sat there starving for days.

"Sorry for the delay," an exhausted Shelby finally said when she set the platters of burgers, fries, and onion rings in front of us.

"No worries, doll," I assured her. "We're not in a rush." Her eyes were exhausted when they met mine. "You have to be worn out," I commiserated with her. She surprised me by sitting down in the booth next to me.

"You know it! Geesh! My dogs are barking! This is the first time I have sat down all night." She sighed with a smile and then a puzzled expression swept into her face. "You look really familiar." She squinted her eyes at me and tilted her head, trying to pinpoint the reason for her deja vu.

I straightened, pretending to adjust a bow tie and preen myself. "Then you must spend a lot of time at the Kansas State Correctional Center."

She chuckled. "Now I remember! You're the Funologist!" she blurted, snapping her fingers. "Freddie… something."

"Freddie Angel," Cora finished for her in a sweet, slightly starstruck way that made me tingle with pride.

"Yes!" Shelby exclaimed. "I saw you a few weeks ago at the Punch Line. You were hilarious. Those bits about your mom? I almost peed."

Occasionally, I would get a double glance from people when I was at Walmart buying eggs or running into the gas station. But this was the first time someone recognized me in public, and it humbled me.

"You know, Shelby, the pee-o-meter truly is the most accurate scientific method of comedic prowess," I said with a smile and pressed my hand to my heart.

"Someday, when you're a guest on *Jimmy Bravo*, I'll get to say, 'I knew him way back when.'"

Jimmy Bravo was the holy grail of late night. A pie-in-the-sky dream for any comedian if there ever was one. A true career launcher.

"You're too kind," I said as she left to go seat another group that had gathered in front of the hostess station.

"Look at you! I didn't know I was having dinner with a celebrity." Cora reached across the table to shove my shoulder.

A twinge of disappointment tightened in my chest. I didn't realize until right then how much I wished she'd used the word date. I tried to play it off, scanning for a quick self-deprecating joke I could spit out to soften the silence, but came up empty.

A few painfully silent moments later, Shelby dropped off

the leather pouch with our bill that came to twenty-seven dollars. I winked at the waitress and asked, "Let me guess. Just the tip?" and all the exhaustion wiped clean from her face as it lit up with a huge smile.

"You know it," Shelby said.

I scooped it up, having to tear it away from Cora's quick hands.

"Let me at least pay for half," she begged.

"Your money is no good here, woman! I'm a recognized celebrity now. Paying for my entourage comes with the territory."

"I'm in your entourage now?" she asked. "I thought I would have to prove my loyalty with more feats of physical agility and strength."

A sting of pain stabbed my heart as I recalled the little boy in the garage holding the barbell above his head, and I worked to brush it away. "*I'm going to make a man out of you*," Dad's voice hissed, and I had to focus to push it to the back of my brain.

"Nah," I said with a forced smile. "You're in."

She excused herself to go to the bathroom.

I signed the bill with a flourish, then pulled out the money clip and counted out ten beautiful Benjamins. The giddy thrill rushed up my throat as I wrote the hashtags on the bottom and took a photo for my own viewing pleasure, tucking the warm memory away for when the voices came calling.

"*Look at the big man, throwing his money around like a big shot*," Dad hissed again, deep in my mind.

"Shut up," I said out loud and pressed my hands to my ears, grateful for the distraction when Cora walked out of the bathroom and drove me home. I focused on her profile as she steered us down the streets. The desire built within me to feel the softness of her lips with the pad of my thumb, and I wanted to trace the planes of her pixie-like face with my fingers. She pulled up to the house, unfastened her seatbelt, and turned toward me. My stomach flipped and churned as a thrill shot up my torso.

The kiss.

This was usually the point where dates went horribly wrong for me. Where, in my awkwardness, I accidentally head-butted my date. Or when I went in for a smooch and she offered up her cheek, delivering me to my typical friend-zoned fate.

"I had a great time," I started in, trying to fill the silence with words and feeling heat crawling up my neck and resting in my cheekbones. The sudden shyness made me freeze and dampened the words to almost a whisper.

"I did, too," she said shyly as she leaned closer to me, waving me in like an airplane on the tarmac. It thawed me enough to meet her halfway, and even with my *Steak and Shake* onion ring breath, it was still the single best kiss of my entire life.

THIRTEEN

I slept deeply for the first time in two weeks without needing the entire fifth of vodka that was far past becoming a bad habit. Visions of Cora's creamy white skin, feeling her lips pressing on mine gave me morning wood so hard even Paul Bunyon's ax couldn't cut through it. I laid in bed reliving the best evening I'd had in a long time and pondered one of life's most challenging questions.

When is the best time to text after a great date? Should I call instead?

My witty banter definitely held up a lot better when I had time to consider each word more carefully. Being put on the spot with an actual conversation made it too easy to put my foot in my mouth. It was much safer to text. Quickly, the worries and anxieties over the next step made my erection disappear, and I was able to take a piss. I hummed to myself, making long loopy circles in the air as I peed. Nothing could kill my buoyant mood.

Searching for my phone, I craned my neck, detecting the faint sound of it vibrating. Then it started in again, and again.

"What in the hell?" I asked out loud. Rifling through the

clutter on my bed and nightstand, playing hot and cold with it as it hummed louder and louder, I finally discovered its hiding place, sitting aloft on the pile of dirty clothes in a hamper.

I tapped the home screen that was completely filled with notifications. Scrolling down them with my index finger, they went on and on as the phone continued to blow up and vibrate even more. I was confused as all get out, trying to put the pieces together. Instagram, Facebook, Twitter. Follows, likes, tags, shares. Something was blowing up on social, and I needed to find out what the hell it was.

Four texts from Cora were mixed in with the Instagram notifications and Facebook tags. I opened Facebook and tapped on a post I was tagged in. The cause of the ruckus was Shelby Witaker posting a photo of my receipt last night from Steak and Shake.

"The Funologist left me 'just the tip'! I had the pleasure of serving Freddie Angel and his lovely date at work last night. What he doesn't know is that I was going to be evicted from my apartment. Medical bills were piling up for my son's breathing treatments, and we were days away from being homeless. Freddie Angel worked a miracle for my family. Thank you, Freddie! Go catch his set at The Punch Line."

Little bursts in my chest filled me with happiness, like champagne bubbling up, effervescent and light. The post was going viral, shared over a hundred thousand times in less than eleven hours. Two-hundred and forty-two comments, likes, and shout-outs. Thousands of new followers on Instagram.

It was a virtual love fest, and I read through every single comment, savoring them all one at a time as I feasted on the praise. I basked in the glow of adoration from complete strangers.

They love me. They really love me.

I opened up Instagram and was stunned to learn I'd gained nine thousand followers overnight. New Facebook fans took my page from 225 likes to over two thousand. It was pure insanity. The phone in my hand vibrated with a call coming in. Seeing Cora's name pop up made my heart hammer and my mouth dry up.

"Well, damn, Freddie, now you *are* a real celebrity." She laughed into the phone. "I can't believe you didn't tell me you left a tip like that. You hear about this kind of thing happening, but never to someone you know."

"It was supposed to be a secret."

"Welp, I'd say the cat is *definitely* out of the bag."

"I guess it is," I confirmed, her excitement making me gain new confidence. I rode the wave of it and boldly stated, "I had such a great time with you last night." But the shyness dropped my voice an octave lower and made me hesitate for a brief second before saying, "I was hoping you would want to do it again."

"Do it again? Isn't that the very textbook definition of insanity?" Her musical laugh tickled my ear. Out of all the people I entertained, Cora was the only one that mattered. "Are you kidding? To have the undivided attention of *the* Freddie Angel? Sign me up!"

"I admire your enthusiasm! We'll make a real plan tonight at the club."

"You got it!" she said and hung up the phone.

I wandered through the fresh messages that were rolling in nearly every thirty seconds. "Set up a Venmo account!"

"The world needs more Funologists" "God bless you, Freddie Angel." I thought Ma would be especially pleased with that one.

Win column. Check. Check. Check.

I strolled over to Venmo and created an account with the code @thefunologist. I had no plan, no idea what I was doing. I just did it.

Give the people what they want.

I posted the handle to the new Venmo account on the viral post of Shelby's, and you could have knocked me over with a feather when, within two minutes, I got a notification that a payment of $50 was added to the account. A minute later, another $25.

The instant gratification sent me running up the stairs two at a time. "Ma!" I said, shouting for her. "Ma!"

"What on earth is going on, Freddie? Is the house on fire?" Washing dishes at the sink, she was dressed in another house dress and tattered slippers. She spun toward me, sending clumps of tiny bubbles flying from her rubber gloves.

"You're never going to believe this! Something amazing has happened." I pulled her gloved hand from the sink and peeled the plastic orange gloves off, discarding them on the countertop. Astonished, she broke out into a smile as I twirled her toward me, something I hadn't done in years.

Ma loved to dance. When I was really little, and Dad wasn't such a dick, he would take her out on the town one Friday night a month, and she would get to go dancing. She'd come home afterward and tuck me in, and I would pretend to be sleeping while she brushed my hair from my forehead and kissed my cheek, still humming one of the Sinatra ballads she loved so much.

I know it sounds lame, but Ma taught me how to dance in the living room before my first boy-girl dance in junior high school. I was literally forced to participate in one of those cheesy *Footloose*-inspired awkward montages. I'd never admit it to her, but my opportunities to put that knowledge into practice were few and far between. The only gal I got to twirl around the floor up to this point was Ma.

She laughed as I spun her around, humming "Strangers in the Night" in my goofy Sinatra-inspired baritone, and then reeled her back into my arms as we both rocked side to side.

"What has come over you?" she asked, her cheeks pink and her eyes lively. "I can't remember the last time I saw you this excited about anything."

I took the phone out of my pocket that had not stopped vibrating, opened the Facebook post, and gave it to her to read. Her jaw dropped and her eyes widened as she scrolled through each post one by one. "Oh, my word." She read and read, her smile getting bigger with each message.

"And look at this!" I showed her the new Venmo account that I was shocked to see had been filled with nearly two thousand dollars in only ten minutes.

"Wow. Freddie, I can't believe it. What are you going to do with all that money?"

"I was thinking I could continue the Funologist movement. Find more people who need a helping hand, people that truly deserve it."

"You have such a beautiful heart."

"I just know what it's like to get kicked in the teeth. It's happened to me a time or two."

"I know, sweetheart." She handed me back the phone. "That's admirable."

I read a few more messages, stunned at the outpouring of love. "I'm going to make it my mission to spread this money and love out to deserving people as far and as wide as I can!" I found another gushing comment and tipped the phone to her. "Did you see this? Steven Miller said, "God Bless you, Freddie Angel." Mom reached out and cradled my face in her hands.

"I always knew you were destined for great things!"

"You were the only one!" I joked and hugged her tight. She was tiny in my arms. I closed my eyes and savored her words dancing in my childhood kitchen with my biggest fan. Sucking it in deeply, I let the feeling wash over me and coat me with a peace and joy that I had never known.

This was living. This was why I was put here. This was a life full of purpose and passion. It had taken me forty years to find my place in this world, but I finally had, and that revelation made me feel so worthy and so loved that the wetness coursing down my cheeks didn't register at first.

Tears of joy.

That's what people called them. Tears of joy, and it was the first time I had ever cried them in my entire life.

You can love life again... all of it.

FOURTEEN

Ten thousand.
Then twelve.
Then sixteen.

The notifications were rolling in so fast and furious that I could almost dance to the music of the ringtone. I was in such high spirits that when Tommy called that after-noon, I answered on the first ring. When I realized who it was, there wasn't the heart-plummeting dread I usually experienced.

"Fritzy, look at you. A star," Tommy said condescendingly. "You must think you're hot shit now."

"Well, I'm definitely not cold shit!" I quipped. "Thank you, Seattle. I'll be here all week."

"Your comedy still blows goats." He resorted to immediate insults and chortled into the phone an obnoxious sound that was like fingernails on a chalkboard for me.

"Did you need something?" I blurted, cutting him off. "I've got a big day." I snapped my fingers impatiently. "Time is money and money is time, and right now, you are costing me both, son," I demanded, irritated, wanting him to get to the point of this phone call. I jiggled my leg up and down and then got to my feet and paced in my bedroom.

"We need to sign some paperwork to get Mom on the waiting list for Golden Oaks."

"If Ma wants to go, I will support her decision," I said diplomatically. Now that I had options and could survive without relying on Ma, it was an easier transition to support. I felt a pinprick of guilt stab the back of my neck at that admission.

"Wow. Put a little money in your pocket, and even a blind dog can find a bone," Tommy chimed in, then quickly changed tacks, "Hey, bro, I need to ask you for a favor."

Bro? Really? Puke.

My anger prickled up at the word. "What? A favor? Why does King Crossfit need a favor from poor little me?" The money was making me ballsy, giving me the confidence to say things I never would have had the guts to say before.

"Listen here, dickwad, I've helped bail you out more than once," he sneered. "I only need a couple thou." He hesitated for a moment then continued sheepishly, "I may have gotten myself into a little bind."

"You? The golden child?" I feigned shock unabashedly, rubbing it in. "Mr. Perfect. With the perfect life and perfect family?" I yanked the silver spoon out of his mouth and was taking delight in eating up his discomfort with it.

"Please," he pleaded quietly. His voice took on a begging quality that was so personally gratifying I almost came in my jeans.

"That's rich," I said. "Now you come to me with your hat in your hand, and I'm supposed to just bend over and let you take what you want?" I gripped the phone in my hand and continued, "If you'd have just once been supportive of my career, it would be a different story. I'd love to help you, but I can't. The Funologist has one cardinal rule. Only help deserving people," I spit into the phone, surveying my new kingdom boldly from my high horse. "And I am sorry to say that you do not qualify. Have a great day, Tommy." I punched the red button to end the call and tucked the phone back into my pocket.

I victory-punched the air. Double jab, uppercut, and roundhouse. Dancing around my mattress on the balls of my feet amongst the piles of dirty laundry and damp towels like a boxer in the ring.

Float like a butterfly.

I was unstoppable.

If Tommy was here, I would have dropped him like a rock.

FIFTEEN

The high from my interaction with Tommy surged through me all day. I was on fire with energy to burn. I peeled off all my clothes, down to a wife beater and my skivvies, and started another mammoth run on laundry. Most of it was already clean, but to be sure, I laundered it again. Then I pulled everything out of the closet and scrubbed the floor on my hands and knees. Hunkered down, my ass in the air, I enjoyed the cool concrete on my shins. My face was inches away from the floor as I scoured with an old rag from the bucket next to me. The smell of pine-sol stung my nostrils.

"That's the power of Pine-sol, baby!" a voice screeched in my ears, making me laugh.

I found an old toothbrush, and in the corner of the closet began to scrub the filthy track between the trim and the floor. Scrub, scrub, scrub. The water turned gray as I pressed harder and harder. It was vigorous work that made me sweat. I wiped it away with the back of my forearm and kept going.

Scrub, scrub, scrub! That's the power of Pine-sol, baby.

The catchphrase looped over and over in my mind on

repeat. I heard a weak ding and tossed the toothbrush back into the bucket, then raced up the steps to the dryer. Scooping up my third load of clean laundry, I walked it downstairs and threw it onto the mattress. I folded each t-shirt and each pair of jeans into obsessively perfect piles. When my stack of t-shirts was transformed into a tight column of perfectly symmetrical squares, I stacked them into the freshly cleaned closet one at a time. Walk to the bed, pick up a shirt with two hands, walk to the closet, line up the shirt on the pile. Repeat.

Normies would consider this a waste of effort and energy, to which I would argue that it is the only way to complete the task correctly, allowing me to move onto the next one unfettered by crippling anxiety.

Finally, at six in the evening, instead of taking the bus, with energy surging, I started a light jog to The Punch Line.

Why don't I jog more? Jogging is good for you. I want to do things that are good for me. Why don't I jog more?

I ran and ran, my lungs on fire, adrenaline coursing through me, finally rounding the corner by the club when the most delicious smell hit my nostrils. Out of breath, I stopped on the sidewalk, my hands clutching my knees and massaging the side ache that began two blocks prior as I gasped for breath.

Yum. The scent of fried chicken filled the air—and it was making my mouth water. The Chicken Coop was a downtown dinner staple across the street from The Punch Line.

You can be the Chicky Sandy Genie! That will make them love you!

So, I bellied up to the greasy counter where I ordered twenty original chicken sandwiches and twenty bottles of water. I took a quick photo and added the hashtags #thefunologist, #freddieangelisthefunologist, and #thefunologiststrikesagain and posted it to my social media profiles. Immediately, the now-familiar chorus of vibrations cued up, each little notification injecting a burst of dopamine that bubbled to the top and sent me flying. I picked up the bags of food and exploded through the door.

I should have a cape. I wonder where I can get a cape? What color cape should the Funologist wear? Blue? Purple? Yellow?

The cold air cooled me off as I picked my way down the dirty sidewalks. Every year, it seemed like more folks who were down on their luck gathered in the doorways of the shops downtown after closing time to seek shelter. The homeless were multiplying, and so many times I bolted by without making eye contact, afraid of any interaction. Terrified their reality would somehow rub off on me, knowing I was only one step removed from being homeless myself. Living in Mom's basement wasn't a dream, but it also gave me three hots and a cot. More than most of these people had in years.

I spread my arms like an airplane and ran down the sidewalk with the bags in hand, landing in front of three older men tucked into a doorway with a skinny dog. They were wearing layers of grungy clothing and lying on a shabby blue blanket next to an old cart of "treasures" overflowing with empty pop cans and folded-up tarps. My nose rankled as the combined scent of cigarette smoke, urine and B.O. twisted in a sad tang of hopelessness.

Breathing through my mouth, I bent down and opened the bag. "Are you guys hungry?" I didn't even get the full sentence out before their desperate eyes swung to mine, three weary pairs filled with longing. I pulled one sandwich out of the bag for each of them and handed them an extra for the dog along with three bottles of water. They were missing teeth, wearing dirty clothes, and smelled like a distillery. If

Tommy ever got his way, I knew this would be my fate. The brutal reality was a thought that made me shiver.

"Who's this?" I asked, scratching the mutt behind his ears as his leg twitched up and down in response.

"Shadow."

"Well, hello, Shadow, I'm Freddie," I said, talking to the dog. I always found it easier to talk to animals than to people.

"I know you," said one of the men, his dark hair hanging limp in front of his glassy eyes. He flashed a crooked smile that revealed teeth that had been ravaged by meth. He tugged the last cigarette from a wrinkled pack, stuffed it in his mouth, and lit it. Then he sucked on it like it was the only oxygen in the area. "You're that guy… the… the Funologist, right?"

Shocked, I jumped back, my brow crinkled in concentration. "You've heard of me?"

"Just the tip!" the other two men next to him said and cracked up, elbowing each other. Mouths full of chewed-up chicken as toothless glee washed across their faces.

A genuine smile broke out across my face. "I can't believe you know who I am! How?"

"You mean how do homeless guys get into a comedy club?"

"That sounds like the set-up for a joke. Three homeless guys walk into a bar…" I started in, then felt guilty until they came to life laughing at the idea.

Win column. Check.

"Old buildings, you know, the holes in the walls don't just let the rats in. They let the sound out. If we hang out in the alley, we can hear the show." He took another long drag on his cigarette, exhaling a puffy cloud of smoke that hung in the air between us.

"You can?" I was dumbfounded.

"I know this might be hard to believe, but I wasn't always this disaster you see standing in front of you," he said with a wry grin.

"What's your name?"

"Bob." He offered me a dirty, calloused hand, and I shook it. "This is Larry and Bill."

"It's nice to meet you guys."

"Can we have another?" Bob asked. "We haven't eaten anything in a week."

A week. Heartbreaking.

"Sure, I pulled out three more and another for the dog, worried it was going to make him sick, but sick was better than starving. "I think I can do better than that," I said to them. "I might be able to get you a shower and a warm bed for the night." Their eyes popped up hollow and hopeful. I looked down at the bag. "Let me give away the rest of these and I'll circle back for you."

Fear flickered across their faces. These were men who were used to being disappointed, who swam in the deep sludge of personal failure and found themselves stuck, living a life that was all about survival. Trapped in a world of what's next. When is my next meal, my next fix, where is the next warm place to lay my head? "I'll be back," I said. "I promise."

Knowing they were counting on me filled me with energy. It chased away the dark clouds that normally hovered low and tight and were impossible to shake. Having a purpose parted the clouds and gave me the drive to keep going.

I walked down the street, stopping at every lost person in a doorway and handing them a warm sandwich and a bottle of water. One man looked dead and smelled like he was, for sure. I laid it up by his head, hoping I was wrong and he was just resting.

I looped back and found them again.

"You came back," Bob said, stunned.

"I promised you I would."

My answer made him crack wide open. After a life of existing on crumbs, of being perpetually let down, his expectations were finally so low that seeing me follow through and step up for him brought tears to his eyes.

He looked down quickly to hide them.

"I know someone at the Tropical Breeze," I told them. "It's a hole in the wall—a real no-tell motel, if you catch my drift, but it is warm and you can shower and sleep on a real mattress for a night. And I think the manager will turn a blind eye to Shadow." I offered a hand to him and pulled him to his feet. "Come on."

They followed me, three men in various stages of intoxication, pushing a rickety old cart and walking a skinny old dog. I ran from side to side on the sidewalk, flapping my arms until we reached the motel. I'm sure we made quite the spectacle—a parade of lunatics.

"Stay here." I hid the guys from the view of the office and walked in, noticing the hourly rate sign taped to the glass.

Classy.

Sheila sat in an army green armchair, giving off an air of inconvenience, glued to an ancient TV with rabbit ears. Boxy and beaten with the ugly stick, she had an unfortunate number of brown moles with hairs sticking out at odd angles.

"Sheila, darling, I'd like a room for some friends for the night." I pulled out my money clip, grabbing Sheila's attention instantly. "How much?"

"Where'd you get all that cash, big spender?" She shot me a fake smile, and I noticed chunks of pepper lodged in her yellow teeth.

"Haven't you heard the latest? Life is looking up for

Freddie Angel." I pulled out the phone and showed her the viral post.

"Wow. We have a bonafide celebrity in our midst. How will I ever be able to contain my excitement?" she dead-panned, the sarcasm so thick you needed a knife and fork to cut it. "Sixty-five," she answered, trying to wrap up this inter-action as fast as possible.

"What's the friends and family rate?"

"For you—eighty-five." Her face was stony, not even a wisp of a change in her expression. I dropped a big bill on the desk as she slid the key to room eighteen toward me.

"Can I get a couple of extra towels?"

"Fine." She turned to get change, and when she held it out for me, I squeezed her hairy hand shut.

"No, that's for you, sweetheart."

"Gee, thanks." She rolled her eyes. "You're a peach."

"I bet you say that to all the guys." I scooped up the key and towels and let myself out as the door jingled in my wake. I slipped around the corner and walked them to room eigh-teen, then opened the door and they rolled the shopping cart inside.

"Alright, guys, you can shower up and get a good night's sleep, but you have to be out by eleven."

"Thank you, Freddie," Bob said.

"You're most welcome."

He saluted me, and I closed the door behind them and then walked over to The Punch Line.

SIXTEEN

It was a full house, and Cora was slammed. An ass held down every stool and the long side of the main bar was already three people deep. She was running around slinging drinks flitting from one end to the other like a bumblebee in the fall.

"What in the world?" I wondered out loud as I headed to the comedian's lounge to get my head right for the stage. Paulie made a beeline for me with a huge smile on his face. I was puzzled, trying to decipher an expression that could only be interpreted as overjoyed to see me. An expression I had never seen on his face before.

"My man!" He clapped me hard on the back, and my shoulders tensed up, edging closer to my ears. I quickly glanced over my shoulder, trying to figure out who he was speaking to. "I'm talking to you, you old rascal." He jostled my shoulders playfully like men do who weren't hugged enough as children, but then grow up starved for physical touch. "We haven't had a crowd like this since… God, I don't know… since forever."

"Are you giving away free beer? Let me guess… did you install complimentary glory holes in the bathrooms?"

"No, you big sicko!" He smiled widely, and it bordered on bizarre. "They are here to see you, Freddie Angel the Funologist!"

"Really?" I asked incredulously looking around the room in shock and disbelief.

"Can you perform a longer set?" he asked. "I'm going to bump Phil. He's been bombing lately."

I felt a stab of empathy for Phil. I had been bumped before and knew firsthand it made you feel shitty. "Yeah, I've been working on some new material."

"You're the headliner, baby!" He buttered me up, suddenly becoming my best friend. "I bet you never thought you'd hear me say that after the stunt you pulled last time."

"True," I agreed and then said, "I've got to get ready for my set." I couldn't wait to get away from Paulie. His complete one-eighty personality shift was difficult to digest.

"Do you need some quiet?" he offered. "You can use my office. Hell, I'll even send Cora in with your favorite libation. I know you're sweet on her."

My face reddened. I hated that I was so transparent. "Oh, okay," I answered, not wanting to sound too excited about the prospect of having Cora to myself.

"But don't keep her too long," he warned.

Keep her? Did he forget she's her own woman? You don't 'keep' a woman like Cora, she keeps you.

"Of course," I answered anyway, knowing that was what he wanted to hear.

Paulie settled me into the chair in his office and rubbed my shoulders like a boxer's manager does for his prize winner before a big fight. The act made my skin crawl, and I had to fight the urge to physically recoil from the contact.

"I've got to focus," I said, desperate to get him out of there. "Can you send Cora in with a screwdriver?"

"Of course. Whatever the Funologist wants, the Funologist gets," he agreed with a wink and then left, pulling the door shut behind him quietly.

Cora came through the door with my drink next. She set it down on his desk and pulled up a rickety chair next to me. "Can you believe this? I'm exhausted, but the tips are amazing. I'll make more tonight than I have the entire last month. All because of you!"

Her praise leveled me and made my heart accelerate. I was fidgety, so I stood and started pacing the small office in circles.

"What if I bomb?"

"What if you don't?" she reasoned and walked up to me, grabbing my forearms. "You have nothing to worry about. They love you already! I'll go out there and keep plying them with booze, and by the time you take the stage, you will be able to do no wrong." She pulled me in for a hug, and I wrapped my arms around her, keeping them high on her waist. Respectable. I pulled back and looked down at her, and she surprised me by brushing her lips across mine quickly before she left.

Forty minutes later, a low rumbling started and began to swell louder and louder. Thundering applause punctuated by indiscernible chanting. I pressed my ear to the door to try to make it out, the sound forcing the cracked walls to vibrate and come alive.

"Fre-ddie! Fre-ddie! Fre-ddie!"

"*Die! Fred! Die! Fred!*" a voice hissed deep within that barely registered, and I forced myself to ignore it.

The chanting intensified, and I heard Paulie's voice next,

muffled through the wood. Opening the door a crack, I caught the tail end of his introduction and was swept onto the stage to thunderous applause. For the first time ever, The Punch Line was standing room only. Packed to the gills. I took a deep breath, letting the crowd's energy rev me up. It was intense and electric and spun me up like a top.

I grabbed the microphone and took a long, deep breath before looking out into the crowd again. There in the front row, nursing a beer, was Darlene from the bus. She gave me a little wave, and my heart bloomed with joy.

"Helllllooooo!" I shouted into the microphone as I used my hands to hush the crowd. "Holy cow!" I pressed my hand to my heart. "I tell you what, you tell one bus full of people that you'll buy them a beer..." The crowd chuckled and stomped and clapped.

"Looking back, it probably wasn't the smartest decision to tell a crowded bus full of strangers I won the lottery, but hey, I never claimed to be a brainiac."

I turned to the bar. "See that cute little redhead over there?" I pointed at Cora, who quickly bowed. "Freddie Angel is a man of his word. I am going to make good on my promise. Cora! Give these fine people a thick pour of your most mediocre draft beer. And don't forget to give her..."

I pointed the microphone to the audience, who roared, "Just the tip!" I laughed into the newfound ease, savoring the love.

"You got it, boss!" Cora shouted out.

"Boss?" I asked, pressing my luck on stage. "Let's remember who's boss when we get back to my bedroom tonight, sweetheart." She shook her head at me as the room erupted into applause, and I walked to the other end of the stage.

"Dar-lene, Darlene, Darlene, Darleee-eene," I sang poorly, a sad imitation of Dolly's iconic hit *Jolene* into the microphone as I walked toward her and then giggled. "I promise that is the full extent of my vocal stylings you will be subjected to tonight." I pointed at her and beckoned her forward with my finger. "Come up here, sweetheart." She stood and walked up the steps to the stage. Wearing ortho-pedic shoes and a striped seersucker pantsuit, her fingers were covered in gold rings with colorful gemstones. "Why don't you tell these beautiful people how we met?"

She smiled and said, "We met on the bus, where you were escorting your giant check home."

"Escorting—that truly is the most accurate word you could use." I turned back to the audience. "Let me paint the picture for you. I'd just left the lottery headquarters and got on the bus with the giant check they use for publicity photos. It was a thing of beauty. A true masterpiece. I never thought I would see my name scrawled across one of those. So, I'd be damned if I was going to leave it behind." I smiled sweetly. "I was stroking it and cuddling it." I mimed a loving face, pretending to kiss it. "I love you the most." Then the pantomime quickly morphed into holding the fake check in my hands and dry humping it as the audience lost it. Darlene covered her eyes laughing as I pulled an ugly orgasm face while the crowd's hysterics egged me on. "Sorry, Mom. I'm done, you can look now."

Uncovering her eyes, she glanced up at me again, her face glowing with a sweet smile as I continued. "Yes, it's true. I won the lottery, folks. Fifty thousand dollars!" Then I softly muttered into the microphone, "Thirty-seven-point-five after Uncle Sam rapes you without the Vaseline." Darlene laughed, her cheeks turning pink. "And what did you say?" I tipped the microphone toward her.

"I asked how you were going to spend it," she said timidly.

"And how did I answer?"

"Hookers and blow," she answered matter of factly, as the crowd roared, at the irreverent words coming from the mouth of a sweet little old lady.

"Have you ever been to a comedy show?"

"Why, heavens no." She shook her head.

"And after being here, be honest, you're never coming back, are you?" I winked at her as she laughed. "You've been a good sport. What can I get you to drink, sweetheart?" I asked.

"A Blue Moon?"

"Absolutely. Cora, can you see that Darlene gets a Blue Moon and add it to my tab?" I turned to the audience. "That's a little trick I picked up from Bill Cosby." The crowd went wild, and Darlene shook her finger at me and laughed. "Let's give Darlene a hand!" She waved at the crowd and then got settled in her seat, and Cora brought her beer over.

"The lottery… Man, it changes you," I commiserated with the crowd. "But I decided to flip the script. I'm going to give it all away." I stopped and leaned on the mic stand and looked back out to the audience. "Every penny," I looked out into the crowd, "and I started to do that and you know what happened?" I paused again. "Venmo." I covered the mic and my mouth with my hand, obscuring it from the audience. "Shameless plug alert, you can be a part of the movement by donating **@thefunologist**," I murmured into the mic as the audience laughed. "After the Steak and Shake waitress's post went viral, someone suggested I set up a Venmo account, so I did, just for shits and giggles… a kind of social experiment if you will." I rocked the stand back and forth. "And in seconds, money started to flow into the account. I was floored."

"So, I decided I am going to give that away, too." I waited. "But here's the caveat. No charities, no government agencies, I am talking about putting it into the hands of real people who need it."

The crowd clapped and stomped so loud I had to wait a full minute for it to be quiet enough to continue.

"I'm gonna stretch this fifteen-minutes-of-fame into at least thirty, and as long as there is money in the Venmo account, I will be out there in the wild, spreading the fundamentals of Funology like chlamydia on a Naval base."

The rest of my set killed. I barely remember it. I said the words, and the audience rolled and roared. After what felt like seconds, but was more like half an hour, I walked off the stage on a high still basking in the afterglow. The adoration you feel on stage is like no other feeling in the entire world. They loved me. I was a comedy god. Freddie Angel was finally somebody.

After the set at The Punch Line, Instagram swelled and the Venmo account ballooned to a massive twenty-seven thousand dollars overnight. It was impossible to sleep. I'd refresh the screen to find twenty more followers by the second, then I'd search the hashtags and scroll through all the posts, reading the comments and responding. Hours would go by and my eyes would get bloodshot and red, and I'd settle down to try and sleep, but then I'd hit refresh or head over to twitter and get sucked right back into the social media love bubble.

They loved me. Actual real people took time out of their days to read my posts and share them on Insta and Tik-Tok. Even Darlene made the cut with her hookers and blow comment; her video post cameo landed over four thousand shares in twenty-four hours. I jumped up and did fifty jumping jacks and then what was going to be fifty pushups, but that only turned into ten feeble attempts with the last two being the modified lady version. I had energy for days. Giving money away invigorated me. I was finally relevant. I did important things that people actually cared about. My star was rising, and I was enjoying the rocket ride into the stratosphere.

At three a.m, I ordered one hundred I Love Porn bumper stickers, a case of whoopee cushions, and an air horn. I had special plans for Paulie's chair for that one. I bought Ma some new slippers and some Lindt truffles. I ordered some leather pants and two pairs of sunglasses, a diamond pinky ring, and a case of that spray-on hair stuff from Billy Mays from a late-night infomercial I watched to try to calm my mind.

Inside, my brain surged and spun like a superhighway in India. Chaos and horns, screaming and whispering. Reckless drivers speeding and slamming on the brakes headed nowhere. When I was fully immersed in the moment, giving things away or on stage, it quieted. When I was home alone, the insanity symphony raged on. I pulled out my notebook and began to write feverishly, pressing the pen to the paper so hard it left an imprint on the next three pages.

Sweaty and spent, I looked over my handwriting. Cramped and tiny, it filled the pages haphazardly in a manic fashion no one else would be able to interpret. It looked like hieroglyphics and needed a translator. I patted myself on the back.

Good job. That way, no one will be able to steal my jokes.

"Yeah, doofus, they will be a secret, even from you," a man interrupted. *"Great plan, Einstein!"*

Shut up.

I wrote another page worth of jokes and laughed my ass off when I read them back out loud, delighted and ready to trot them out at my next performance at The Punch Line. My thoughts ran wild on circular tracks in my mind, solving all the world's problems eight at a time. I didn't need to sleep. I needed to get these ideas on paper. I needed to write these jokes down before I lost them. It would be a disservice to the act of comedy itself if they never saw the light of day.

SEVENTEEN

Wanting to keep the momentum up and spend a little time with my best girl, I reached out to Cora. Later that night, she drove over and was sitting in her car, idling at the curb.

"Freddie, your meds!" Ma called out and ran outside in her pajamas and slippers. She offered me a glass of water and dropped the pills into my outstretched hand. I tucked them under my tongue and took a sip of water from the glass she offered.

Taking notice of Cora in the car, she asked, "Can I meet your friend?"

"Sure," I answered then turned my head and coughed, spitting the bitter pills into my hand and shoving the disintegrating tablets deep into the pockets of my jeans. I pulled open the door and leaned down. "Cora, someone is dying to meet you." I pulled Ma into her field of vision, and she reached into the car to shake her hand. "Ma, this is Cora."

"It's nice to meet you." She smiled. "What do you two have planned tonight?"

"That's a good question," Cora answered. "What *do* we have planned tonight, Freddie?"

"A top-secret Funologist mission," I said and held my finger to my lips to shush them both. "I'll tell you all about it later, Ma, I promise." I squeezed her in my arms and said, "Love you, Ma, but we gotta go."

"Have fun, you two." Then she watched us drive away, waving at the curb in her fleece pajamas.

"Ready for a little field trip?" I asked, turning back to Cora.

"What did you have in mind?"

"Drive me to Barnes and Noble, woman!" I ordered, edging my words with playfulness.

"That's funny. I didn't peg you as the literary type."

"There's a lot you don't know about me," I offered. "But I prefer to remain a man of mystery."

Cora parked the car, and I pulled out my phone and started a video. "It's Freddie Angel here at Barnes and Noble on Claremont with this gorgeous creature, Cora." I turned the camera toward her. "Say a little something for the camera."

"A little something for the camera," Cora drawled on repeat, her face pinking up from the attention. I chuckled and turned the camera back toward me.

"We are here to encourage reading by carefully placing some of these beautiful babies inside books." I pulled a thick stack of two-hundred teal envelopes from my coat pocket that each held a crisp twenty-dollar bill inside. I zoomed in on the envelopes so they could read the words. Printed on the front of the envelope was, "The Funologist wants to buy you this book. Follow him on social." I turned the camera back to my face and wrapped up, "So, come on down and enjoy a literary treasure hunt courtesy of the Funologist." I ended the video and turned to Cora. "Ready to get this party started?"

"Let's do it!" she enthused as she got out of the car and ran over to entwine her fingers in mine. It was a sweet gesture that spawned a thrill deep in my belly.

Once inside the store, I handed half the envelopes to Cora and walked her over to a stack of Children's books. I pulled one off the shelf and tucked an envelope inside a copy of Robinson's *Crusoe* and book twenty-five of the Hardy Boys mystery series.

"Let's spread out and cover more of the store," I told Cora, who smiled and saluted me. She giggled and pulled out a few brightly colored children's books, quickly tucking an envelope inside each one before returning them to the shelf.

I couldn't resist the end cap of shirtless Fabio look-a-likes coating the glossy front covers of the smutty paperback section. Then I popped over to the cooking section and hit up *The Joy of Cooking*. Not to be outdone, I tucked one carefully into every copy of *The Joy of Sex* and a book on Kama Sutra I found on the shelves. With all my envelopes gone, I searched for Cora in the aisles on my tiptoes and finally found her. I snuck up behind her as she was staring at the new releases in the business section, preparing to bury an envelope deep inside a thick business book. Coming up behind her, I said sternly in her ear, "Don't you even think about it! I forbid it!" She jumped and laughed, and I used the opportunity to wrap my arms around her and hug her from behind. She fit perfectly in my arms, so little my chin rested on the top of her head. A thick stack of envelopes remained in her hand.

"Let's leave these greedy bastards behind, and head over to the self-help section. Those are the people who really need a boost," I explained and she nodded as she followed me. We stuffed more envelopes into the books in the psychology and self-help sections. One was inserted into a thick copy of *The Power of Positive Thinking*, another into *Awaken the Giant*

Within, and one more behind the orange cover of *The Subtle Art of Not Giving a Fuck.*

"The rest of these are going to the kids," I said. "I spent so many hours in this bookstore, sitting in comfy chairs reading books I couldn't afford. Let's plaster that section with the rest of them."

Twenty minutes later, we were finished.

"One second." I pulled out my phone and posted the video we made earlier to Tik-Tok, Facebook, and Instagram with all the hashtags.

"Want a treat to celebrate?" I suggested and pulled Cora by the hand to the Starbucks in the corner.

She hemmed and hawed over the menu. "Five bucks for a latte? That's ridiculous."

"My girl gets anything she wants." I wrapped an arm around her shoulder and bent down to plant a kiss at her temple. "You're worth a five-dollar latte. In fact, you're worth double that."

"Your girl?" she tested me, her eyes flashing.

"I mean… if… if that's what you want," I stammered, backtracking, feeling warmth surge to my cheeks.

She considered it for a moment, each second gnawing like an eternity. "I think it is." She reached out and squeezed my hand and then turned to the aproned barista and ordered a pumpkin spice latte with an extra shot of espresso. I proudly paid for my girlfriend's outrageously expensive coffee and then covered the next fifty peoples' orders who would come up to the counter behind us by dropping a couple more hundies on the counter.

I pulled Cora toward a cafe table in the corner. "And now we wait," I said, sipping on my mocha with a triple shot. The caffeine shot through me as I watched people start to stream through the store. Throngs of children and teenagers dragging their beleaguered moms behind them filtered in, and as the envelopes began to be discovered, I heard whoops of joy in the aisles. The store's energy crackled with excitement and shouts of glee. Kids ran through the aisles of the store with their mothers in tow, desperate to find a teal envelope.

More and more people flooded the store on the hunt. I overheard employees talking amongst themselves.

"What in the world is going on?"

"This is a bigger crowd than we usually have on Black Friday."

"I've been following this guy. He calls himself the Funologist. He just posted a video that he hid envelopes full of money all over the store, and it's going viral."

"He's amazing. Did you see the post of him tipping that waitress? Wish *we* worked for tips."

It didn't take long for me to be discovered. "That's him!" One mom waved an envelope at me as a group of people developed behind her. She walked up to me with her two kids in tow, each clutching a teal envelope and a book to their chests. "Will you take a picture with us?"

"Of course!" I said and proudly stood next to her and her kids while Cora snapped away on my phone and hers. To the right, a line started to form as a small mass of humanity waited to have a picture taken with me. I spoke to all the little kids whose excitement was the reason I wanted to do this in the first place. The nerdy emo pre-teens wearing eyeliner, jacked-up platform boots, and spiked collars. The bone-weary mothers cracked small smiles of gratitude that there was finally a reason for their kids to enter a bookstore. I hammed it up with the Barnes and Noble staff, a collection of super nerds that wrapped their arms around me, and then I bought them a round at Starbucks. The line kept growing and growing—an endless chain of animated adults and children.

"Freddie, don't you think we should wind this down?' Cora asked.

"I can't tell them no, not when they've been waiting to see me," I said. "Just a little longer, sweetheart, and then we can go? These are my fans."

"Of course," she answered and continued to take photos and corral children.

I smiled until my face felt like it was going to crack. They adored me. Enough to line up and wait for hours to take a photo with me. And by God, I was bound and determined that I would stay there until the last envelope was found. I was not going to disappoint my public.

EIGHTEEN

All night long, after Cora dropped me off, my mind spun.

What's next? How can you top the bookstore? You gotta stay on top, Freddie Angel. You gotta blow their minds.

I poured a shot of vodka, just enough to take the edge off, and scrolled through social media that was becoming an even bigger addiction than the vodka in my hand. Only a swipe away, gushy messages from people who loved me could be accessed 24/7. I swiped and swiped so much a tender spot formed on my index finger and tingles crawled up my forearm from all the repetitive swiping.

The bookstore giveaway was a hit and amplified the online chatter. Each event came with an immediate surge of online activity, rushing endorphins to my head and heart. But even eight hours later, the surge dwindled to a trickle and I had to continually feed the fame machine to stay relevant.

When my shenanigans began, the internet chatter was focused locally, but as each act picked up more online momentum, I noticed messages were coming in from Canada and states as far-flung as Delaware and California. I'd love to say that the attention didn't go to my head, but it did. It was changing the way I thought about myself, giving me the wings to dream about a future that I had long ago thought were clipped.

Each night, I would lie in bed and read through the messages, one by one, responding to them individually. Hours and hours would tick by in this fashion. Responding to every message was a blessing and a curse; it created even more messages which created an even bigger need to respond. It was like running on a treadmill. They just kept coming, and I was running so fast I didn't know how to stop or even if I wanted to. Around sunrise, I got an epiphany while standing at the kitchen sink eating a fudge-filled Drumstick that I called breakfast.

Ice cream. Everyone loves ice cream.

The next day, Paulie hooked me up with one of his friends who owned an ice cream truck. Diego was skinny and lanky with a dark goatee that he endlessly stroked with his thumb and forefinger.

"You want to do what?" he asked, his arms folded across his chest, sizing me up. The extra scrutiny made me edgy.

"*He knows,*" Dad shrieked in my ear. I blinked long and slow, clenching my jaw and grinding my teeth. "*He knows what a screw-up you are! You want to be the ice cream man? The kid that couldn't even decide what kind he likes is now going to drive a truck full of it to the ghetto and give it away? That'll never happen.*" I sighed and pushed Dad to the deep recesses of my mind again.

"I want to rent your ice cream truck for a night. Pay you to drive it and head to the crappiest neighborhoods in the city, and I'll give ice cream away to the people that live there."

"You crazy, Ese," Diego said with a quick smile, a flash of pearly white dancing across his brown face.

"How's five-hundred cash to drive me for the night and another fifteen hundred for inventory?"

He shook his head as a slow smile spread across his face, then he extended a hand toward me. "You've got yourself a deal."

Two days later, I was standing at the curb with a blind-folded Cora.

"Is this really necessary?" She pawed the air with her hands, searching for me. "At least hold my hand." I laced my fingers through hers with a squeeze.

"Come on, it's an adventure," I declared. "He'll be here any minute."

"Who?" she asked as Diego pulled up and hopped out.

"Right on time. You can look now." At my statement, Cora ripped off the blindfold and looked at the ice cream truck with confusion. "Ta-Da!" I sang out and waved both my hands at the truck and an uncomfortable Diego.

"Cora, I'd like you to meet Diego. He will be our driver during tonight's Funology excursion." Diego extended a caramel-colored hand that Cora shook, then shoved it deep into the pocket of his Levi's.

"Can we?" I waved a handful of windshield markers at Diego.

"Sure," he agreed with a shrug, and I passed markers out and wrote on the sides of the white truck. FREE ICE CREAM, #thefunologist, and #freddieangelisthefunologist were scrawled in huge letters on the back and sides of the truck. Diego revealed his hidden graffiti talent and kicked it up a notch with killer lettering and hand-drawn ice cream cones. I got lost working behind him, coloring our mobile canvas.

"Will you take a photo for us?" I asked and handed the phone to Diego, pulling Cora closer to me. Smiling widely, he fired off two shots that I posted to my social media. I pressed the video button on my phone. "Hey, Kansas City! If you see this truck, you better come running because it is packed full with ice cream and treats, and we are giving it all away. Be on the lookout for us in your neighborhood. Free ice cream is incoming! And thank you to everyone who has donated to make this possible. If you want me to continue doing outrageous acts of kindness like this, you can help fund the mission @thefunologist on Venmo. I scream, you scream, we all scream for ice cream!" I pressed the end button and posted to Facebook, twitter, Tik-Tok, and Instagram. Then I turned toward Cora. "You ready, gorgeous?"

She smiled at the compliment as we jumped into the truck, and Diego pulled out and headed to our first stop. After he exited the highway, he turned on the carnival music that streamed out of the speakers as we turned down a dark street lined with old row houses that sunk into the ground, decrepit and leaning. Many were missing windows and doors, and sometimes entire swatches of the roofs were gone from a forgotten storm and years of neglect. Cora squeezed my hand, and I glanced over at her biting her lip, her expression pinched and worried.

"It's okay. We're perfectly safe here, sweetheart."

I pulled the PA to my mouth and began to speak. "Hello, Elmwood! The Funologist is here! Who's ready for some free ice cream? Come and get it!" The music continued to repeat and spin as the first porch lights came on and doors creaked open. Diego continued to cruise down the street and stopped at the end of the cul-de-sac. I handed stickers to Cora and Diego. "Slap these on the treats. Never know where that big break is going to come from."

"Probably not from here, but whatever you want, man.

I'm yours for the next three hours," Diego replied as he began to stick the stickers on popsicles and drumsticks.

I opened the serving window on the side of the truck and saw the first swarm of people walking toward us. Teenage girls with babies on their hips or dragging boyfriends behind them, grandmothers with little ones following behind them like ducklings. In ten minutes, we were slammed. Cora and Diego handed out drumsticks and ice cream sandwiches, and I stood outside the truck like a carnival barker entertaining the masses.

"Step right up!" I shouted right into the loudspeaker. "Get your sweet treat!" I recorded little video snippets of the groups of children with huge smiles on their faces and posted them to social media. When there was a break in the action, we climbed back into the truck and went to the next neighborhood. The posts were picking up steam on the interwebs and being shared like a virus. At our next stop, the crowd was twice as big, and it was obvious we were going to run out of ice cream after only three stops.

"I'm down at Hidden Hills, where your donations are putting happy smiles on the faces of kids here. If you want to help the Funologist continue his work, hit me up on Venmo @thefunologist. You never know where I'll end up next."

I was engrossed in posting the video to all my social channels when I heard a gravelly voice behind me, "The Funologist, huh?" I whipped around to see the barrel of a handgun pointed at my face.

Cora screamed, and I heard the serving window slam shut behind me. My heart accelerated as the fight or flight mechanism kicked in. My eyes darted around, thankful the line of kids had disappeared and the streets were clearing out as porch lights clicked off.

"Give me the money," he demanded.

"You've got the wrong truck, buddy. There isn't any. We gave all the ice cream away for free," I explained, looking for an opening. He shoved me roughly up against the truck, and my skull cracked against the metal, sending a jarring shooting pain to the back of my head. He was eye to eye with me, with skin so white it was bordering on albino. I smelled cigarettes on his breath. His eyes were ringed in red and bloodshot, and his thumb clicked on the hammer of the gun.

"Go ahead," I said boldly. "Pull the trigger." With wild eyes, I dared him, and behind me through the metal of the van, I heard Cora begin to cry.

"Don't think I won't," he sneered.

"If you're gonna do it, then get on with it," I stated impulsively as he continued to stare me down. "You're not doing anything I haven't already thought about doing myself," I confessed. "I've got a fully loaded shotgun in the back of my closet right now, ready and waiting, but my Ma always said I had a shitty work ethic," I deadpanned. "Go ahead, save me a bullet."

His hand slid up to my throat and squeezed, and I could feel the tremors in his grip.

He was afraid. I felt fear and desperation oozing from him.

"What are you waiting for? Send me out with a bang," I taunted him, croaking out the words thick in my throat, taking small gasps of air through my contracted windpipe.

Completely confused, he stared me down, weighing his options. His pale eyebrows furrowed.

"Why are you doing this?" I asked him. He released his death grip on my throat, and I coughed as blessed air rushed in.

"Got to get mine," he answered defensively, still pointing the gun at me.

"You're scared," I revealed to him like I was reading his tarot. "You live in fear and think you're invisible," I whispered as I tapped into his feelings like I was reading a book, and it rattled him. "Without that piece, you think no one will listen to anything you have to say, but you're wrong."

He pressed his forearm across my chest, pinning me to the truck. In the distance, I heard a siren wailing and hoped it was heading closer.

"I will," I said bravely. "I will listen."

"People stopped noticing me a long time ago. This is the only way to get their full attention." He waved the gun at me.

"I don't know about other people, but you have mine," I said. "What do you want?" He was cutting off my air supply again, leaning in so close I could feel his warm breath on my cheek. Out of the corner of my eye, I saw movement. A four-year-old little beautiful ebony girl, with rows of beaded braids clutching a pink blanket, was running toward the truck, and terror seized me. In a few short seconds, she would reach us. I didn't have time to think, just to react. I head-butted him, and he yelped, biting through his lip and staining his lips crimson as he dropped to the ground and the gun went flying. I kicked it under the truck, and Diego opened the door and grabbed it.

The sirens were closing in. "Get in," I said roughly and yanked open the door for him. Stunned, he hesitated for a moment.

"Now!" I shouted. "The cops will be here any minute."

He sprang into action, and I jumped in behind him and slammed the door shut.

"Drive!" I shouted at Diego as Cora sat paralyzed in the seat, pressed up against the back of the truck silently. Her face ghostly white and pale, she clutched her hands to her heart. Diego peeled out of the neighborhood and took several turns as the sirens faded behind us.

I handed the bleeding man a napkin. "Here, put this on it." I passed him a small bag of ice from the cooler.

"What's your name?" I asked him.

"Jerry," he muttered. "Where are you taking me?"

"Wherever you want to go. Are you hungry?"

His eyes shifted to mine, and without answering, his eyes welled up with tears. He buried his face in his hands and began to sob. Uncomfortable, I decided for him. "Let's get a pizza. Diego, can you drop me and my new friend at Giovanni's?"

"Sure, Ese." Diego pulled up to Giovanni's twenty minutes later and left the truck running.

"You want to grab a bite with us?" I asked Diego.

"Nah, man, you crazy," he said with a lopsided grin. "I need to go home and change my boxers. Pretty sure I shit myself back there."

"Go inside and get us a table," I told Jerry, who collected himself enough on the drive over to follow my directions.

I turned back to Diego, pulled my money clip out of my pocket, and gave him an extra three hundred dollars. "Sorry this took a turn, but we made a lot of kids happy tonight."

"What are you going to do with that guy?" Diego asked.

"Love him," I said. "He's just as messed up as the rest of us. Don't worry, I'm really good at reading people. He's not going to hurt anyone. He doesn't have it in him."

"Can you take her home?" I nodded my head at Cora, who was still in shock, silent in the back of the truck. "And get rid of that gun."

"Sweet Jesus," Diego muttered under his breath and made the sign of the cross, but nodded in agreement. I crawled into the back to where Cora sat frozen and whimpering. As I pulled her into my arms, I felt her tremble.

"Everything is okay, sweetheart. Diego is going to drive you home."

"Don't leave me," she whispered as I pulled her in closer. Her hands were so cold. I rubbed my hands on hers to warm them up.

"I don't think anything else is going to happen tonight, but I can't be certain and I won't put you at risk." I kissed the top of her head. "Go home, curl up in bed, and try to get some rest. You have to admit, it was big fun before all the drama, wasn't it?"

Cora didn't answer me, clinging more tightly to my t-shirt balled in her fists. I gently extracted myself and cupped her face in my palms. "Get some sleep, sweetheart, and I'll message you later." Then I brushed my lips across her clammy forehead. "You're okay. It's all over," I whispered, and she finally nodded.

"Come on!" I egged on Diego. "Admit it, you had a blast!"

"I guess so," Diego answered. "It *was* a crazy night. But I have a feeling crazy follows you wherever you go."

"You might be right about that."

"I'll get her home," he promised and pulled away from the curb, leaving a cloud of exhaust behind. I walked into the restaurant and sat down in the booth opposite Jerry.

"Pepperoni and a couple of beers?" I asked and he nodded.

A waitress took our order and immediately returned and set two bottles in front of us. Jerry pulled his to his mouth and sucked on it eagerly. He rubbed his weary face in his hands, rubbing his eyes with the balls of his fists. I studied him as he fought exhaustion.

"Just tell me why," I asked. "It will stay between us, I promise."

"I don't know how I got here. I'm exhausted," he confessed. "Fighting my way through life, while watching other people glide through it." He took another long sip on his beer, and then the pizza was slid onto the stainless-steel stand and I served him the first piece. He shook the powdered parmesan over it until it looked like it snowed and then took a bite and yelped when the hot cheese burned the top of his lip. Fanning his mouth, he inhaled air and tried to push it around with his tongue to cool it off enough to swallow, but I was pretty sure he just succeeded in scalding his entire mouth.

I served myself a piece and waited. Sitting back in the booth, the adrenaline from being held at gunpoint finally dissipated enough to allow me to relax.

"Ever feel like a black cloud follows you wherever you go?" He asked.

"I know a thing or two about that," I admitted and took my first bite.

"It's been a real shitstorm for the last two years. My wife got cancer and passed away and the only promise I made to her, to take care of our daughter, is one I can't keep. Then I lost my job and after six months exhausted my unemployment benefits. And don't even get me started on the cost of child care in this country!" Anger filled his eyes again, and he pushed it down to continue bitterly. "So I'm reduced to stealing bread from gas stations and picking up pop cans to try to feed my kid. I've missed two house payments." He took another bite. "They repossessed my car last week, so we can't even live in it when we get evicted."

"That's rough," I said.

"When your back's against the wall, you have nothing to lose. And when you have nothing to lose, suddenly those options you would have never exercised before seem perfectly normal." He chewed on the crust, and I signaled the waitress for a couple more beers. Peeling the label, refusing to make eye contact, Jerry's shoulders drooped and he continued, "Christmas is coming. The idea of seeing her eyes on Christmas morning, so hopeful and then empty, it just kills me."

"How old is your daughter?" I asked.

"Five. It's hard because she goes to school now, and she talks to other kids. Pretty soon, she's going to learn that Santa is just a big fat disappointment." He hung his head low. "And shortly after that, she'll learn her dad is, too."

I pulled my money clip from my pocket under the table and counted out the bills. Then I laid them on the table in front of him and pushed the stack toward him. "How about he comes a little early for you?" I whispered. "It's four thousand. Get caught up on your mortgage and then make a special Christmas for your girl."

He gasped, afraid to grab the money and put it in his pocket, yet afraid not to.

"Go on, it's okay," I said and nudged the money toward him.

"What do I have to do?" His eyes magnetized to the stack finally lifted and met mine.

"Never put another gun in another man's face," I said, looking deep in his eyes, and in seconds, he crumpled. Holding his face in his hands, sobs racked his body. "You might think life is rough now, but if the police had shown up a few minutes earlier, you wouldn't be going home to your daughter tonight. You'd be sitting in jail, and she'd probably be put in the system."

"Why are you doing this for me?" he asked as tears trickled down his pasty cheeks.

"Everyone needs a little help sometimes," I said to him. "Truth is, until recently, I was one step away from where you are and it nearly destroyed me. I didn't even have a daughter watching. So, I understand where you are at, brother."

The waitress brought two more beers, and I lifted mine. "Can we make a toast?"

"Sure," he replied, uncertain.

"To new beginnings and better days." He reached out and tapped his glass bottle against mine. He repeated the phrase, letting it roll off his tongue. "I know it's hard to believe in those, but they are coming. I hope tonight helps you see that."

"You're a saint."

"Nah, far from it." I pulled another piece of pizza onto my plate. "Just trying to buy my way back into the big guy's good graces."

"Thank you," he said solemnly.

We finished our pizza, and then I called for an Uber. I dropped him off at his house and then, as the driver headed home, I pulled out my phone that I had shut off during dinner. Notifications rained down, dinging and ringing, sounding like a slot machine in Vegas winning the jackpot. "Oh, shit," I said as I scrolled through social media. Videos and photos of us giving away ice cream to the kids were everywhere. I stopped to watch a video that had been uploaded to *YouTube* titled, "The Funologist Strikes Back" that was picking up likes, shares, and comments. Fascinated, I was riveted to the footage of a dark fuzzy form headbutting Jerry and kicking the gun under the truck. It was a surreal, out-of-body experience, and hard to believe I was watching real footage of real events that had happened only a few hours before. From a glance, it looked more like an episode of *Cops*.

Totally out of character. Look at you, big man!

Pride surged through me followed by fear, knowing that

Cora had been in the crossfire. I scrolled through more messages, and there were three from her. I didn't want to wake her up, but in case she was up, I sent a text.

All is well. Headed home. Will text you in the morning.

I checked the hashtags and discovered the video had been uploaded everywhere: Youtube, Facebook, and sketchy news sites. #thefunologist hashtag was trending on Twitter.

Then I opened my Venmo account and dropped the phone, my hands shaking so violently it was hard to make out the numbers at first. *Forty-nine thousand dollars in one night.*

I kept giving it away, and what was left multiplied like bunnies in the springtime. I was going to have to step up my game in a major way in order to give away all this money. Fame was rocketing me from obscurity to the milky way of celebrity, and the love bomb of notifications rolling in every minute went straight to my head.

"Marry me, Freddie."

"Freddie Angel is an Angel."

"I love you, Freddie Angel."

It was the highest high of my life. Love pouring in from strangers across the country validated me. I wish I was one of those people who didn't care what people thought. That I didn't spend my days slaving for the approval of other people. But I cared. *Deeply.* And to finally feel that kind of love and acceptance wash over me was like being offered a cup of water in the desert, and I never wanted to live without it again.

NINETEEN

I face-planted into the mattress for three hours after enough Trazodone and Melatonin to take down an elephant. It was the first stretch of real sleep I'd had in a week.

"Sleep? Sleep is for pussies. You have important work to do. You can sleep when you're dead."

From far away, I heard the old rotary phone Ma still used trilling. She was the only person I knew who still had a land-line. A cordless phone would have made her life so much easier and stepped her into the twentieth century, but she wouldn't have it. Replacing something that still had useful life was a sacrilege to her. It rang and rang endlessly, and through the ceiling, I heard the muffled sound of her voice like the teachers on *Charlie Brown*, but I couldn't make out any of the words.

The door cracked open, and a shaft of light spilled down the stairs. "Freddie! Are you up?" she called down the stairs. "I need you to come up here." The phone rang again, and she let it ring over and over, a sound that grated on my brain. The thick vestiges of medicated sleep left me groggy and disori-ented. I slid my feet to the cold concrete, chugged the last inch of a warm 7-Up in the can by my bed, pulled on a faded Grateful Dead t-shirt, and crawled up the stairs.

"Good, you're up! What happened last night? The phone has been ringing off the hook this morning."

"Well…" I bit the inside of my cheek, trying to figure out how much I should tell her. I hated lying to my mom, but I didn't want to scare her either.

The phone rang again, distracting her, a wall-mounted blue plastic number with the curlicued cord. The grating ring was relentless, desperate for a reprieve, I walked over and slid the lever to turn the ringer off. Tucked in my pocket, the cell phone vibrated non-stop. I stood at the sink as Ma placed a cup of decaf in my hand and kissed my cheek. Sipping the bitter coffee slowly, I pushed the yellowing curtain to the side at the window and looked out onto the street, expecting the familiar daily view that hadn't changed since I was seven. In shock, the mug hit the stainless steel sink with a *clink*.

"Holy shit!"

"What, Freddie?" Ma's voice was pinched as she ran over from the table and looked out the window over my shoulder. "What in the world?" There were several white news vans with station letters emblazoned on them boldly parked across the street.

I jumped back and pulled the curtain closed to kill their view, which was starting to feel claustrophobic. I couldn't shake the feeling of being a specimen on glass getting slid under a microscope.

"You have to tell me what is going on, right now, mister," Mom urged as she poured a bowl of honey nut Cheerios in a bowl and then added milk and a splash of heavy cream for me. I pulled out a chair and sat at the table, my mind spinning.

This was what I always wanted, wasn't it? For people to know my name?

"Be careful what you ask for."

She sat down and waited for me to explain.

"Well, I rented an ice cream truck and gave away ice cream to some kids last night."

"That's nice, dear," she said as she patted my hand. "But what does that have to do with all the news vans parked outside?"

"I've been looking for bigger ways to spread the love with my lottery winnings," I continued, "and I thought it was a good idea. I mean, who doesn't love ice cream?" I paused and then added, "But it took a little turn and the videos went viral."

"What's this viral business?" She scrunched her face. "I don't understand it at all."

"It's okay, Mama, you don't have to. Basically, it's just a post or a video that goes crazy on the internet, spreading like a virus. People share it, and then more people share it, and it takes on a life of its own."

She nodded, finally making the connection. I decided to change the subject and not divulge the full details of the night.

"Guessing the media is looking for a feel-good story to close the six o'clock news."

She set her spoonful of shredded mini-wheats back down in the bowl and assessed me, her gaze penetrating mine searching for signs of the first hints of mania.

I changed the subject quickly to pull her focus away. "You should have seen the looks on the kids' faces. It felt so good."

She reached out to squeeze my hand. "You've always had a big heart." Thinking that was the end of the story, she moved on. "Those boxes came for you." She pointed to a huge stack of cardboard boxes by the door, the sheer volume of which even surprised me.

"Ooh, Mama! I got you something!" I sang out like a little kid who spends his last dollar at the dollar store on his mom. I ran over to the stack, pawing through the boxes, stopping to shake them, then diving into the next stack.

"You did?" Her interest was piqued. I'm sad to admit, it was a rare occurrence. The gifts I'd given her up to this point consisted of the occasional bouquet of ditch flowers I picked on the side of the road.

I ripped open the boxes in a frenzy like a kindergartner on Christmas morning, quickly discarding them one by one until I found the one for her. "New slippers with memory foam for you, a heated mattress pad, and some of those chocolate-covered cherries you love so much."

"It's not even my birthday!" she gasped. "Oh, sweetheart, you should have kept your money." She studied my face that was beaming. "Are you feeling okay?" she asked and pressed her hand to my forehead. I pushed it away, instantly incensed.

"I'm fine, Ma!" Defensiveness bubbled up from my belly. "Why can't I ever be excited? Why does it always have to indicate a psychotic episode?"

"It's just that…" She paused, not wanting to spell it out, but with enough experience to know she had to. "Dr. McGivern says this kind of spending can be a symptom of mania."

"Jesus Christ!" I sighed, exasperated. "It's *not* mania. This is the first time I've had more than two nickels to rub together, and I wanted to spoil my mom a little. What's the harm in that?"

"You're right." She backtracked, trying to soothe me, then brushed the rest of what she wanted to say in the pile with her hand that was busy sweeping breakfast crumbs into a paper towel. "I'm sorry, honey." She shot me an apologetic smile. "I almost forgot! Channel nine called and said they needed to speak to you as soon as possible. They want to set up an interview with the Funologist." Her forehead crinkled up in confusion. "What's the Funologist?" she asked and without waiting for an answer continued. "I told her I'd take the message, but honestly, I had no idea what she was even talking about." Ma shuffled to the little table by the phone, searching for a note. "I wrote down the number here some-where…. Oh, here it is." She waved an old envelope in the air with digits scrawled on the back of it in her handwriting.

"No way!" I said, joy bubbling up in my belly. "That's me, Mama," I sang out and performed the running man in the kitchen in my stockinged feet to dispel some of the energy that was ramping up. "*I'm* the Funologist." She handed me the envelope with the number on it. "I'm gonna be famous! You were right all along."

"That's nice, dear," she dismissed, moving quickly to the most important question of the day. "Did you take your meds?"

"Sweet Jesus, Ma, you're relentless," I said, exasperated. "Yes," I lied. Technically, I always took them. I took them from her and flushed them down the toilet, or I took them and buried them deep in the trash. "Stop worrying. I feel better than I have in years, maybe better than I have ever felt my entire life." Her eyes bored into mine, searching for clues, and I knew she wanted to say something more, but she just reached out and patted my hand instead.

But faintly, I heard a little warning bell begin to ring. I was well-versed in the signs of mania. This was far from my first psychiatric rodeo. Part of me welcomed the surge of energy, part of me welcomed the burst of focus and brilliance that accompanied a less-medicated psyche. During bouts of mania, I always wrote my best jokes. My creativity flourished without the numbing woodenness of over-prescribed pharmacology. I didn't want anything to hold me back from greatness anymore.

It was time to claim my rightful place in the world without the baggage that had weighed me down for so long. It was finally my time to shine. The stars were starting to align. I was the chosen one. I was going to be famous.

TWENTY

Normally, Ma took the flo-bee to my hair once every six weeks like clockwork whether I needed it or not, but if there were going to be press appearances and television interviews in my near future, I figured it was time to invest in my look.

Later that morning, I decided to take my style game up a notch and headed to Great Clips. The chatty twenty-year-old girl assigned to cut my hair ended up recognizing me and insisted on taking a picture after she trimmed my hair close to the scalp and added a warm towel to my neck. I had to admit, after forty-five minutes in her chair, it was a huge improvement. I finally understood why celebrities had glam squads. The reflection looking back at me in the mirror was hardly recognizable. I was a brand new man.

Is it really this easy to reinvent yourself? Can you just wake up one day, turn your back on your old life, and begin again? Fresh and new? The idea of wadding up my old useless existence like my life was disposable was oddly comforting. Shedding it like old skin and leaving it in the dirt. For so long, I'd felt shackled to the path I was on, but now, a brand new direction was laid out in front of me. I was ready to come out of my cocoon. To emerge fresh and shiny and fly.

It started with a text from Cora.

Cora: *I need to see you.*

Glee flooded my chest, and I immediately responded.

Me: *You do? Heart-eyed emoticon. What did you have in mind?*
Cora: *Just an easy night in? We can order some takeout?*
Me: *I'll be there at six.*

Now that I was taking pride in my appearance, showering, preening, and grooming took much longer. I methodically cleaned every inch of my skin, hair, and nails and then shaved everything, and I mean everything. I manscaped for the first time in my life for Cora because this was *the* crucial date.

The third date. The sex date.

At least, that's what the *Cosmo* I read standing in line at the grocery store said. I slapped some newly acquired Polo on my freshly shaven cheeks. It stung when it settled into the two cuts that were covered with a wad of toilet paper, like putting lemon juice in an open wound. Down below I attempted to manscape for the first time. Big mistake. My unskilled over-eager maiden voyage into the land of penile grooming garnered a pretty deep cut on my balls that bled forever. Not thinking, I swiped some aftershave down there, and it might be the single worst idea I have ever had in my entire life. If I thought the cuts on my chin were bad, this was a million times worse. Imagine your tenderest places exposed and sliced wide open and then *voluntarily* rubbing the equivalent of rubbing alcohol into the fresh wound. The screaming from the burning was so loud Ma made it all the way down the steps to check on me.

It's so much fun talking to your mother about your burning balls through a door. No, really. You know those parents that say, 'My kids and I, we talk about *everything*. I'm an open book.' Some books should remain shut. Some books should be padlocked and thrown into the river. This was such a book.

"You're wasting your time. Aftershave won't make you any less ugly, dumbass."

Ignoring the voice that cracked in my ear, I squirted blue gel into the palms of my hands and rubbed it into my freshly shortened hair the way the girl from Great Clips taught me.

Obnoxious laughter rang out behind me, and I tuned it out.

I pulled out the pleather pants from the box, bit the tag off with my teeth, spit it out, and began to tug them up my skinny legs and over my wounded junk. The process was lengthy, included a lot of jumping, and should be counted as cardio, because at the end of it, my heart was pounding from effort. Finally, after my legs were successfully encased in buttery black pleather, I donned a V-neck t-shirt and a black jacket. All courtesy of Amazon. The pants were skintight, hugging my flat behind, and cinched in tight at the waist, squeezing all the extra up and over the waistband, which significantly increased my paunch. One look in the mirror, and I could see I looked like I was about six months pregnant.

You look like a busted ass can of biscuits.

I tucked and untucked the t-shirt. I sucked it in and stood on the toilet in the cramped bathroom, trying to catch a glimpse of my freshly pleathered behind, then I just gave up and ordered an Uber that would take me to Cora's house. I needed to see her with my own eyes and make sure she was okay after the night we had. I gave her address to the driver and settled in the backseat, my knees jiggling up and down to dispel the nervous energy as we sped toward her apartment.

At Cora's door, I knocked and waited. Not sure I was at the right door, my eyes darted around as I hesitated and then gently knocked again. Finally, I heard footsteps and the door opened. Cora's eyes were red-rimmed like she had been crying.

"Hey," she said with a pained smile as she leaned on the open door. Her eyes washed down the length of my body. "Wait… Are those…?" She pointed at my pants. "Freddie Angel, are you wearing leather pants?" She stifled a giggle.

I turned around and bent over to show off my ass(ets). "Be honest. It's turning you on, isn't it?" I said over my shoulder with a wink.

"I'm not sure how I feel about it." She laughed. Her navy sweatshirt was slashed with diagonal cutouts. Her skinny legs were wrapped in galaxy leggings and white combat boots. "Come in, weirdo," she said and pulled me in for a hug I wasn't ready for that made me stumble into her arms. "You scared me," she accused. "Don't ever do that again."

"Do what?"

"Headbutt a guy with a gun in your face."

"Admittedly not my most brilliant moment, but it worked, didn't it?" I answered.

"This time," she warned as she turned to lead me down the hallway and into her living room.

The pants made a plastic squeaking noise as my thighs rubbed together when I walked. Panicked with warmth surging up my torso, I froze, and the noise stopped. Having no choice, I followed her into the living room, and the sound started up again. Scrunch. Scrunch. Scrunch.

"What is that noise?" she asked. "Do you hear that?"

Squeak, scrunch, squeak, scrunch.

"There it is again. That." She craned her neck to listen, holding up her index finger to shush me.

I stopped and the sound stopped. "No," I lied.

She turned around and waved me closer. I hesitated with a grimace, then started walking toward her as the quacking noise began again.

"Wait, is that *you*?" Her eyes widened and darted from my pants to my face. "I think it's those ridiculous pants."

My face flushed red, and I radiated heat which made the pants chafe. The friction was brutal against my already wounded junk. I grimaced. "May-be?" I said, waving jazz hands at her. "You wouldn't happen to have any baby powder laying around here, do you?"

"Lemme check… Ah, do you see any babies around here?" She put her hands on her hips as she glanced around the room. Her eyebrows lifted, and a silly smirk teased the corners of her mouth.

"I do not," I admitted and walked to the sofa bowlegged as if I'd just gotten off a thoroughbred after a day on horseback, stepping as lightly as possible to muffle the scrunching noise.

She sat down. "That's a whole new look. Not gonna lie, it's going to take some getting used to." She leaned in. "Who are you tryin' to impress?"

"You," I confessed. The truth was the easiest choice, but the crushing vulnerability it created left me scrambling. Needing something to do, I sat next to her, my shiny leg touching hers, and the warmth that radiated from hip to kneecap was a jolt to my center.

She blinked a few times and nodded then began in a small voice. "I wanted to talk to you about…"

I shifted on the sofa and the pants scrunched loudly again

flushing my cheeks in embarrassment. I watched as Cora's lips disappeared while she pressed them together to bite back a giggle.

"Okay, I can't take you seriously in those leather pants."

"It's pleather, darling. The finest pleather direct from the Ningbo region of China." I bobbed my head at her and teased.

She snorted and then threw her head back and laughed a deep throaty laugh.

"You have the best laugh," I told her. "Did you know it's one of my favorite sounds in the whole world?"

"Did you know that's one of the sweetest things anyone has ever said to me?"

Win column, check.

Cora leaned in closer, and it shored up my confidence.

"I have some big news." The secret was bubbling up inside me, ready to spill over. I was dying to tell her.

One of her delicate eyebrows arched up. "Do tell."

"Channel nine wants to do a story on me."

"Really?" She tucked her feet up under her and sat on them. "Are you going to do it?"

"I can't really become a household name if I don't show them this face." I traced one hand down my cheek. "What do you think? Do I have a shot at *People Magazine*'s Sexiest Man Alive next year?"

"That depends," she answered with a grin. "Are you going to be wearing those pants?"

"Unless you take them off of me." The words left my mouth before I could stop them, blurted impulsively, and I instantly wished I could take them back. I gulped to calm the hammering of my heart.

She stood and held her hand out palm up, curling her fingers in three times while her eyes were locked on mine. Surprisingly, I acted. The old me would have remained frozen, waiting for an actual engraved invitation, thinking I had no chance in hell with a woman like Cora. The new me took risks and followed her down the hall into her bedroom, the damned pleather squeaking all the way. Her bed sat in the middle of the room, unmade and filled with too many pillows. I waited at the edge of it, unsure and unwilling to break the spell, like when you're riding your bike on a trail and you pop up onto a doe with two baby fawns. I didn't want to spook her. Even my breath I controlled, barely letting it escape my lips, but between the shallow breathing and the tight pants, I was quickly becoming lightheaded.

I felt her fingers at the button of my pants, and then blessed relief when the unfastening of the button allowed my belly room to expand. Cora yanked them down, wrestling the jumble of my legs to pull them off. Huffing with effort and dissolving into a pile of giggles, clutching her stomach, she said, "It's like taking the casing off a sausage. Lie back." She pushed me down onto the bed and finally peeled them off and then unbuttoned her shirt. Swinging it around her head in the air like a striptease, she threw it, and it landed on a lamp in the corner, tipping the shade askew. A white lacey bralette covered her chest in triangles.

"Look at you, channeling your inner brothel trollop," I praised with a smile, resting on my elbows. I sat up to yank off my t-shirt and pulled her to me, eager to feel her bare skin on mine. I traced my fingers up her ribs slowly, one at a time, relishing in the softness of her skin. I exhaled and closed my eyes as she stroked my chest with her fingertips. Her long creamy neck was graceful like a swan. "Beautiful," I breathed into her skin. My thumbs rubbed in circles at her cheekbones, pulling her lips to mine. Soft and sweet, she was like a luscious peach. I explored her body, devouring her with kisses, and she began to tremble.

"Are you okay?" I asked her, suddenly worried and stuck in my head.

"*You're doing it wrong,*" a man with a low voice mocked me.

"*Bad lay,*" a woman said, and my dick softened.

"Freddie?" Cora asked, my name on her lips the only sound that mattered as the others faded away. "Can you hold me for a minute?"

"Of course," I said and pulled her down onto her bed and into the crook of my shoulder.

"*I knew she wouldn't fuck you,*" a man's voice said from deep inside.

"Do you really have a loaded gun in the back of your closet?" she asked softly, a question so innocent and fearful it took my breath away.

"Of course not," I lied, hating myself for it. "I was just trying to diffuse the situation."

"I'm so grateful no one was hurt." She traced her finger through the wisps of hair on my chest.

"Me too," I whispered into her hair. "You know we don't have to do anything more than this," I said as I tickled her hip and then her lower back. "Just lying next to you makes me ridiculously happy."

"Let's not get hasty," she teased and snuggled to me, conforming her body to wrap into mine. I didn't know where she stopped and I began. We were fused at the hip by something stronger than lust. It was the beginning of love. At least, that's what it felt like in my limited experience. After several long serene minutes that were stunningly quiet in my mind, she climbed on top of me, bringing my hands to the small mounds on her chest. I found everything I had been searching for in her eyes. Of all men in the world, she wanted me.

Me!

Afterward, the room was still and quiet, and her legs were tangled in mine as I adjusted the sheet to cover her up. "Are you warm enough?" I whispered into her temple.

"Mmhmm," she murmured sleepily. "I'm so tired. Didn't sleep a wink last night."

"You're so beautiful," I said out loud as she tried to dodge the sandman. My fingers tickled her back as her breathing slowed and lengthened. "Rest now, sweetheart. I'll be here when you wake up." Tears gathered at the corners of my eyes.

"Crying after sex. Jesus, you're a pussy," a man hissed somewhere in the silence.

I laid there for an hour, savoring the softness of her skin, and then Cora started to stir. Like a sleepy kitten, she stretched her skinny arms and legs and then opened her eyes and stared into mine.

"Have you been watching me sleep?"

"Is that weird?"

"I can't decide if it's creepy or sweet."

"I think you should go with sweet," I replied as Cora sat up and tucked the sheet around herself as I playfully tagged at the corner I was allotted. "You know, if you're gonna hog all the covers, we're going to have some serious problems."

She yanked it back with a flirty smile.

"Looks like someone might have some control issues," I teased with a sing-song voice then stood up, trying to find my clothing. Seeing the wadded-up pleather on the floor, I groaned and grimaced when I realized I had to put them back on. "Not my smartest purchase," I admitted, and she snorted again and collected her own discarded clothing, and then began to get dressed.

Finding my phone, I turned the ringer back on and it immediately sounded a crescendo of jingling notifications spiraling on the home screen in my hand. "This is nuts." I looked down and Cora came up behind me to see. "Last night is blowing up, and the Venmo account is filling faster than I can spend it." I opened the app and was startled to see the number climbing past sixty thousand. "We need to think bigger."

"We?" she asked shyly.

"Yes, we," I confirmed. "We're a team."

Her expression brightened. "What did you have in mind?"

"I was thinking a Christmas shopping spree for the kids at the Agape Shelter."

"Is that the one that only allows women and children?"

"That's the one."

"I love that idea."

"You know, I would be nothing without my Ma," I said. "She sacrificed to make sure I had a place to live and food on the table after Dad died. She worked hard, but there wasn't a lot left over for things like toys and games. The gifts under our tree on Christmas mornings were always pretty meager."

"Why didn't she remarry?"

"Dad was such a dick, she probably didn't want to take another chance. I don't think she even went on a date, I mean, that I know of." For the first time, it occurred to me that she might have but never brought them home to meet me. You don't really know anyone outside yourself; even your own mother could be an enigma. She could have been living a secret life that I never knew about. "I'm not sure if she did that on purpose to protect me or just wasn't interested."

"There are a lot of women who have very little room in their life for men after they've been hurt," Cora said. "I don't blame her. Hell, I was practically there myself."

My head popped up to meet her eyes, hoping to hear her proclaim, "But all that has changed now." She didn't and I swallowed my disappointment.

"She was probably saving you from a monster. When a kid gets abused, it's often the stepfather."

"Looks like someone has been watching too much *Dateline* again."

She rolled her eyes and steered the conversation back to the shopping spree. "I think it's an awesome idea, and the chances of a repeat of last night are slim to none. We should be safe in a toy store."

"It all worked out in the end. He was in a desperate place, and it was making him do desperate things."

"That doesn't give him the right to act out like that. Plenty of people deal with hardship and adversity and don't go drawing weapons on people that are trying to help."

"I think we're all capable of great lapses of character and judgment when under pressure like that. Forgive and forget," I said and kissed her cheek. Her body was tight and frustrated in obvious disagreement with me. "You're adorable when you're angry," I said, trying to lighten the mood. "Like a pissed-off little elf."

"Fine," she agreed. "I'll forgive, but I'll never forget. You get one chance with me." Her shoulders set in a hard line and her lips pressed together.

"Duly noted, love."

"*You're going to fuck this up.*" Dad's voice was summoned from the dark recesses of my mind. "*Like you destroy everything.*"

TWENTY-ONE

I was fidgety standing in front of Fiddlesticks Toy Emporium, a mom-and-pop toy store on the verge of collapsing after being undercut for years by the internet and big box stores. Cora reached out and squeezed my hand.

"You ready?"

"As I'll ever be." I exhaled a hot breath, and we walked to customer service to find the owner.

"I can't believe it," the balding shop owner enthused. He held out a hand to me and pumped it up and down like I was the mayor. "It's been a rough year. I thought we were going to have to close our doors and then you called." He teared up, and his neck flushed red. "I just don't know how to thank you."

"No thanks necessary. I've always been a huge fan of the underdog," I answered, "having been one my entire life."

A channel nine news van pulled up, and a well-dressed woman and a denim-clad cameraman crawled out of it and walked toward me. I brushed my fingers across my forehead and pasted a smile on my face that felt fake, but that Ma always said made me more approachable.

"Marcia Moore." The woman introduced herself confidently as her immaculately groomed hand popped out from the crisp cuff of her red power suit.

"Marcia! Marcia! Marcia!" I teased in my best Jan Brady voice. It didn't land. I had miscalculated her age, rendering my pithy pop culture reference invalid. She blinked at me, and the air got sucked out of my lungs.

Loss Column. Check.

"Freddie Angel," I pushed on. "Gotta say, I am a little nervous. I've never been on TV before. I know that's hard to believe with a face like this."

A small smile played at the corners of her mouth, and I was able to breathe again.

Nice recovery.

The cameraman busied himself finding the correct lighting and setting up his tripod as Marcia gave me instructions. "Just answer the questions calmly and slowly. When people get nervous, they tend to talk faster. This story has a lot of heart, so we just need to get out of the way and let it shine."

Two extended vans from Agape Shelter downtown pulled up, and mothers with small children alighted from them and lined up outside the store. Babies on hips, little boys with buzz cuts and dirty shoes. Frazzled mothers who were equal parts exhausted and wary. The roadmap of lines on their faces revealed a life of struggle, and worry lines chiseled deep elevens into their foreheads.

Marcia was in stark contrast, her perfectly pressed suit, immaculate and shiny dark hair cut into a chic bob. I watched her fish a red lipstick from her designer bag and begin to professionally apply it, holding up a small compact mirror for reference. Then she tucked it away and grabbed her microphone.

"Let's go get some interviews from the women," she barked her order at the cameraman as the women and children shuffled into a haphazard line at the front of the store.

For the next twenty minutes, she interviewed them for sound bytes as I watched, trying to calm my nervousness.

"Freddie, this is amazing!" Cora said as she looked over at the women in line. "These kids are going to have a real Christmas this year all because of you."

"I hope so," I admitted. "I have to say, this is the best part of giving it all away." I locked eyes with a little boy no more than four standing in line with his mother. He waved at me, and I gave him a salute and a smile.

"Do you have a plan?"

"I was kind of thinking of making it a game. Giving each kid a five-minute timed shopping spree, you know, like grocery games."

"That's so much fun." Cora smiled. "And *crazy* expensive." She grimaced.

"That's the thing. The money keeps flowing in faster than I can spend it. It's like I am a conduit, directing it, but it's the donations from fans that allow this to happen."

Marcia finally finished with the women and landed back in front of me. "Are you ready for your interview?"

"Never been more ready." I gave her a charming smile as my heart fluttered in my chest.

She waved the cameraman over, and he turned on his video light that reminded me of the stage light at The Punch Line.

"I'm here at Fiddlesticks Toy Emporium with Freddie Angel, who you might know as the Funologist." She turned slightly and swept her manicured hand back toward the line of women and children gathered behind her. "He's spreading early Christmas spirit in an incredible way today. Behind us are residents of the Agape Women's Shelter who have been gifted a generous shopping spree. Freddie, can you tell me how this all came together?"

"Sure, Marcia." I smiled at the camera, impressed with how smooth my delivery sounded. "I was fortunate enough to win the lottery on a scratch-off ticket, so I got the idea to spread the joy far and wide and give away all the proceeds. It's been a challenge and a joy to try to pull that off."

"You're giving it *all* away?" She asked. If her forehead wasn't immobilized by Botox, I'm sure it would have crinkled in surprise.

"Yes," I answered. "That was the original plan when the ticket was a winner, but something else happened. A photo of a tip I gave a waitress went viral, so a fan told me to create a Venmo account. Almost immediately, donations starting flying in from all over the country. The account has ballooned to the point that we can help bring a very merry Christmas to these women and children."

"What's the Venmo account handle if our viewers wanted to donate?"

I answered, "@thefunologist. I can personally guarantee that all donations will be used to fund community outreaches like this one."

"That's incredible."

"It *is* kind of a modern-day miracle," I mused. "It's humbling, actually, to be in a position to help people that need it."

"Can you tell us about the video that went viral with the ice cream truck?"

"Who doesn't love ice cream?" I asked. "Well, a few days ago, I had the crazy idea to rent an ice cream truck, fill it with treats, drive down to the neediest neighborhoods, and give it away until it was gone."

"And you were rewarded for this act of generosity by being held up at gunpoint?" she expertly questioned, leading me through the interview.

"That *did* happen. But I have to say that almost anyone is capable of a violent act when pushed into a corner." I looked down, then back up to answer. "He just needed someone to hear him. The poor are invisible in our country. The only way to get people's attention sometimes is to act out. That's all it was."

"And you aren't going to press charges?"

"No. First of all, I have to stress that no one was hurt, just a little shook up. And I know I've made plenty of mistakes in my life, and if I had to pay the piper for each one, I wouldn't be standing here talking to you today. Sometimes people just need a pass. Sometimes good people make bad mistakes."

"Well, you're a better man than I am," she jibbed with a smile, revealing perfect whitened teeth, then continued, "You're a stand-up comedian?"

"Yes. You can find me at The Punch Line on Sycamore a couple of nights a week," I offered.

"This funny man turned philanthropist is exactly the kind of Christmas spirit Kansas City needs right now," Marcia summed it all up neatly in one sound byte, turning to the camera with a practiced smile. "If you'd like to be part of the Funologist movement, send your Venmo donations to @the-funologist. Thank you, Freddie Angel. I know this won't be the last time we hear from you."

I smiled, and then Marcia said, "That's a wrap." She turned to me again. "This is exactly the kind of feel-good story our viewers love. I hope it has legs."

"Whatever happens beyond this is a gift," I told her. "Are we ready to get started?"

"I'm going to stick around and do some filming. But yes, the interview portion is over."

"Thanks, Marcia." I shook her hand one more time and then stepped in front of the line of women and children.

"Okay, my friends, today is going to blow your mind. Each child is going to get a five-minute shopping spree. Moms, you're in charge of pushing the carts, kids, your job is to fill 'em up. Run fast!" I said, addressing the kids. "You want to make every second count. The only rule is that you can only put one of each item in your cart. We have to make sure that there are enough Xboxes to go around for everyone. Got it?"

"Yeah!" It was a chorus of excitement as the children grew more animated. They chattered to each other and craned their necks to see what was in each aisle. Planning their attack, the crowd was smiling and the moms were wiping happy tears away from weary faces.

"Okay, let's do this!"

A young blonde woman and her dark-haired five-year-old son were up first. I pulled up the timer on my phone and set it for five minutes. Kneeling so I could look him square in the eyes, I asked, "Are you ready, my man?" He was keyed up and jumping. "Run as fast as you can, grab what you want, and fill that cart! You must return to the checkout line before the clock runs out, got it?"

The boy nodded solemnly.

I added a taped starting line to the floor, and he squatted down behind it like he was queued up on blocks to run the fifty-yard dash. "On your mark, get set, go!"

"Let's cheer him on!" I shouted to the crowd, sweeping my arms up like I'd seen hype men at concerts do. "Runnnnnn!"

He ran from aisle to aisle, his mom trailing behind him

pushing the cart, and he filled it in record time. "Five seconds left! Get to the checkout," I shouted. Ending his dash, he stood proudly next to his filled cart, out of breath and red-faced. The lights in his mom's eyes turned on, and she smiled a real smile that made my heart burst.

Twelve more kids ran the gauntlet, throwing in toys as fast as they could. Cora and I took turns running cart duty for the moms with toddlers and infants, running up and down the aisles, cheering them, on and filling them to the brim. Those sixty minutes were the most cardio I had done in a decade. My heart was exploding from the effort, but more from the absolute joy on their faces. The kids checked out one by one, and Marcia met me at the register.

"Twenty-nine thousand, four hundred, and eleven dollars," the manager said, wincing slightly.

"Actually, I'm surprised it wasn't more. I feel like I got away cheap!" I pulled out my Venmo credit card with a flourish and swiped it as the camera rolled, thankful Cora had the foresight to call Venmo about the sizable transaction for pre-approval. How embarrassing would it have been to have my card declined on camera?

The register spit out a massive receipt that I scrawled a signature across and then I headed over to the families whose moods had totally transformed in the two hours since they had first gotten out of the vans.

"Did everyone get what they wanted?" I asked the families, and they roared back in choruses of, "Yes!"

"You kids were running so fast, and everyone scored such an impressive pile of loot, looks like we might have to make a few trips to get you guys home."

The kids were jumping up and down, screaming and hugging their gifts to their bellies. Several had tears streaming down their faces.

"This is the first real Christmas he's had."

"Last year, I couldn't give him any presents."

"It's so hard to tell a kid that Santa skipped his house when, at school, their friends are getting huge hauls."

"You made her dream come true."

I was on fire, bursting with joy and pride. Seeing the physical manifestation of joy on the faces of kids who hadn't seen much of it in their short lives wrecked me in the best way. The energy crackled through me, and I fed off their excitement that surged on a track from me to them and back again. Humility and gratitude crashed over me in waves, and I have never felt more complete and more at peace.

"This experience gave me as much as it gave your kids." I was getting choked up. "I will never forget this day." My voice cracked. "The squeals of delight and complete happiness coming from these kids is a gift that I will take to my grave. Thank you for being part of one of the best days of my life."

Cora reached out and squeezed my hand. Not ready to end the lovefest, I walked with a fresh burst of inspiration over to the shelter representatives that were standing by.

"I'd like to do something for these moms," I told them. "I know it sounds silly, but I was thinking maybe makeovers? I recently discovered how a haircut and a new outfit can make you feel like a new person. Do you think we could arrange something like that for them?" I was just spit-balling an idea, but I hoped it would land.

"Mr. Angel, that is incredibly generous."

The utter respect that dripped from their words puffed me up like a peacock.

"We'll work out all the details. Cora, can you help me find a salon and a boutique that can help us out?"

"Absolutely." She smiled up at me.

I walked back over to the moms who were celebrating with their kids and said, "The Funologist has one more surprise in store for you!"

An excited squeal of excitement rose from the kids.

"This one is for all the mamas!" I ran down the line, high-fiving anyone who extended a hand for one. "Moms are the glue of the family, holding everything together. My Ma, she's a saint, especially for putting up with the likes of me, so I was thinking…" I stopped for a minute to catch my breath and watched their eyes filled with hope. I dragged out the tension until the kids began to chant.

"Tell us! Tell Us!" It grew louder and louder as I stood and played conductor, cranking up the excitement to a fevered pitch until they couldn't stand it anymore. Then I ran over to the first woman in line.

"You get a makeover!" I shouted out like Oprah on the episode where she gave away cars to the entire studio audience. "You get a makeover! And *you* get a makeover! And you!" I shouted out as I walked down the line, pointing at each woman.

Four of the women burst into immediate tears, making their children anxiously stare up at me. "It's okay, kids. This is a good thing. I promise. Some tears are happy tears. You got spoiled today, and soon, your mamas are going to get a chance to be spoiled. Don't you think they deserve it?"

Marcia appeared at my side. "That was amazing. Can we tag along, do an exclusive story on the Mommy Makeovers?"

"Sure," I said, unaware of just how crazy the media circus was going to become after her story was aired. Life as I knew it was about to change completely.

TWENTY-TWO

Marcia said the interview was going to air in seven days, so I busied myself making good on my promise for the mommy makeovers. Cora did all the heavy lifting. She booked the salon, and she approached the owner of the boutique, but the credit always shot my way. When I tried to put it on her shoulders, she just pushed it back on mine.

"You're the one they come to see, Freddie. You're the Funologist. I'm just helping you out."

When you eliminate sleeping, suddenly your days become fifty percent more productive. Every morning started the same way, counting the remaining cash in the briefcase, organizing it by denomination, and making sure all the bills faced the same way. Then faithfully recording the amount remaining on the steno notebook tucked into the front flap. Anxiety was my constant companion and always lodged deep in my gut, but as I passed the faded bills from my left to right hands, the tension began to subside. My shoulders that were ever hunched tight around my ears would relax and shift downward.

I was euphoric the morning of the makeovers, standing in front of the mirror, dragging the black plastic comb downward from crown to forehead. My ritual demanded fifty strokes counted by twos until it was perfect, then I was allowed to move to the next section. Fifty more strokes on the right side, fifty strokes on the left side and fifty on the back. If I lost count, or was interrupted, or, worse yet, I landed on an odd number, I had to start over. Complete laser focus was required, but once I finished the task, I could move on to the next one.

I yanked on a pair of jeans and a shiny leather jacket. After the painful lesson I learned about chafing with the pleather pants, wearing leather was forever restricted to the upper body. The only people over forty who can pull off leather pants are the aging members of Aerosmith and Brett Michaels. My pleather pants found a permanent home stuffed in the back of my closet where they would never see the light of day. Finally ready, I took the stairs two at a time, counting by twos in my head, and landed at the top with a jump.

"I've got a surprise for you," I sang to Ma while she was working on a sudoku puzzle at the kitchen table. A cup of cold coffee stained a circle on the paper towel next to her.

"You do?" she asked absentmindedly as she tried to solve the puzzle. "Ah-ha!" she blurted triumphantly, licking the tip of her pencil and tracing a seven neatly into the fourth box of the third row. I never understood why she always had to actually taste graphite before committing to an answer.

"I made a promise to all the moms from the shelter, and Marcia Moore from channel nine wants to do a story on it."

Her eyebrows lifted, and she immediately set down her pencil, shut the book, and burrowed into my eyes, digging for clues about my current state of wellbeing. "Another one?"

she asked. "But we haven't even seen the first yet. I don't know, Freddie," she cautioned. "This sounds…"

"You only have to wait a few more days. It airs on Friday," I interrupted, sitting in the empty chair across from her. "I wish you could have been there, Ma." I leaned onto my elbows closer to her, excitement creeping into my voice, energy surging to my limbs. I forced myself to remain still, knowing that her radar would go up if I got too animated. "Winning the lottery was my destiny!" I declared. "I started out just wanting to give it away, but it's grown into a completely different animal. It's bigger than just that ticket now—it's a freaking movement! I have the chance to make a real difference in real people's lives, and I plan on carrying it out for as long as the donations come rolling in." I knit my fingers together to keep them from flying out. "Say you'll come with me," I begged. "You have to see what it's like first hand, then you'll understand."

"Me?" she asked as she pulled her smudged glasses from her face, exhaled on the lenses, and rubbed the fresh condensation pooled there with her thumbs wrapped in a fold of cotton from her house dress.

"Yes, *you*, silly. I'm giving these moms the royal treatment, and no mom deserves it more than you."

"Aww, Freddie. You don't have to do that. I have everything I need." She shooed away the attention with a flick of her fingers.

"But I want to," I urged. "Cora found a salon that wants to be part of the movement, and we are going to gift makeovers and massages to all the women from the shelter. A boutique is going to step in and help style the women and put together a professional look for their job interviews. It's going to be awesome."

"Wow, sweetheart." She pressed her hand to her heart.

"What an incredible idea! You're giving them a fresh start. It's so generous."

"Now that's the spirit!" I exclaimed. "Ma, seeing those kids running down the aisles and the utter joy on their faces, I just knew I had to do more. These moms, they have been through it. They deserve a day of pampering."

"I'm so proud of you," she gushed, smiling up at me as she reached her hand up to cup under my chin. "So proud." Her eyes crinkled and her cheekbones popped as the smile danced across her face.

Proud. The word leveled me, and instant tears pricked the corners of my eyes. I craved hearing it so intensely. I wondered if it had been written on each of my cells inside the womb. The need was a deep-seated, primal ache that became a festering wound as the failures began to stack up in my life. It took on an elusive patina, something I could endlessly strive for yet never attain. I didn't do many things to make anyone proud. Not myself and definitely not my mother.

"Thanks, Ma," I said sheepishly, swiping at my eyes. "Go take a shower and get dressed. The limo is arriving at eleven."

"Limo?" she exclaimed, shocked. "Freddie, that's a little…" her voice trailed off.

"Extravagant, I know, but I decided to go all out. This money is coming in as fast as I can spend it."

She stared at me unblinking, lips slightly pursed. Her head tilted this way and that in confusion, narrowing her blue eyes as she searched my eyes for signs, looking for hints and clues. Always considering and weighing my behaviors against the list of known symptoms of mania in bipolar adults with OCD.

"I've got a whole new way of thinking. If one can afford

to shower their mother with extravagance from time to time, one should do it."

"You're such a sweet boy." I could see her crumple up her worries like tissue and push away her doubts with the puzzle book as she leaned closer to hug me. "Then I won't get in the way of that. Looks like I better get ready for an incredible day."

———

An hour later, the stretch limo I'd ordered was stationed in front of our house. Marcia's news van was parked behind it, and Cora stood with me waiting for Ma to emerge.

"Simon, were you able to get the bouquets?" I asked the spry chauffeur dressed in a black suit and hat holding the door open for me.

"Yes, sir."

"Thank you, my good man." I pulled out a fifty for him before sliding onto the soft leather seats and dragging Cora into the darkened car by her hand.

Resting on the bench seating that wrapped around the interior were fourteen bouquets of yellow roses, Ma's favorite. I pulled one of them out and handed it to Cora, who blushed.

When it comes to women, flowers are magic.

"Can you open the sunroof for me?" I asked Simon, and he responded with a swift nod.

The motorized whir of the sunroof sliding open made me giddy. I slid to the center of it and popped up like toast as Ma walked out of the house. "I've wanted to do this since I saw Richard Gere pull it off in *Pretty Woman*," I said to Cora. "Come here. Come see how the other half lives." I beckoned her with my fingers, and she crammed into the rest of the space and hugged me, waving at Ma.

"Holla at your boy, Ma!" I shouted out, waving like a moron, while she smiled with the whiff of an eye-roll she always gave me whenever I used terms she called "street vernacular." It was a dynamic that had been playing out since I was little. Always pushing the edge of outrageousness to make her laugh.

The chauffeur opened the door for her, so I crawled down, scooped up one of the bouquets, and landed it square in Ma's arms.

"Flowers? For me?" she gasped. "Oh my! I can't remember the last time I got flowers." I felt a pang of guilt.

I have taken this woman for granted.

She pulled the bouquet to her nose and inhaled, and her eyes twinkled.

"They smell so good, honey. Thank you."

"Anything for you, Mama." I was swollen with pride. Feeling like a man, a real man for the first time in my entire life.

We settled in and enjoyed the drive to the shelter, heading deeper into the belly of the city. The streets grew grimier and grittier the further we went. Check cashing businesses, vape stores, and bail bondsmen filled the neglected storefronts. Heavy bars were curtained at the sides of convenience stores, waiting for the end of the night lockdown to begin.

I pulled out my phone and began a video. "It's Freddie Angel, the Funologist, heading to Agape Shelter where your donations are going to help me pamper some deserving mamas." I swung the camera to Ma's face. "This is my beautiful Ma. Say hi, Ma!" I instructed. She waved and parroted my response. Knowing I was making her uncomfortable, I panned to the bouquets of flowers resting on the seat. "We're arriving in style and going to present each of these women with a bouquet, then whisk them away for a massage and a makeover. It's your donations that help fund this mission, so if you want me to continue, send a little donation via Venmo to @thefunologist. You never know where I'm going to turn up next." I added the hashtags and uploaded it to all my social profiles, then waved the phone at Ma to show her the notifications as minutes later, the first thumbs up and donations started rolling in.

"That's all you have to do?" she asked incredulously.

"That's it. That's the power of social media," Cora answered for me.

"Wow." She struggled to grasp the concept.

"When you have a raving fan base like mine, you have the power to change lives." The words puffed me up like a peacock. I was so damn proud.

"Hmm." Ma considered my words, biting on the side of her cheek like she wanted to say something, but was afraid to ruin the moment.

The driver eased us to the curb. "Ready?" I looked at Ma and gathered up as many bouquets as I could, wincing when a thorn dug into my palm. "Can you grab the rest?"

The driver opened the door for us as the women began to file out of the shelter, excited with bright smiles on their faces. I handed them each a bouquet and introduced them to my mom. Cora faded into the background, but I was too distracted to notice.

"Can you take a group photo for me?" I asked Simon, holding out my phone.

"Of course."

"Photo op!" I exclaimed. "Squeeze in, everyone. Ma, you get the special spot, front and center."

She squeezed in beside me and wrapped her arms around

my waist. The spicy floral scent of the roses washed toward me in a wave.

"Whoa, whoa, whoa! Wait! Where's my other best girl?" I asked, looking around for Cora. My eyes finally lit on hers at the edge of the group, hiding in the back.

"Get over here, gorgeous." I insisted and the group adjusted to give her space. I was an Oreo, flanked by the two women I loved most in the world.

"On the count of three, say Funologist!" I instructed as Simon snapped off three photos of our group in front of the limo. Crushed in the center of this warm puddle of feminine energy, I joked, "I think we're looking a little more Utah right now than Missouri. Everyone, take a moment to introduce yourself to your sister wives! You're going to want to set up our sleepover schedule amongst yourselves. Don't worry, ladies, there's enough of Freddie to go around." There was a ripple of laughter as Ma protested with a smack to my chest, but cracked a smile anyway.

Win column. Check.

I felt Cora stiffen against my back.

"Yeah, you have yourself a real harem, Freddie. You probably have to pay for even one of these desperate chicks to bang you," a voice hissed as the women dispersed and began sliding into the limo, chattering amongst themselves in excitement.

I settled in next to Ma, who reached out to squeeze my hand.

"Look at you, big man. Still holding your mama's hand in a limo full of available women! You're forty years old, not a preschooler needing to cross the street." I gently extracted my hand from hers and forced a smile.

We stopped in front of a salon where the owner was out front waiting with a tray filled with champagne flutes with bobbing strawberries as I had instructed. Behind her, ten stylists stood in a V formation like birds fleeing the cold in the fall, dressed from head to toe in black with their arms folded behind them. I pulled out my phone and turned the camera on video mode.

"Hey, guys! It's the Funologist here with Lauren, the owner of Bombshell Salon and Spa, who is giving these lovely ladies a makeover and day of pampering." I scanned over the crowd and then focused in on Lauren. "Thank you, Lauren, for helping make this day possible."

"It's our pleasure," she said. "We've been following your story since the waitress post went viral. Never underestimate the power of an hour in your stylist's chair. It's better than therapy, it's hair-apy!"

Next door, Sylvie, the rail-thin boutique owner, stood in front of her shop with her two assistants. I turned the video back on and started recording. "These ladies are in luck because we've also partnered with Main Street Boutique, who are going to style each of these women so they are ready to re-enter the workforce. Thank you, Sylvie, for being part of this!"

"We're just as excited as you are, Freddie. Putting on the right outfit is like wearing confidence. We want these women to kill at those interviews. Change your outfit, change your life!"

"No doubt they will!"

I posted the videos on Tik-Tok, Instagram, and Facebook, hash-tagging it and then tucked the phone away.

"Lauren, can you take extra special care of this one?" I said as I wrapped my arm around Ma's shoulders and guided her over.

"Of course." She escorted Ma into the salon. I searched

for Cora, finding her cleaning up the loose flower petals in the back of the limo.

"I don't know if you noticed, but we have a guy for that."

"I know, Freddie. I hired the guy. Remember?"

"I'm sorry, sweetheart. Don't be mad at me."

"I'm not. I just don't live for the spotlight like you do. We're different people."

"Opposites attract," I offered as a weak explanation. Something was wrong. It was the hard set of her lips. She was more stingy with her smiles.

Do something. You're going to lose her.

"Did you want a massage?" I asked. "I can set you up."

"No. I'd feel too guilty using your donations for personal gain."

"I'd be happy to pay for it out of my own money to thank you for coordinating this event. You know we wouldn't be here at all if it wasn't for your handiwork." The praise melted her, and her shoulders unclenched. She put her hand in mine as relief flooded in.

"You know, we have a few hours and a limo that's free… We could have Simon take us anywhere we want. And these windows are tinted if you catch my drift."

"Drift caught." She laughed with an eye roll. "That would be the scandal of the century. Tonight on *Inside Edition*, An exclusive look into the Funologist's Polygamist Cult."

I pulled her closer to me and kissed her neck while she protested.

"Careful, I don't think we negotiated this special time with the other sister wives. They're going to be so jealous," she said, her words tingling with an edge that filled me with fear.

I kissed her on the mouth, knowing I was pushing my luck. "But you would be the legal one. The first one. The most important one," I murmured into her lips, feeling them soften and turn up into a smile.

"I better be," she said and kissed me.

———

Three hours later, the women were unrecognizable. They glowed, lit up from within, and their flowing hair was smooth, shiny, and bright. They radiated happiness. Dressed in heels and suits. Jeans and sweater sets.

I turned to Cora, both of our mouths wide open, jaws on the floor.

"Seriously, these are *not* the women who first showed up here."

"Never underestimate the power of a little concealer, a good haircut, and the right pair of jeans," Cora said knowingly.

"I've got an idea. Catwalk time!" I shouted out eagerly. "Who's ready to strut? Cora, can you pull up some runway jams?"

"You got it." She scrolled through some options, landing on "I'm Too Sexy."

"Classic. Good choice."

One by one, the women strutted down the sidewalk toward me as I crouched low for an artistic angle. Some of them stopped at the end and shot me a pose. Hands to hips. Hunching their shoulders forward and laughing at themselves. Some of the women were more shy, walking carefully and blowing me a kiss when they landed in front of the camera. Some of them stomped like they had watched too many episodes of *America's Next Top Model*, like pissed-off giraffes, all legs.

"Where's Ma?" I asked Cora. "I'm dying to see Ma's new look."

"Dottie! Dottie! Dottie!" I started the chant, and Cora and the other women joined in. And then I saw her. Dressed in a lavender pantsuit that picked up the slight purple cast to her salon-whitened hair, she was illuminated as she slowly walked toward me, smiling wide. The women lined up on either side of the catwalk began chanting her name. "Dot-tie! Dot-tie! Dot-tie!"

She landed at the end of our impromptu catwalk and blew me a kiss before turning to stride back. Halfway there, she whipped a shoulder around and blew me another kiss, and the girls went wild, clapping and screaming and chanting her name. She disappeared into the group, enveloped by a throng of arms clad in poplin and lace.

I turned the phone to face me. "Who knew I had such a hot mama? Aren't they gorgeous?" I panned back to the building and Lauren and Sylvie. "Special thanks to Bombshell Salon and Main Street Boutique, our partners in crime. Come support these local businesses. Your donations and the generous gift of their time and talent have truly transformed these women from the inside out. You're all amazing."

I clicked the camera off, tucked it away, and found Ma and Cora surrounded by the women. Simon stood at the limo with the door propped open. It was a sea of perfect blowouts and coordinated wrap dresses and jackets. I was scooped into a group hug, pulled to the center of the circle in a cloud of Moroccan oil-scented hairspray. Love bloomed there, along with acceptance and joy. It spiraled me up higher and higher making me feel like a king. The jubilant energy synergized and swirled, coming together in a rush of sweetness and glee. A lump formed in my throat as my eyes moved slowly from woman to woman, piecing together the faces I met at the shelter with the radiant beauty that now lived in each one of them. I swallowed hard to keep myself from crying, and when my eyes landed on Cora's, her head tipped so slightly and her gaze softened. I felt a knot loosen in the deepest center of my soul that had been constricting me since birth. She mouthed the words, "I love you."

"I love you, too," I mouthed back to her. I closed my eyes for a moment, savoring it, recording it in my mental memory, and when I opened my eyes, I saw Ma dab along the bottom of her lashes. She blew me a kiss that I plucked from the air with my fingers. I exhaled and laughed at myself. "I'm a big, sentimental baby," I admitted to the women. "Don't tell anyone."

Choruses of, "Aww," surrounded me as the women linked their arms and hugged me, and another knot loosened.

Their impromptu group hug was a force of love so strong, I choked on a sob, needing a full minute to regain my composure. I swiped at my tears and laughed at myself and finally was able to say, "We have to head back now, but I just want to thank you for sharing this day with us. I know, to most people, what we did today was superficial, but it was much more than a haircut."

"I know life for you ladies has not been easy. Today, I got the chance to hear some of your stories, and it was a truly humbling experience. You are survivors, you are warriors, you are selfless human beings that consistently put the needs of everyone else above your own. My Ma has been doing that for decades. I hope today you learned that at any moment you can re-invent yourself, that if something isn't working in your life, you can change it. I hope you return home and can go back out in the world feeling more confident. Feeling stronger, and beautiful, and capable, and worthy. Because every one of you deserved the star treatment you received today. I hope you return to your lives with the understanding that, even in your darkest days, life can still surprise you. Today was a great day, and I am so grateful I got to share it with you."

I waited as the women filed into the car and then paid the bill at the salon and the boutique. I waved an extra $500 in cash at the stylists, and was rewarded with a chorus of, "Wait? Is that just the tip?"

"What else could it possibly be?" I responded with a huge smile and walked out of there bursting with joy.

TWENTY-THREE

After the story aired was when the shit really hit the fan. The phone started ringing off the hook, and donations exploded on a nearly second by second basis. I was on fire, and my star was shooting into the stratosphere. I was white-knuckling it with all I had, knowing you only get one ride on the rocket to fame.

"Just ignore it, Ma." I came by and kissed her cheek.

"It's just such insanity, Freddie! All these people, I can't believe it. You're a sensation."

The Venmo account was close to hitting six figures, even after the Christmas shopping spree with the kids and the mommy makeovers. Fast and furious, money was rolling in at all hours of the day and night, so much so I had to set the phone to silent after I drank enough to finally fall asleep for two hours. When I woke up the next morning, it was like spinning the wheel on *The Price is Right* to zip through the thousands of payment notifications, messages, and social media tags that appeared overnight.

And then came the call I had been waiting for my entire life—the big time. Jimmy Bravo's assistant called and asked to book me for an appearance on the show. *The* Jimmy Bravo. A comedy god whose show was taped live in New York, whose monologue I'd studied every day since the first time I stood on a stage. It was the kind of life-changing opportunity that usually passed me by. A pie-in-the-sky dream I tucked deep in my heart years ago finally floated into my reality. I was being touched by the hand of God. My moment had arrived. Everything I had worked so hard at for so long was now within my grasp.

They wanted to fly me to New York and offered me a six-minute set on the show. *Late Night with Jimmy Bravo* was one of the only LIVE shows left in existence; most late-night television is taped in the middle of the day. Jimmy fought to do things his way and on his terms and successfully negotiated this caveat into his latest contract with the network. That's the kind of power you have when your weekly viewership is ten million people. Normally, you have to go through the audition process with a tape, but after my last few appearances getting a million views on YouTube and the Funologist posts going viral, I was riding high on the fast track—a thundering, unstoppable train. It catapulted me from obscurity into becoming a recognizable quasi-celebrity overnight. Suddenly, the doors that had all been locked, that I stood outside beating on until my fists were bloody, were flying open.

Win Column. Colossal check. Biggest check of them all.

The phone call from his assistant left me trembling, and I called Cora immediately.

"Hey you," she said into the phone.

"You're never going to believe this. I got a call from *Late Night with Jimmy Bravo*."

"What?" She shrieked, "Holy shit, Freddie! I'm speechless."

"I can't stop shaking," I admitted. "They want to fly me to New York next week!" I paused, "And I am doing a six-minute set. Can you believe this?" I laughed into the phone, the joy rushing up, higher and higher, leaving me breathless and my heart pounding. Then an impulsive thought flashed through my mind and came out of my mouth. "Come with me."

"Me?" she asked. "I wish I could, but I can't afford it."

"I need your moral support, and I still have some of my lottery winnings, so I'd love to fly you over. Maybe we could see a Broadway show, eat somewhere extravagant and over-the-top where they brûlée shit?"

She laughed. "Are you serious? That sounds incredible."

"Yeah?" I asked. "I'm probably going to need you to talk me off the ledge before I go on. Request a crystal dish filled with only green M & M's. You know, the usual."

"Of course, you will." She laughed. "But a vacation? Man, you don't know how long it's been!"

I was already planning it in my head. We could stay at the Baccarat—a five-star hotel I saw once in an episode of *Lifestyles of the Rich and Famous* when I was a kid. Eat at Le Cirque, take in *The Book of Mormon*. It would cost a pretty penny, but hey, you can't take it with you. We were going to paint the town and do it up right.

"So that's a yes?" I asked. "Don't worry about anything. Pack a bag and I'll take care of all the details."

"It's a yes!" she exclaimed into the phone.

"I'll see you tonight at the club?"

"The way your star is rising, you won't be playing little rinky-dink hole in the walls like The Punch Line for much longer."

That thought hadn't crossed my mind at all, but once it had, it left me reeling, unhinged, and undone. Suddenly, the life I had been living was too small and restrictive. I felt the pull toward more, to become more, and then the fear rushed in. Like the ocean at high tide, the force of the fear was a panicked surge that felt like the floor was dropping out from under me. The mundane and normal life I was living was disappearing and morphing into something different. It was time to shed the old skin to make room for the new.

The excitement was electric, turning me into a livewire that crackled and short-circuited. I had boundless energy with this opportunity on the horizon; it was a good thing I wasn't numbed out and medicated anymore. I was tack sharp and had enough stamina for ten men, and I needed it. This was a big break, the biggest of my entire life, and I needed the extra energy and drive to perfect my six minutes.

We said our goodbyes and I pulled out my notebook and racked my busy brain for the next several minutes. Staring at the blank white expanse of my notebook, I felt blocked and stuck. I read through my material and my existing set, but for the upcoming big show, none of the jokes seemed to have the "it" factor. The thing that made them punchy and vibrant and memorable.

"This is all shite," I said aloud in my best Scottish accent. I would have to start from ground zero.

"Ma!" I ran upstairs two at a time.

Two. Four. Six. Eight. Ten.

"Ma!"

"Judas Priest, is the house on fire?" She walked toward me with a cracked plastic hamper balanced on her hip.

"Almost!" I said with a crazed smile. "You're never going to believe this! Jimmy Bravo called. They invited me to New York!"

"What?" She dropped the basket in shock, both hands covering her mouth. "That's amazing!"

"They want me to do a set."

"Of course, they do! My beautiful boy." She squeezed my shoulders and pulled me in for a hug. "Your star is rising. Enjoy every second of this. You earned it."

There was a sheen of sweat on my forehead when she touched it. "Did you take your meds?"

"Of course," I lied.

"Good. You don't want to let your condition ruin this opportunity for you. You've worked too hard for a big break like this. We can't have anything go wrong now."

TWENTY-FOUR

I picked up the call. I know I shouldn't have, but a big part of me needed to gloat. Tommy lorded his successes over me my whole life, so to get a chance to shove mine down his throat was an opportunity I just couldn't pass up.

"Tommy," I responded, my voice oozing new confidence it never had before.

"Fritzy," he replied. "Surprised you stooped so low to pick up my phone call."

"You definitely put the *bother* in brother, but what can I say? I am feeling extra generous lately."

"Yeah, I can see that. Better be careful or you're asking for another gun in your face. Personally, I wish he would have just pulled the trigger and rid me of a problem that has plagued me my entire life."

Dick.

"Look, I really need your help," he pleaded, changing gears so fast it was comical and I had to call him out.

"You've got to be kidding me!" I exclaimed, gripping the phone tightly. "In the span of ten seconds, you go from gleefully hoping for my homicide to begging for my help? The answer is no."

"Don't be an asshole. I'm going to lose everything."

"I'm sorry to hear that," I offered a half-assed response, but then rethought it immediately.

His insult incensed me. "Wait, no, I'm not," I spit into the phone. "Maybe you'll finally get a taste of what struggle feels like. You've needed a reality check for a long time. It's called karma, jack-leg! Besides, with the way things are going for me, Mom might be in the market for a new roommate soon."

"Live in Mom's basement?" he scoffed at the thought. "Absolutely fucking not. I would kill myself before I did that."

Not the worst idea you've ever had, Jackass.

I didn't say it, but by God, I wanted to.

"I have a responsibility to my fans," I bragged into the phone. "They didn't donate money for me to use to bail my brother out of his shitty decisions."

"Fans?" he sneered with contempt. "Is *that* what you're calling them?"

I sighed, wishing I hadn't picked up the phone after all.

"How about a couple thou?" he asked. "Just enough to get me by until I can make other arrangements?"

"How about you take a long walk off a short pier?" I retorted. "You made your bed, now you have to lie in it." I lectured. "Isn't that what you always told me?" I closed my eyes and pinched my nose in frustration. "You know, Tommy, if you would have shown me one shred of decency, one iota of compassion, I might have been compelled to say yes."

"You're an asshole. Fuck you, Freddie."

The dial tone stung my ears. Smug and satisfied, it was sweet to see him finally get his comeuppance. My whole life, he acted like I was something he'd scraped off the bottom of his shoe, but now that he needed me, the tables had turned and a self-righteous thrill swept through me.

———

The phone call spun me up. With energy to burn, I walked and walked, not really having a destination in mind, but ended up at one of my favorite haunts—Cal's Pet Emporium. Some days, I'd randomly swing in to pet the cats in plexiglass cages up for adoption. I've always had a soft spot for animals, they never let you down.

The bell jingled on the door as I walked in, and the sharp ammonia tang of animal piss on cedar chips stung my nostrils. Squeaks, squawks, and zings punctuated the space as the animals went about their days on full display in their enclosures. I squatted down to watch one particularly rotund hamster running on a wheel.

I rubbed one finger down the aquarium, leaving a trail of fingerprints on the glass.

You got this, little fat man.

It occurred to me that I felt like this my whole life. Stuck in a cage, running and running on the track to nowhere. Waiting for someone to choose me. To take me home and love me, endlessly performing for their approval and acceptance.

"You're an asshole," a falsetto voice said. I glanced around, searching for the source of it, this time unsure if it came from inside my head or from someone else. To the side, I noticed a large gray bird with its talons clutching a tree branch. I walked over to the enclosure and saw a tag identifying him as Alvin, an African Grey Parrot whose age was estimated at seventeen, and his cost was a staggering fifteen hundred dollars.

"You're an asshole." I heard it again, and this time, the teenager in the blue smock that was stocking shelves said, "Sorry about that. Alvin is a rescue and he's kind of a dick."

"That was the *bird*?"

"Unfortunately," he said. "Once a bird learns a phrase, you're stuck with it forever. His owner let him watch too much HBO."

Alvin whistled and then ducked his head under his wing, preening for me.

"They do that?" I asked, shocked.

"Yeah, it's pretty incredible. Watch this." He pulled out his phone and pressed a couple of buttons, and then Queen's smash hit "Another One Bites the Dust" started playing through the phone. Alvin began to bob up and down, shuffling along the length of his perch, and then bobbing in tune to the music.

I laughed because it was pretty impressive. "Okay, that's just awesome. Does he say anything else?"

"He's got an extensive vocabulary, but most of it is cuss words. Not exactly the perfect family pet and probably why he's been with us for over a year." He turned to the bird. "Who's a pretty boy?"

"Alvin is," he squawked back. "Eat a bag of dicks. Bwakkk!"

I snorted. "Did he just tell you to eat a bag of dicks?"

"Yeah." The boy shook his head. "Sorry about that."

"Dude, don't apologize!" I exclaimed. "This bird is my spirit animal." Alvin turned his head and chirped as his one dark eye bored into mine. Blinking. Stuck in his cage, unwanted and misunderstood. "I have to have him."

"You do know these guys live forever, right?"

"Uh. Of course," I lied.

"Like to be eighty years old."

"Wow. He might outlive me." I calculated. "What do they eat?" I asked.

"Pellets, but they also love fresh veggies and fruit and seeds. Like kale and broccoli."

"No wonder they live forever. I'd live forever if I ate a diet of kale and apples."

Alvin bobbed his head up and down while walking up and down the stick in his habitat. His long claws squeezed and released. He was a performer, another characteristic we shared. I loved that about him.

"You're the man," he blurted out, making me laugh.

"So, which is it, Alvin? Am I an asshole or the man?"

"You're an asshole," he answered quickly, punctuating his response with a click and a purr.

"Well, now that I know he isn't just trying to butter me up, I *have* to have him." Mind made up, I followed the teenager to the cash register.

"We can deliver him to you, set up his habitat, and get you all stocked with food and toys."

Alvin rang the bell, and I took it as a sign. "Looks like we have a winner," I said. "Ring me up."

Two thousand six-hundred dollars later, I was set. They would deliver the bird when I got home from New York.

TWENTY-FIVE

Less than a week later, I signaled to the stewardess, who appeared with two warm towels and glasses of champagne for us on a silver tray.

"I've never flown first-class before," Cora enthused as she took the flute she was offered. "A girl could get used to this." She unfolded the warm towel and pressed it to her face and hands.

"Oh my God." Cora moaned through the towel draped over her face. "I am never leaving this seat." When she removed the towel, her skin was dewy and pinked.

I felt like a million bucks, swelling with pride at ten thousand feet with my best girl sitting next to me. For the first time in my life, I didn't feel like a fuck up. I felt electric, in the flow, aligned, or some shit. I didn't know exactly what it was, but I felt unstoppable.

"All the pieces are coming together," I beamed and settled into the spacious seat, leaning back and stretching my legs with a yawn.

"Are you tired?" Cora gazed at me with concern in her eyes.

"Not really. I don't need much sleep to function," I bragged, trying to remember when was the last time I strung more than four hours together at one time, and I couldn't.

"Are you nervous?" she asked.

"Not yet," I answered, "but I will be. I've been working on some new material."

"Isn't that risky to bust out new material on live television and in front of a studio audience?"

"Life is a risk, baby. It's go big or go home time."

An hour later, the wheels touched down and the first of my surprises for Cora was waiting. A dapper chauffeur holding a card with her name written on it was waiting for us in front of baggage claim. Closer to sixty than fifty, he was in full uniform, his white shirt pressed perfectly and outfitted in a black jacket and bowtie. He had a quick smile and flashed his incredibly white teeth that were long and straight and contrasted richly with his ebony skin.

"What's this?" she asked, her eyes sparkling and wide when she saw the card.

"I pulled out all the stops," I told her with a grin as I strode proudly to the chauffeur, dragging our carry-ons on their tiny squealing wheels behind us.

"Hello, my good sir. I believe you are here to provide us safe passage to our hotel. This is Ms. Cora Butler, and I am Freddie Angel. Pleased to make your acquaintance."

"Freddie Angel..." he mused. "That name is so familiar. Where have I heard it?"

"See, darling? My reputation precedes itself." I turned toward him. "You might know me as The Funologist."

He snapped his fingers together as a giant smile spread across his features. "Yes! That's it. You're that guy who drove an ice cream truck to the ghetto and had a gun stuck in his face."

"Ah, yes," I said with a little bow. "Among other things, but for some reason, that event seems to stick in people's minds."

"What brings you to the Big Apple?"

"I have an appearance on *Late Night with Jimmy Bravo*."

"That's incredible. I watch him every night." He walked closer. "Let me take care of these for you, Mr. Angel. My name is Lewis, and I will be your driver today."

I leaned in closer to Cora and then whispered, "Hear that? I love being called Mr. Angel." I squeezed her shoulder and then asked, "Are you ready to have the time of your life?"

She let out a little squeal, and I grabbed her hand and followed him out into the cold December air. Our breath huffed out into the frigid morning, like puffs of smoke.

Lewis opened the door to the sleek town car for us, and Cora slid in. I followed suit, sliding across the leather upholstery to land practically in her lap. "We have arrived." I surveyed the drinks that waited for us on the mini-bar set up in the back.

"Allow me to serve you, *Mr. Angel*," she said with a wink, pouring us two mimosas barely tinged with orange juice, just enough to change the color to the palest orange. She handed me a glass and a napkin, and we sipped on them as the car slipped into traffic. New York is stop-and-go, and there is a lot of waiting in between. I tapped my fingers, thumb to ring finger, counting by twos.

Two, Four, Six, Eight. Who do we appreciate?

I chanted the phrase over and over in my mind, my mood elevating higher and higher, getting myself pumped up. Cora leaned toward the windows, her breath fogging them up. She drank in all the sights as Lewis guided us through traffic smoothly like butter on a warm slice of bread. Finally, he pulled up to the elaborate entrance at The Baccarat.

"Whoa." Cora's eyes were huge and fixated on the impressive entrance of the five-star hotel as we waited on the curb for Lewis to pull our luggage out of the trunk. She looked down at the puffy jacket and yoga pants she'd worn on the plane. "This place is fancy."

"Of course, it is. You're with a fancy man, now," I explained.

She grimaced. "I don't think… I'm not dressed right for this." Her fingers trembled as she swiped her hair and tucked a few of the short stragglers behind her ear.

"Oh, pshaw!" I dismissed. "You're fine. You always look great to me."

She exhaled hot and heavy and took the handle of her rolling carry-on from Lewis. I pulled my money clip from my pocket and handed him two crisp one-hundred-dollar bills.

"Thank you, sir," he responded. "Can we take a photo together? It's kind of a hobby. I collect photos with celebrities."

Celebrities? Is that what I was now? Hearing him use the word validated me, and I stood taller and widened my stance, confidence surging. That's what winners did. They commanded every room they walked into. They owned it and took up space. I had cowered in the corner long enough.

Lewis held out his phone and took a selfie with me as Cora took one on my phone. The social media monster demanded to be fed at least once a day. I had to post often to stay relevant.

"Lewis, it's been a pleasure," I told the driver as I pumped his hand, and then I rolled my rickety suitcase into the hotel through a gold door that was held open by a proper doorman. The entire front façade was covered in golden, elongated prisms that drenched the sidewalks in amber-hued rainbow light. Dripping in crystals from chandeliers, the hotel lobby was opulent in rich reds and gold leaf accents. Cora was spinning in a circle, looking up with her mouth agape, her eyes bugging out of her head. A hand-blown glass installation filled the gold-leafed ceiling. She tripped on her suitcase and flew forward, her hands breaking her fall on the ground, then popped up in record time red-faced and laughing at herself.

She recovered and we waltzed to the concierge, an impeccably groomed elegant man with thick silver hair and manicured fingernails, on his wrist sat a platinum timepiece—not a watch, *a timepiece*. He studied us through haughty, half-closed eyes. A gold name tag identified him as Niles.

"May I help you?" he asked with a nasally voice that barely concealed the disdain.

"Why, as a matter of fact, I believe you can." I pulled out my phone. "We have a reservation for this evening."

He hid his shock quickly. "Last name."

"Angel, Freddie Angel," I boasted. "You might know who I am."

"I assure you, sir, I do not." His voice was tinged with contempt and a slight English upper-crust accent.

"After Friday night, you will. I've been invited to perform on *Late Night with Jimmy Bravo*."

His eyes opened fully with that tasty tidbit of information, and his voice was infused with warmth when he said the next words. "Here it is. One night in our Huntington Suite. I am going to upgrade you and your guest to the Penthouse."

"Thank you, my good man." I pulled out the money clip and dropped another Benjamin at him.

He swiped my credit card, then handed me the keys and called the bellhop to take us up. Darwin, a fact gathered from his name tag, was a spry twenty-something, dressed like one of those monkeys with the cymbals, complete with the captain's hat.

"Mr. Angel, follow me." He took our luggage from us and led us through the lobby to a private elevator, requiring him to swipe the key card before use. Cora was silent and speechless, but I could tell from her animated expression that, inside, she was squealing as much as I was. We were both so far out of our league it was hysterical. Her hand found mine and squeezed in the back of the mirrored and crystal-covered elevator. Her eyes choreographed, '*Can you believe this is happening?*' Which just made me smile wider.

The elevator doors opened into a bright walnut burl-covered suite. Daylight poured in from an enormous bank of floor-to-ceiling windows. The walls were trimmed in a rich, warm wood that had been lacquered to a high gloss. Low-slung mushroom-colored furniture with clean modern lines and sparkling glass and crystal accents were everywhere, and in smart little circles, there were pops of red in the form of fresh red roses in small, wide vases.

Cora ran around the room, flitting like a butterfly from the crystal glasses on the tray beside the bed, to the harlequin-patterned lap pool and hot tub on the other side of the ensuite bathroom. "Freddie! A private pool! This must have cost a fortune." Darwin stood and waited at the door after tucking our luggage into the closet, presumably for a tip, clearly enjoying Cora's reaction as much as I was. Every exclamation from her made the corners of his mouth twitch up. I peeled off a twenty and handed it to him.

"Thank you, sir. Please enjoy your stay with us," he said and then quietly closed the door behind him.

I found Cora in the bedroom, spellbound by the layers of white linens and feather pillows three feet deep at the head of the bed. I took off my shoes and coat and threw them in a pile on the floor, then climbed up on the bed. "Come on! This bed was made for jumping." She hesitated for only a split second, then climbed on the bed and we started to jump. The pillows slid and fell on the floor, but the four-poster bed was rock solid, not even a squeak, just a thick pillow top of spongey memory foam. Out of breath, I flopped down onto my back, and Cora landed next to me, her head kissing mine as she stared up at the gold-leaf ceiling.

"This place is coated in gold," she pointed out. "Have you ever seen a hotel more beautiful? I shudder to think what you're paying for the night here."

I pulled her hand to my mouth and kissed the back of it. "Why don't you let me worry about that? Come on!" I sat up and yanked her toward the pool. Running to it, I jumped in fully clothed while she stood on the edge, waiting. "Come on in, the water is nice. It's actually warmer than I thought it would be."

I pulled the damp phone from my pocket, blew on the lens, and turned on the video function. "This is the Funologist live in NEW YORK!" I shouted into the phone. "God, I have always wanted to say that! I'm in town getting ready to make an appearance on *Jimmy Bravo* tomorrow evening. Here with Cora, the sweetest girl from Kansas City. Say hi, Cora." I turned it toward her.

"Hi, Cora!" she repeated with a smirk.

"It's a good thing that one won't be on stage tomorrow, am I right?" I laughed into the phone. "We are staying in a swanky, wanky hotel suite with a private pool! Can you believe it? That would explain why I currently look like a drowned rat." I turned the camera to scan the room. "This place is dripping in luxury. Don't worry, I covered this on my own. I wouldn't dare misappropriate any of your donations for my own amusement. Or would I?" I joked inserting an evil laugh "Stay tuned!" I turned it off and added the hashtags and posted to social media.

"I would be careful," Cora warned. "The public is very fickle. Sure, they love you now, but public opinion can change on a dime. Gotta be careful what you say and how you say it."

"I have to be me," I replied. "I'm not going to change who I am to fit into someone else's box."

"You never were one for fitting into boxes, were you?"

"Not anymore."

I got out of the pool and stripped down to my skivvies. Giggling, I pulled them up my crack, completely exposing my butt cheeks, and turned around, shimmying my hips from side to side. "Does the lady see anything she likes?" I bent forward and tried to twerk, gaining a new respect for strippers, which just made Cora squeal with laughter. "Turns out, exotic dancers are more athletic than I thought."

I laughed and then turned around, sticking my belly out as far as it would go in front of her. "Oh no!" I looked down in despair, distending my belly out and palming it like a woman who's eight months pregnant and can't stop herself from rubbing her swollen belly. "What's happened to me, Cora?"

"Looks like about two cases of Vodka and ten gallons of mashed potatoes." She giggled as she poked my belly button. I pulled her into a soggy embrace, holding her tighter to me while she groaned and fought me off. "Freddie!"

"Hot tub?" I asked as I started to unbutton her jeans. "First a little soak to rid us of the stench of travel, and then we can get out there and enjoy the city?"

"I have a feeling you won't take no for an answer."

"I always knew you were a genius." I leaned in and kissed her.

TWENTY-SIX

Later that evening, the doorman hailed a cab for us as I stood clutching Cora's hand on the sidewalk. It was nice having someone do things for me; that was what money did for you. It was a tool that opened doors and forced respect, two things I had struggled with my entire life. Finally, I understood its power.

Wearing the puffy down jacket over her dress, Cora was quiet, watching impeccably dressed women coated in the finest wool depart the golden door confidently as their Jimmy Choos clicked out a morse code on the pavement. I watched her shrink in their presence, and I hated it.

Our taxi pulled up and we climbed in. I gave the instructions to the driver. He eased out into traffic, and I studied Cora looking out the window.

"A penny for your thoughts," I whispered.

"Sorry," she answered quickly and then turned toward me. "I'm not sure I'm cut out for the limelight like you are." She glanced back out onto the street of immaculate designer showrooms and boutiques ostensibly to prove her point. "I mean, I don't even know who Michael Kors *is*. I'm a fish out of water here." She shifted in the seat, and I pulled her cool hand into mine and gave it a reassuring squeeze.

"Try to look at it as an adventure, sweetheart," I offered. "We are so far away from our normal life, no one knows who we are, so we can reinvent ourselves and be anyone we want to be here."

"But I'm just fine with who I am," she argued. "My simple life back home is enough for me."

"Hmm." I settled back into the seat, contemplating her statement.

Was it enough for me? I wasn't sure anymore. If I chased my dream to fill auditoriums and clubs in every city, where would Cora fit in? Would she even want to fit in at all?

The darkened streets sped by as I turned over these questions in my mind. In twenty minutes, our driver pulled up to Impresso, the most highly rated new restaurant in New York. I bribed the hoity-toity concierge to get us a table, and he came through. Another opened door thanks to the ease of my two new best friends—Ms. Fame and Mr. Money.

Cora's eyes widened as she looked out onto the street. I tipped the driver, and he sped away, leaving us in front of the restaurant. Masses of people rushed by on the sidewalk with earbuds in their ears, lost in their podcasts and music. Weaving in and out in figure-eights, they sped on foot to their individual destinations. We were enveloped in a sea of people, and yet everyone reeked of loneliness. Cora glanced at the menu posted on the wall outside the restaurant and gasped.

"One hundred and twenty-five dollars for a steak? That's insanity."

"We're splurging tonight," I dismissed. "Stop worrying about it."

"I don't want you to spend your hard-earned money on me like this."

"What if I told you I'm using some of my easily earned money? The kind that just dropped in my lap? Would that make it easier to stomach?" I flashed a lopsided grin at her and pulled her into the open door that was being held open for us by the hostess.

It took a moment for our eyes to adjust to the candlelight. At a cherry wood stand, an angular hostess with a high pony-tail and cheekbones that were slashed from granite narrowed her eyes at us.

"Niles from the Baccarat said you would be holding a table for us."

"Ah, yes. Follow me." She stomped between the tables like it was a runway at a Versace show, leading us to a booth with high benches that would ensconce us in velvet luxury. Warm light spilled from the candles in crystal votives as we struggled out of our coats and placed them in her arms. Her nose wrinkled in disgust, carrying our dirty jackets, but she fought her way through it and stomped away.

Cora opened the menu, overwhelmed immediately at the wine list and entrees listed with the words 'market price' instead of a dollar amount. I gently pulled the menu from her hands with a flourish.

"Allow me," I said, glancing at the appetizers. Our waiter appeared dressed in all black, wearing a long apron with a towel draped over his arm.

"Welcome to the Impresso. I am Dustin, and I will be taking care of you this evening."

I smiled up at him.

"Tonight, the chef's special is fresh sea scallops in a cream and saffron reduction with baby leeks that have been flash-fried, served on a bed of pork belly."

"Yum," I said, even though I had no idea what half of what he said even meant.

"I see you are perusing our wine list. Have you made a selection?"

I closed my eyes, swirled my finger above it, and randomly landed on one. "This?"

"Great choice. I'll return with the bottle."

Cora laughed. "This place is so fancy. Do you even know what a saffron reduction is? Or pork belly?"

"My lady, pork belly is bacon for those with a highly sophisticated palate," I said in my most haughty tone. "We cannot be expected to lower our standards to eating the poor man's breakfast meat. Oh no! We must elevate it and call it something entirely different to prove our status." I pronounced the last word "state-us" in a terrible English accent.

"You sound like Niles." Cora relaxed with the joke. "I think I'd rather just have bacon," she admitted. "The word belly makes it a skoosh cannibalistic, don't you think?"

"We can leave if you're uncomfortable," I offered. "Or —" I tipped my head and paused with a smile, "—we can blow a wad here and have one of those once in a lifetime experiences." I paused. "That's got my vote."

"You're right," Cora relented. "I have nothing to prove to these people."

"Damn right you don't!"

She picked up her water glass and held it delicately with her pinky out. "Freddie Dahling," she said with a breathy English accent. "I must have the pork belly. I am simply famished."

"That's my girl." I encouraged her with a smile.

The waiter returned and made a huge show of opening the wine and handing the cork to me. "Why are you handing me your garbage? Is there a trash can under here?" I asked and swept the table cloth to the side to look under the table. Stunned, Dustin looked at me robotically and blinked.

"Do you not wish to smell the cork, sir?"

"But of course." I enthused and hoisted the reddened end to my nostril, inhaling like I was shooting an eight-ball of cocaine that made Cora giggle and the waiter's eyes twitch.

He poured a tiny serving into my glass. "Why you gotta be so stingy, Dustin? I bought the whole bottle, didn't I?"

His forehead wrinkled, but he pushed through the confusion and answered, "Why, for you to taste and approve, sir." I had to hand it to Dustin, the man was unflappable.

"Well, considering that my two requirements for drinks are that they are wet and can get me drunk, I'm going to go out on a limb and say that this will work just fine."

"Of course," he muttered as he filled our glasses and then rested the bottle wrapped in its white linen cocoon on the table and promptly left.

Looking around the poshly appointed restaurant at all the muckity mucks sipping champagne and gorging themselves on frog legs and caviar inspired me. I pulled out my phone and tapped on the fart machine app. I tucked the phone between my legs, cued it up, and added a thirty-second timer while Cora studied the menu, trying to decode what the hell Prix Fixe meant. She was distracted by her calculations and questions as our server glided back to the table with a basket of bread, olive oil, and parmesan cheese. He deposited it between us and said he'd be back to take our orders when, seconds later, the first loud fart burst through the undercurrent hum of the restaurant's ambient noise, amplified by the wooden bench I was sitting on. Cora jumped, and I started to shake with repressed laughter as Cora's eyes snapped to mine. The patrons around us went silent, searching for the source of the offensive sound.

"Freddie," she hissed and then started to chuckle herself. I took it as a sign she wanted me to continue, so I pressed another thirty-second delay and waited.

Thirty seconds later, an even louder and longer flagellation filled the air. This time Cora and I clamped hands on our mouths to prevent the shrieks of laughter from escaping. I looked up in time to see the stomping hostess drilling us with a death glare, and it just egged me on. I pressed the button one more time, and a squeaky, moist, burbling, gassy fart burst through the speaker. I stifled my giggles, enjoying watching Cora's nostrils flare and seeing her shake with effort to contain her laughter.

"You're gonna make me pee," Cora said, clutching her stomach. "It hurts."

Win column. Check.

The angry gazelle appeared at my side. "Sir. If you continue to disturb our other diners, you will be asked to leave."

"I'm so sorry, I had a colonoscopy yesterday and I can't help it." I smiled sweetly at her. "It's a bodily function."

"One more complaint and you are going to have to tend to your *bodily function* elsewhere," she said before swinging her high ponytail away and stomping back to her perch, where she continued to shoot us daggers with her eyes.

Cora's face was reddening from embarrassment and repressed laughter. She sighed and shook her head at me. "You're crazy."

"Just for you, sweetheart."

Dustin appeared at my side, no doubt summoned by the angry gazelle's instructions to get us in and out. "Have you made your selections?"

"We both would like to try the Prix Fix-E thingy," I answered.

"You mean the Prix Fixe?" he corrected with obvious disdain.

"Yes, my good man." I skooched my fingers away, encouraging him to leave as soon as possible.

Cora was becoming shifty and uncomfortable. "I feel like we're an exhibit at the zoo," she said softly out of earshot of the other guests whose eyes kept darting our direction.

"Screw 'em!" I said and hoisted up my glass with a flourish and sipped thoughtfully.

Three courses later, we were stuffed with fancy food and escorted out the backdoor of the restaurant like a dirty secret. I pulled Cora's hand into mine and started walking to the park where there was a line of carriages set up and waiting for tourists like us.

"Fancy a ride?" I asked her, and she nodded eagerly. The driver got us settled into the carriage and offered us hot chocolate from a thermos and a warm blanket. Cora snuggled in next to me with a contented sigh as the driver eased the horse out onto the road, and it began its jerky trek down the moonlit streets. Fat snowflakes began to gently fall from the dark sky, lit by rogue stars and a bright crescent moon.

"It's just like in a movie!" Cora cried as she stuck her tongue out, tasting a flake.

"Might want to be careful there, darlin'. This is New York snow—smoggy and smoky, not the pristine, fresh Midwest snow you're used to."

"You might have a point there." She laughed as the big flakes settled on my head, and she brushed them off. The horse continued to pick his way down the streets. The wheels creaking under our weight, his horseshoes clicked and clacked on the pavement while the blanket was warm and toasty across our laps.

This is it. Kiss her, you fool. It doesn't get any better than this.

It *was* perfect, so I decided to go for it. In the middle of a New York snow globe, riding in a horse-drawn carriage, during the most romantic moment of my life, I delicately clasped her hand in mine. I leaned in to gently place my lips on hers, and at that precise fairytale moment, when all the stars had aligned, the horse decided to take a royal shit. The sheer quantity of which stunned even me. It just kept coming and coming; impressive black piles hit the pavement and splattered out onto the ground. Seconds later, the stench hit us like a tidal wave, a scent so pungent and thick you could almost taste it. It flooded our nostrils as Cora snorted in laughter.

"Cock blocker!" I shouted at the horse, plugging my nose. Cora's giggles were muffled by her hands that covered her mouth and nose and neither of us could stop laughing. We'd stop and then the giggles would start up again, unable to be contained. My abdominal muscles shook and strained from the effort. Twenty minutes later, the driver deposited us right where we started and offered Cora a red rose that she brought to her nose to inhale its sweetness.

"Now? You give that to her now?" I asked. "Dude, where were you with that a few minutes ago? That's when we really could have used it!" He just shrugged his shoulders, flipped open the door, and pulled the makeshift stair out for us to descend.

I held a hand up to help Cora alight from the carriage and then tucked her hand into my arm to escort her back to the hotel. "How are your feet? Should we get an Uber?"

"Let's walk," she said. "It's not far, and New York with its jewel box lights gleaming in the skyscrapers is so pretty in the snow."

"It is. Covers up the dirt and stench of this cesspool. Almost makes it beautiful," I agreed.

We walked quietly as the snow kept falling.

"You know what I've always wanted to do?" Cora asked.

"Get a tattoo that says Property of Freddie Angel on your ass?"

She yanked her arm from my bicep and punched me with it. "No, goofball. One of my favorite childhood traditions was watching them light up the Christmas tree at Rockefeller Center." Her voice took on this misty milky quality that pierced my heart. "They would pan down to the people skating on the ice rink, and it just looked so dreamy and romantic." Her eyes flickered across to mine as her lips turned up in a quick smile. "Is that stupid?"

"Not at all! Let's do it!" I offered eagerly.

"Really?" she cried. "Do you even know how to ice skate?'

"How hard can it be?' I asked. I hailed a cab, and thirty minutes later, we were standing in the long looping line for skates at Rockefeller Center. Cora's face softened and her eyes glinted with excitement watching skaters circle the ice. I brushed a flake of snow from her cheek, then paid for our tickets when we finally arrived at the front of the line, then we hauled our rented skates to benches where we sat to put them on. I laced up my skates as Sinatra swooned, "You Make Me Feel So Young."

Perfect moment, perfect song. Win column, check.

The stars were out in force, poking through the black satiny cover of night, littered casually across the sky. "Look, Freddie. Have you ever seen anything so beautiful?" There was a wistfulness in her voice that I had never heard before, reducing her to a little girl. She stood shakily on her skates, her ankles leaning in as she walked to the ice, and I struggled to catch up. Walking on a narrow metal blade definitely isn't as easy as the hockey players make it look. I stumbled then caught myself, then tentatively inched out one shaky foot onto the ice as I watched Cora take off. She glided effortlessly over the ice while I pushed off with one foot a little too fervently and lost my balance clawing my hands in the air like a cartoon, before landing hard on the ice with a crunch.

"That's going to leave a mark," I mumbled under my breath.

"*You're a disaster*," a voice screamed from the back of my mind. I pushed it away and crawled to my knees and then to a precarious standing position, scanning the crowd of skaters for Cora. A few seconds later, she glided next to me, and I was so excited to see her, I lost my balance again and scissored down into the worst splits an adult male has ever attempted. All my joints snapped, crackled, and popped in protest.

Cora dissolved into a pile of giggles, and I reached out a hand to her.

"Help me," I begged. "I think I'm stuck, and I definitely pulled a groin muscle."

She struggled to pull me to my feet, and I clutched her like a drowning man.

"You realize, if one of us goes down, we are both going down, right?"

Not wanting to hurt her, I pulled my hand away and willed my feet forward on the bumpy ice. "I have to say, I thought it would be a lot smoother," I admitted, marveling at the pock-marked ice sliced with grooves from the hundreds of skaters that had taken to it before us. "Isn't smooth as ice a thing?" I mused out loud. "I swear it's a thing."

I followed her lead in the counterclockwise circle that we traveled in, tentatively increasing my speed to keep up. My thighs and calves burned from the concentrated effort that felt foreign to them. I hadn't physically exerted myself like this in almost a decade. "Don't let me hold you back," I shouted into the void. "Skate your heart out until you're tired, then come find the old guy who brought you here."

"Are you sure?" she asked. "I am fine hanging back and skating with you."

"I insist," I said with a little bow that was my chivalrous downfall and collapsed onto the ice again, this time taking out a four-year-old who came up behind me too quickly.

"Freddie!" Cora shouted over her shoulder. "Do you need help?"

"Save yourself. I'm fine." I helped the stunned kid find his feet, and he disappeared into the mass of skaters circling around me.

She skated away into the crowd, and I got up onto all fours and then placed my skates back on the ice and pushed off. My ankles were exhausted and tight.

How do hockey players do this for hours?

"You're no hockey player, dumb ass," a woman cackled. *"Maybe a* hokey *player."*

"Shut up," I mumbled.

I skated two more looping circles and then found a bench to sit on to wait for Cora to come circling around again. I rested and rubbed my knee, which was starting to ache. Cora zoomed by and then surprised me by executing a perfect spin in front of me.

"Bravo!" I shouted and stuck two fingers into my mouth and whistled loudly at her. She skated away into the fray again as I waited. Twenty minutes later, she skated to my bench, her face flushed pink with effort and her eyes sparkling.

"You ready?" she asked.

"I can sit longer if you want to close this place down."

"I think I'm tired. Let's head back?"

I was relieved to hear that because I was in dire need of some ibuprofen, but truthfully, I would have sat my frozen ass on that bench as long as Cora wanted me to.

I unlaced my skates and stretched out my toes, slipping them back into my shoes I had a newfound appreciation for. In the span of an hour, the death blades strapped to my feet made even my pinched dress shoes feel like wearing marshmallows.

"Here, I'll return our skates," Cora offered, and she picked up both pairs and ran them back to the counter.

She returned with a smile. "That was awesome. Freddie, I crossed something off my bucket list tonight."

My soft heart burst open and bubbles rushed in. I wasn't used to being the guy who made dreams come true. The way Cora looked at me now put me on a pedestal. Her eyes shone with happiness, and I was the man that put it there. It was the highest high in my entire miserable existence. I wish I had savored that moment more. The problem with highs is that they don't last.

TWENTY-SEVEN

The green room really turned out to be green. An offensive vomit color whose irony wasn't lost on me as my stomach roiled. I knew how much was riding on this appearance; it was *the* pinnacle-defining moment of my career. Cora was swept away by an assistant the minute we arrived and seated in the audience. I was shown to the green room and perched on the edge of a molded resin see-through chair that probably cost more than Ma's car and was uncomfortable as hell. I read through my notebook, repeating punch lines to myself under my breath, preparing my bits, and walking through my set. I didn't sleep a wink last night, but that was okay because I had evolved. I didn't need to sleep anymore. I was becoming super human, paving the way for evolutionary breakthroughs that only happen every few thousand years.

I stayed up all night reading and rereading my notebook, and after listening to a podcast encouraging me to take more risks to earn more rewards, decided to rewrite my entire act on the hotel stationary. I scrawled page after page until my hand was tight and cramping. Genius on every single line.

This six-minute set would launch me into the stratosphere, and by God, I was ready. I deserved it. Worldwide fame was finally going to shine its warm light on Freddie Angel.

The closer we got to the appearance, the more on edge I became. My belly was a stormy sea in a hurricane. I pulled the flask from my jacket and took a nip to calm my nerves and stop the shaking in my hands. My entire life rested on this one moment in time. The terrifying pressure was starting to manifest as hairline cracks.

"Welcome to your downfall."

"This is the end."

"You're out of your league."

It was hard to read my jokes with the chorus of nay-sayers in my head, each louder and more obnoxious than the last.

"Shut up!" I screamed, and then there was a knock on the door before it opened.

"Everything okay in here, sport?" There he was. Jimmy. Fuckin'. Bravo. Clad in a dark grey suit with a teal tie, his hair thick and expertly coiffed. It was a look that screamed 'I am important.' "Are you hearing voices?" he asked with a smirk, as the two handlers wearing headsets and carrying clipboards behind him cackled in response.

"Just a few," I joked honestly, hoping it came off as a lie.

He thrust out a hand, and I put my sweaty one in his.

"Nice to meet you." He said then discreetly wiped his hand on his trousers.

"You're disgusting."

My hands gripped into tight fists at my sides as the urge to wrap them around Jimmy Bravo's smug, self-important throat surged through me. My nostrils flared as I felt myself breaking into pieces that I gathered feverishly to pull back together. Inside, I was disintegrating and terrified, while on the outside, I forced myself to project calm. The contrast of maintaining both realities was a heavy weight that exhausted me.

"So, we'll bring you out to the couch, do a little interview, and talk about the movement. Great name, by the way. The Funologist—you should trademark it." His words were host-snappy perfect like he knew every word that came out of his mouth was going to be quoted for years to come.

My shoulders unclenched with his warm flush of praise, I nodded like I understood what trademark meant. I did not.

"We're live, one of the only shows who's balls enough to do that anymore. So, no matter what, you gotta keep talking. You got it, champ?"

I nodded like it was my job.

"Then we'll have a commercial break, and when we come back, you'll do your stand up. Six minutes, so keep an eye on the camera man. He'll count you in and out. You're gonna be great." He squeezed my arm, then strode out followed by the chattering assistants, and I finally exhaled. The entire exchange lasted about five minutes, and it had worn me out. I pulled the flask from my pocket again and took a long sip to calm the hammering in my heart, and then another just to make sure. The booze made me smile wider and feel like butter. Calm euphoria welled up in my gut.

This is it. This is your time. You have to own this.

―――――

Twenty minutes later, there was a quick knock on the door, and I was urged to follow behind a thin woman dressed in all black. We dodged lighting equipment and old props, a single-file walk down cluttered hallways as the volume of laughter and applause increased. Each step closer amped up the tension in my gut. I shook both my hands out to try to dispel the nervous energy.

"Stand here until you hear your name," the woman whispered close to me, holding an arm in front of me like a gatekeeper. "Then walk out and take a seat in the chair next to Jimmy. Good luck."

"Our next guest is an internet sensation. He calls himself the Funologist. Have you heard about this guy?" There were a couple of whoops and a light smattering of applause from the audience. I exhaled through my mouth and wiped the sweat off my forehead.

"He's been doing some crazy good deeds out there. Let's put him in the hot seat, and he can tell us all about his adventures. Please help me welcome, the Funologist, Freddie Angel."

I walked out onto the stage, smooth and supple, shored up by liquid confidence.

Thank you, vodka.

I thrust out a hand and shook his, then sat down in the seat next to his desk. It was a dark heavy wood surface with a coffee cup and a Venus fly trap. In seconds, the plant grew two inches, like the one in *Little Shop of Horrors*.

Feed me, Seymore.

I shifted away, waiting for it to grow big enough to swallow Jimmy's gigantic head whole, but shockingly, the applause made it shrink instead.

In the corner was a collection of naked Troll Dolls. Crazy-colored hair in tufts of red, orange, and rainbow rose like flames from their heads.

Jimmy was speaking, but his voice was far away. It was like listening to someone who was under water. I rocked and jiggled my leg up and down. My skin felt electric and surging, energy levels soaring.

"*It's over, you moron,*" the red troll doll said with a sneer. He was the leader of the pack, the rest assembled in a shoddy army behind him. The red doll turned around, squatted, and defecated on the desk. Then he picked it up, waving the warm steaming pile and taunting me. "*See this? This is what you are. Shit. Complete and udder shit, and in an hour, everyone will know that.*"

"Freddie?" My eyes snapped back to Jimmy, who was signaling me to answer. I had heard the word lottery and focused on an answer to that question. My brain was firing on nearly one-hundred percent of its capacity. I no longer needed to pay attention to mere mundane tasks like listening. I knew without knowing.

"Yes, I won the lottery, and instead of keeping it all to myself decided to YOLO it and give it all away." I smiled as the audience applauded.

They love me.

"*No, they don't, asshole. Everyone knows what a mess you are. No one has ever loved you, ever,*" the troll doll with the blue hair spit the truth at me.

I jerked away and forced myself to focus on Jimmy's mouth and words. Hearing them through the clamor of angsty voices weaving in and out of my subconscious was proving to be problematic. Piecing together word fragments and deciphering them in front of a live audience will make you shake and sweat.

"You've risked life and limb."

"Yeah, it got pretty dicey the night I brought an ice cream truck to Hidden Hills," I admitted as the audience gasped.

"In case you have been in a hole and have no idea what's been going on, a man pulled a gun on Freddie while he was out giving away ice cream to little kids. Check out this clip."

The viral video popped up, showing me head-butting the

gunman, and the audience went wild. Clapping and screaming my name, "Fred-die, Fred-die!"

"That was a crazy night," Jimmy said.

"You could say that," I responded. "But he was just a regular guy having a bad day."

"Wait," Jimmy scoffed. "Are you defending the gunman?"

"Not defending, just acknowledging his struggle. You don't pull a gun on someone unless you have no other choice."

"Well, that is a bloody incredible way to look at it. Right, guys?" He hammed up to the studio audience. "Don't you think we need to take this Funologist movement to the moon?" The audience clapped and hollered. When they finally settled down, Jimmy flashed a smoothly veneered smile at me. "I'm in for a hundred-thousand to keep this crazy train on the tracks, *and...*" he dragged out the word and paused for effect, "I will match every donation that you receive over the next forty-eight hours! To keep me honest, let's do this right now, live on the show, because we can!" The audience whooped.

He pulled out his phone as the cameraman panned in tighter, and he made his donation right there on the spot in front of me. "I'm pulling up Venmo, @thefunologist, six little numbers, and here it is in black and white." He turned the phone to the camera, showing off his full donation. The audience burst into applause.

"Are you serious?" I was stunned, my jaw dropping open.

"Dead," he said with a smile that oozed confidence, then turned back to the audience. "Freddie here is a stand-up comedian, so how about we give him a six-minute set when we return? Are you guys down with that?" The audience let loose again, chanting my name.

Then he broke to commercial, and his sunny host warmth turned off and his eyes focused on mine.

"Thanks for the shout-out," I exclaimed. I could feel the phone vibrating in my pocket like crazy already and was itching to pull it out and look at it, but didn't dare.

"It's a great cause and good publicity for the show. Now, don't screw this up, and you might be able to turn this fifteen minutes of fame into a real career in comedy."

That comment paralyzed me. Boldly declaring what was on the line, just in case I wasn't already aware. I was whisked to the wings and told to wait, taking the opportunity to turn away and conceal the two long chugs on the flask in my pocket. I wiped my mouth while the team worked feverishly to pull together the set change. An assistant who wired me for sound popped a wireless mic in my hand, then they pulled me onto the stage. A teal velvet curtain hung behind me, and I climbed a small gold stage ringed with layers of incandescent yellow bulbs.

"You're gonna want to stay put," she said. "You have two minutes and then we will count you in."

I stood on the platform, the anxiety mounting, my heart rate climbing higher and higher, the heart palpitations a drum beat that echoed deep in my core. Finally, the warm wishy-washes of vodka spilled over me, and I began to relax.

"We're live in three, two…" Then the cameraman held up a single finger. I stood stunned and blank. He started circling with his hand, trying to get me to speak as another assistant pointed to the red light indicating we were live blinking on the camera. Their eyes and gestures got more and more animated the longer I was silent. I was frozen to the spot, standing in the light, freaking out inside, searching for even one remnant of a joke I could begin with. All the time I had spent in the week leading up to this opportunity, writing and rewriting every joke in my six-minute set had vanished. All that remained was the vast void. A silence I was desperate to fill.

The laughter inside my head was reaching a fevered pitch, evil cackles and passive-aggressive guffaws. My mouth was thick and dry. Blank. Empty. Void. A deep cavern of nothing that spooked me like nothing else ever had.

"White privilege… hashtag me too," I said in the microphone, and the audience gasped with open mouths at the first five words. They were the punchline of a couple jokes, but for some reason, they came rushing out of my mouth the second I opened it. I tapped the microphone. "Is this thing on?" I smiled tightly and dug deeper.

"It's tough being a white man in America," I mused. "Was wondering when that white privilege thing kicks in. Do you have to fill out an application on a website or be nominated by a state senator? Because I have to tell you, I've been over here, standing on the corner, white as hell, and getting my teeth kicked in at every opportunity." It sounded funny in my head, but when the words were released into the wild, they fell flat like boulders crushing me. I heard a low rumbling of boos begin shifting toward me in a wave.

"I'm glad there were no smart phones and video cameras around when I was in my twenties because I don't want to give away any big secrets, but I think that my chances of running for a political office were ruined by the grinding I engaged in on dance floors in the early nineties. Now, you can't even hug a person without being misconstrued. You can't offer anyone sympathy. I don't know where to put my hands anymore. It is quite a conundrum. And forget about telling a woman she's beautiful because God knows that's offensive. It's like we've turned into politically correct and unemotional robots. Now, I'm not saying we gotta go full-on R. Kelly mode, but come on. There's got to be a balance."

Still nothing. The audience was silent, and I felt the hum of a building rage seeping toward me, yet I continued, sure that, eventually, I'd win them over.

"We are all so sensitive now. Aren't we? The really good comics are offensive, they've always been. I grew up watching the classics— Richard Pryor, George Carlin, you know the guys that say the thing that makes you laugh and then you feel like a douche for laughing? And you're thinking, did he really say that? It's so sick and so wrong, but that's what makes it funny." I looked out into the light. "But now, we have to sanitize it all, make it politically correct. We have to be tolerant and woke." My voice faltered as I lost my train of thought.

"You're not giving a TED Talk, dumbass. Make them laugh or you're dead."

"My girlfriend is in the audience now. Cora, give them a little wave, sweetheart." A small round of applause spurred me on. "What initially drew me to Cora was her gorgeous red hair. I mean, it obviously wasn't her rack. The woman is as flat as a pancake." I passed my hand straight down in front of me for emphasis. "Apparently, I'm attracted to women with the same body type as pre-pubescent teenage boys. Not sure what that says about me; I should probably have my head thoroughly examined." I turned to the side and affectionately cupped an entire handful of my own flabby pecs. "But more than a handful is a waste, am I right?" I said to a smattering of nervous giggles. "Waste not, want not," I mumbled into the microphone. "My girlfriend is obviously blind and with a severe mental handicap." I proudly turned from side to side. "She'd have to be to sign up to screw this." I laughed awkwardly as the joke refused to land.

"Up until the last month, it was looking like I'd die in my mom's basement," I said, setting up the next joke. "With the big lottery win, I was thinking I'd level up. Buy myself something nice. A new plastic sheet in case I pissed myself drunk one night. Get the four mil instead of the two. I mean, really make it classy." I pretended to sip a cup of tea with a haughty accent. "For men of a certain age with discriminating tastes, it is *the* Cadillac of rubber sheets, so you can piss yourself in luxury."

Again, dead air, not a single laugh in the room, and I was nosediving, plummeting to earth fast. The ground was rushing up like I had jumped out of the helicopter with a faulty parachute that was tangled and twisted and a harbinger of my imminent demise.

I swear I could hear them blinking, each of my senses now razor-sharp. I was sweating through my clothing; the lights were so hot they burned.

Finish big. Leave them with something memorable.

"The internet crowned me the king of the Funologist movement." I paused. "It sounds like an unfortunate poop, doesn't it—the movement?" I looked down. "Like something that happens the day after you participate in a corn on the cob eating contest chased by a bazillion blue raspberry popsicles." I paused. "It's art. I make art. With my colon. It's a gift."

The audience snickered. It was getting harder to breathe. An immovable weight was lodged on my chest, and my thoughts were swimming, racing past me, and then disintegrating into the abyss. I sipped at the air, shallow peckish breaths, searching for one last bit, one last shiny comedic nugget of brilliance to leave them with.

"*You're fucking up, boy,*" my dad's voice hissed.

I took a step forward toward it and stumbled off the stage, face planting onto the floor as the audience gasped. Landing in a hard pile of twisted fleshy limbs as the surprised cameraman recovered and swung his camera back to Jimmy.

"We'll be right back," Jimmy oozed effortlessly into the camera, not skipping a beat. The house band cued up and jazzy music was the soundtrack of my walk of shame. I pulled myself to a standing position, and the assistant appeared again and removed the wireless mic from me.

"How was it?" I asked with a wince, eager for even a single morsel of praise. Desperately praying it wasn't as bad as I thought it had been.

"*You're overreacting.*" I heard Ma's voice. "*It's fine. Everything is fine.*"

"It was… ah…a little rough," the assistant said brusquely, beckoning me to follow as she walked off the set on sharp stilettos.

"I was afraid of that." I followed her backstage to wait out the end of the show. Going over the performance in my head, trying to separate the facts from the fiction. Piecing together an apology that would get me back in Jimmy's good graces again.

"Let's go, Freddie. Jimmy set up a cab for you."

"Oh, he did?" I stumbled behind her. "But my girlfriend is in the audience."

"Are you sure she's going to still be your girlfriend after that set?" she said to me. "Don't worry, we'll get a cab for her, but I have strict instructions to send you to the hotel ASAP."

"Can you thank Jimmy for me?" I asked.

"Sure," she offered, in an effort to end the conversation as quickly as possible, and I walked out into the cold air. I sucked it in, the sweat under my dress shirt freezing instantly. I stumbled into the car, and the driver sped away back to the hotel. The buzz was wearing thin and the reality was starting to clear in my mind, still swirling, but the overwhelming sense of dread was building. I could barely remember what I said onstage. I pulled my notebook out and paged through it, instantly recalling the words I had practiced, the ones that I planned to say that were now so easily rolling off my tongue.

Traitor.

I cursed my poor performance and pulled out my cell phone to try to reach Cora. I saw the incoming text bubble pop up and waited. Then no answer and it disappeared. I sent two more texts with no response.

She couldn't be mad. Could she? I had thrown her under the bus, but everyone knows that a comic's friends and family are fair game, right? It was all for the laughs, just a joke. She had to know, didn't she?

Twenty minutes later, the taxi pulled up to our new hotel that provided a shuttle to the airport in the morning and a truly terrible continental breakfast. Thick with carbs and little else, it was something tacked on at the end that was supposed to add value to your stay.

I stuck the key into the slot and opened the door, fully expecting to see Cora there waiting. When she wasn't and further texts went unanswered, I pulled out my flask and did a proper post mortem. It was bad. My socials were blowing up. Donations had come to a screeching halt fifteen minutes after I'd said the words "white privilege."

The hate came fast and furious, outing the public as a fickle taskmaster who was riding high with you in the Bentley, but jumped ship when you crashed the ford focus.

Smug over-privileged asshat.
Why is he even famous again?
Worst set ever.

You made the entire state of Missouri cringe, you worthless prick.
Waste of Space
Funologist = Useless Has Been Hack
Go kill yourself.

"Looks like they don't love you no more, Freddie Angel."

There was still almost two-hundred thousand in the Venmo account. An idea broke through the surface. It was hazy at first as I sipped on the last of the vodka in my flask. How fast could the Funologist burn through the last of this money? We were about to find out.

TWENTY-EIGHT

My head pounded when I finally opened my eyes the next morning. Disoriented, it took me a full minute to get my bearings. I was alone in the hotel room. The phone in my hand rang, and I answered immediately, praying it was Cora.

"Cora? I'm so sorry—"

Interrupted, my heart dropped at the first syllable. "Fritzy! You piece of shit! Congratulations on crashing and burning on national television! Takes a special brand of stupid to pull that off. You finally got your big break and you blew it!"

I rubbed at the tension behind my left eye, fantasizing about digging my eye out with a rusty spoon so I could fully access the tender area behind it, and then taking that same rusty spoon and stabbing Tommy with it.

"Did you need something, or did you just call to gloat?"

"Gloating mostly," he admitted, "especially since you've been such a judgmental prick lately." He laughed obnoxiously into the phone as my head throbbed. "You were getting too big for your britches anyway. Nice to see you get brought down a peg. Or should I say a few hundred pegs?" Even his breathing on the other end of the phone irritated me. "Seems like poetic justice to me. I'm just glad I got to see it with my own eyes."

"I'm busy. If you don't need anything, I've got to go. I have a plane to catch."

"Toodles," was the last stupid word I heard before I punched the end call button. As usual, Tommy had to have the last word.

My head rattled with worries and the race track of insults, and destructive thinking revved up. Circular thoughts ran like a Nascar track, faster and faster, burning through my mind.

Why did you bring the flask?

Why did you try new material?

You destroyed your big break.

You humiliated yourself on national television.

Cora hates your guts.

You are a piece of shit.

It's over. All of it.

You'll never amount to anything.

Loser.

Fake.

Phony.

Poser.

Talentless hack.

The insults spiraled and spiraled, nearly paralyzing me. To distract myself, I wandered over to the shitty in-room coffee maker. First order of business, caffeine. Second order of business, find Cora.

I pulled out my phone and pulled up Cora's messages while the weak drip percolated into the lime-stained carafe.

Cora: *Got on a flight late last night. You humiliated me.*

She left without a goodbye. My stomach dropped. In the span of twenty-four hours, we had the best and worst date of my life. Life's cruel pendulum gave it all and then stole it away again.

I didn't know what to say to fix this. I punched out text after text, begging for forgiveness, deleting them all, knowing that any explanation I made at this point was useless.

Me: *Sorry.*

Sorry. The apology seemed weak and tepid. A pathetic attempt to heal what I had so casually destroyed in the name of fame. Cora was the first woman who meant anything to me in a long time and I ruined it. Pathetic, but not surprising.

"It was only a matter of time before something like this happened," a woman reasoned in my head. *"You were punching above your weight."*

Both were true statements. A screw-up like me did not deserve someone like Cora. I didn't have anything real to offer her anymore. The pedestal she put me on was struck by lightning on *Jimmy Bravo,* resulting in a massive crack that sent me sprawling. People like me don't get a happy ending. Everything we touch turns to shit.

I did not want that for her. She was better off without me, and I would have to learn to let her go.

TWENTY-NINE

The airport Chinese food I choked down earlier hardened into a ball of lead in my belly. The driver let me off at the curb, and with a heavy sigh, I trudged up the concrete stoop. Back at home, everything seemed smaller, shabbier, dirtier. The expansiveness of the New York skyscrapers pocketed with brightly lit designer shops contrasted sharply with the mid-century lower-class neighborhood I grew up in.

Back in Ma's basement. Perfect.

You open yourself up for torment when you dare to dream. All the self-improvement gurus tell you "Change your mindset, change your life." Anything is possible. If you can dream it, you can do it. Their videos are full of lies, spewing false platitude after false platitude. It's all bullshit. What they forget to mention is getting a taste of the life you want to live and then having it all ripped away is worse than if you had never had a taste at all. I kicked the door, taking my frustration out on the dirty metal kick plate, then walked into the house and jumped.

Mom was sitting like a statue in the dark, waiting for me.

"Jesus, Ma, you scared me." I pressed a hand to my chest, feeling my heart thrumming as I dragged my luggage into the entryway.

"Come sit down, honey. Let's have a discussion."

"I'm really tired. Can we do this later?" I sagged down on the floral sofa, sighed, and scratched my jaw with my hands. I heard squawking and flapping.

"What in the hell is that?"

"I was hoping you'd tell me. He was delivered today. I told them they had the wrong house. I mean, what in the world would you do with a parrot? But they produced a receipt with your signature."

"You're an asshole," Alvin balked and screeched in the cage.

"Ma, meet Alvin. He's kind of a jerk." Alvin flapped his wings in protest, and I flipped him off. "We have to put a sheet over the cage so he'll settle down."

"In a minute, Freddie. I'm getting concerned. You seem a little undone. Are you having another episode?" Mom asked quietly, and I tried to piece together words that would convince her otherwise. Another committal was on the horizon, I could feel it. I willed my words to come out slowly, knowing speaking too fast was one of my mania tells.

"It was just a rough night, Mama," I mumbled. Ma launched her tired body out of her recliner and sat down next to me, her eyes assessing the damage. I laid back and stared at a crack on the ceiling. She pressed a cool hand to my forehead, and I closed my eyes.

"I'm worried about you, honey," she whispered then asked, "How's Cora?"

"I don't know." I sighed. "She won't answer my calls. I ruined it like I ruin everything. So stupid!" I slammed my fist against my head. In the vast dullness, the pain was welcome. To feel anything, even agony, felt like a gift.

"I guess I'm destined to live here the rest of my life. Me and Tommy. We're going to have to share a bedroom again."

"What?" she asked, confused. "Who are you talking about?" Her forehead crinkled in concentration as she leaned in closer and put a hand on my shoulder to calm me that I shrugged off. I sat up and perched on the edge of the sofa, my legs shaking up and down.

"Tommy," I repeated louder, the frustration setting in. "The golden boy?" I didn't have time for this conversation. I needed to find Cora, to see her in person and beg for forgiveness.

"Who's this Tommy?" she asked.

"C'mon, Ma. My brother, your son—Tommy," I snapped, annoyed, stretching out the words slowly and annunciating each syllable.

"Brother?" Mom was confused. Her face twisted up in a frown, and her forehead crinkled as darts of worry criss-crossed it. "What do you mean, brother?"

"Ma. Seriously, you're killing me," I ranted. "Tommy, my brother Tommy. You know the one you squeezed out two years before me?"

"But Freddie, you don't have a brother." She gripped my hand more tightly, and I felt the energy shift in the room.

A chill crept up my shoulders. A sliver of terror opened up under my ribs, growing and oozing out from my center and expanding into my limbs. Hot tears pricked my eyes. "No, Ma. That's not true. Don't say that."

"Honey, it *is* true," she said gently. "You don't have a brother. You're an only child. I had to have a hysterectomy immediately after you were born."

"But... no... I..." I stammered, still in shock. Tommy

was an asshole, a despicable human being. But the truth emerging from her lips was impossible to accept. "No. I don't believe you. Why are you lying?" I argued and began to pace the short span of the hallway, feeling cornered. I paged through my life, searching for proof, rattling off my reasons one by one.

"He heckled me at The Punch Line. He called me last night. He wants to get you on the list for that assisted living center you love. Why are you doing this? You're trying to make me think I'm crazy. I'm not crazy!" I shouted, pacing faster and faster up and down the hallway. Wiping away hot tears with my hands. "I'm not crazy! Why are you doing this to me?"

"I'm not lying, sweetheart," she cried softly as she walked closer to me. "I need to call Dr. McGivern. You're sick, honey. You're having delusions again."

"I'm not going back there." The sheer terror of going back to the mental hospital began its slow climb inside me, like an elevator rising higher and higher and higher. "I won't go back there. It's a prison. I can't go back there."

The locked-down ward, the mandatory daily body and room searches, not being able to piss without permission. The assortment of pills I'd be forced to swallow that would render me compliant and useless. A blob of overmedicated docile flesh. Sitting in the social room with checkers and crayons, with all the dangerous pens confiscated. The screaming episodes and running orderlies with straitjackets and restraints. The nearly comatose patients in wheelchairs, their chests soaked with drool while they looked out the window at nothing for hours at a time. The forced socialization, sitting in groups and lying about feelings, talking about triggers and self-awareness. Not having control over a single thing—what I ate, what I did, who I talked to. I felt the walls closing in, trapping me, pinning me against them, and my fight or flight instinct kicked in.

I about-faced and ran out of the house like it was on fire.

"Freddie! Come back. Honey, please!" Ma's voice shouted behind me, fading away the further I ran. I ran away from the truth that I was being forced to acknowledge. My legs pumped, my side ached, and my breath was rough and jagged in my chest that was burning from effort as I sucked in the frigid air. I felt like a criminal on the lamb, a desperate cornered creature searching for solace.

When I couldn't run anymore, I walked. The panic began to subside, and I pulled out my phone to see several missed calls and voicemails from Mom. She didn't text, and I couldn't bear to listen to her begging me to come home, pleading with me to go to the hospital again, so I tucked it back into my pocket and kept walking. Each step calmed my terrified brain. Each step away, my decision, giving me the illusion that I was in control of my life.

Eventually, I landed at The Punch Line. At the door, I paused and collected myself. Cora was on the schedule tonight, and I willed the words to come that would soften what I had done. I exhaled and opened the door, walking to the bar as my eyes adjusted to the dim light.

"Well, well, well. Look what the cat dragged in," Paulie said, sitting at the bar reading a newspaper, refusing to make eye contact, and sipping on a rum and Coke. "You really shit the bed this time." He shook the paper out and continued to read.

"Unfortunately, that is an accurate assessment," I admitted. "It wasn't my finest moment. Where's Cora?' I asked, searching the empty bar for her shock of her red hair.

"She quit," Paulie muttered and then took another long sip of his whiskey.

"What?" I gasped. "Why?"

"Really? You have to ask that?" He stared at the paper. "I was making bank at the door and behind the bar, but with that stunt you pulled on *Jimmy Bravo*, it would be suicide to put you on a stage right now." He emptied his glass and slammed it hard on the wooden bar, then stood and finally looked at me. "I think it's best if you take a break. Let the dust settle. Once something else becomes newsworthy and takes the spotlight off you and this debacle, maybe we can talk about getting you on stage again." He walked away without letting me answer, without letting me say a word to defend myself.

You don't need them. You don't need this shitty dive bar. You still have two hundred grand to blow. Fuck 'em.

I walked out of The Punch Line feeling unsettled at first. Feeling like a balloon, floating and bobbing in the frigid night air. Cora had been my string, and without the string, I climbed higher and higher, disappearing into the black night. Unable to stop myself.

THIRTY

I t was late when I finally crawled back home. No job. No
Cora. How could I go from having the world on a string
to this abysmal pit of hell in the span of forty-eight hours? It
was a new record, even for me. The white vans parked on the
street filled with cameramen and reporters had disappeared.
Just like that, I became yesterday's news, the kind that you
line your litter box with and let your cat piss all over. I knew
it couldn't last forever, but if you're lucky enough to land
inside the fame bubble, trust me, you'd sell your soul to stay
there. Your ego takes over and easily doubles in size as the
rest of you shrinks, but when the adoration cools off and
moves to the next shiny thing, you're left behind wondering
what the hell happened.

I stumbled to the flower beds and peeked in the windows.
All was dark and quiet. Ma must have given up and gone to
bed. Picking my way up the uneven stairs, I slowly turned the
doorknob and eased the door open, then tiptoed past Alvin's
cage that was covered with a sheet, fascinated by the whirs
and trills he made as he slept. Crossing the living room, I

eased open the basement door, clutching my favorite sleep aid, a fifth of vodka in a wrinkled brown bag. I half-walked, half-stumbled down the stairs, humming softly to myself, clipping the edge of the wall as I ping-ponged down. The tune was an ear worm—it was a hauntingly familiar song I couldn't place, and then it hit me square between the eyes. It was Sinatra from my ice-skating date with Cora in Rockefeller Center.

Shut up, Old Blue Eyes. There's no more songs to be sung.

I didn't feel young, I felt ancient and decrepit. I was used up and worthless.

Practically farting dust over here.

Toasting the memory, I tipped the bottle up and brought it to my lips, drinking it down until the notes faded away. A few minutes later, I passed out in a dirty, sweaty pile on my sheetless mattress.

A few hours later, my head screaming, I opened my eyes and had the spins. A wave of nausea sent me rushing to the floor, where I crawled on my hands and knees, searching for a trash can to puke in. I vomited until I was trembling, my nose running, eyes red, and hands shaking. Peering into the trash can, I tried to decipher what I had done the night before by the chunks of unidentifiable food and waste piled there. I was fuzzy. After my meeting with Paulie at The Punch Line, the rest of the night was blank. Black-out drunk makes your memory like Swiss cheese. It leaves huge, gaping holes in your space-time continuum that riddles your brain to fill. I scrambled to piece the night together but was so hungover I gave up. Maybe it would come back to me, maybe it wouldn't, and the truth was I just didn't give a shit either way. The only person that mattered was gone. Everything else was just details.

I climbed into the shower and let the hot water rain down on me, scrubbing at my forearms with a rough washcloth until my skin was pink. The cloth was like sandpaper, scratching me, yet I continued to rub until I drew blood, and even then, I couldn't stop.

Two. Four. Six. Eight.

If I performed the action in perfect parallel lines in sets of two, I could move to the other arm when I got to twenty. I swatted at a tingling sensation running up the back of my arms. Huge black cockroaches and Daddy Longlegs with paper-thin appendages trekked up my body en masse. Running up and down my legs. I howled and screamed, swatting them away with the washcloth, only to see the numbers multiply and cover me. My hand was now black, completely covered in delicate insect legs that tickled the hairs on my forearms as they ran up my body. I started to scream, muffling it into my mouth, clamping my hand over my lips. The bugs wanted inside. They wanted to eat my brain and feast on me from the inside out. I pressed my lips together, swatting at them and scratching down my face with my fingernails as my heart hammered on.

Cold water. That will send them scattering. I cranked it to ice cold and they disappeared. Relieved and exhausted, I pulled my towel from the floor and wiped off, my skin tender and inflamed. I yanked on some wrinkled clothes from the pile on the floor and went upstairs, careful to only touch every even-numbered stair in search of breakfast.

Two. Four. Six. Eight.

At the top of the stairs, it was eerily quiet. No coffee brewing, no food being prepared, it was so out of character that the first tingles of worry tickled up the back of my scalp.

"Ma!" I shouted, looking at the clock; it was ten a.m. She

was always glued to the TV with her sudoku puzzle at ten a.m. and never missed the *777 Club*. Pulling back the curtain at the sink, I checked the driveway and saw her car was still parked in its usual spot.

"Not the Mama," Alvin interjected from his fabric ensconced perch. "Bwawk! Not the Mama!"

I rolled my eyes and yanked off the sheet, and he rewarded me by shaking his tail feathers and squawking. His food tray was empty. "In a minute, buddy."

"Ma! Where are you? We have to feed Alvin," I shouted into the quiet. Getting no response, I walked down the hallway to her bedroom. At her door, I paused. "Mom, are you in there?"

Still silent, I knocked with two fingers, and the door slowly opened with a creak. She was still lying in bed.

"Ma? Are you sick?" I asked her, walking closer to the bed where she lay covered in a thick comforter and old quilt her mother had made. I shivered in the cold air.

"Ma?" I whispered extra sweetly, not wanting to jar her awake. I knew she deserved an apology, and I was finally ready to give her one and get out of the doghouse. She laid there facing the wall, sleeping soundly, unmoving. I walked closer and saw her mouth was slack. Her glasses sat on the nightstand next to a bottle of Unisom, and a pale blue glass of water. I reached out and touched her hand. It was cool to the touch.

"Ma?" I pleaded a little louder as I shook her gently. "Come on, Ma, wake up."

My hands were trembling as I leaned over and touched her forehead, confused.

Why isn't she moving?

Her skin was ice cold, buried under layers and layers of

quilted cotton. I passed my hand over her mouth, hoping to feel her warm breath on my palm. My eyes fixed on her chest, willing it to move up and down, examining it for signs of movement. She was utterly still. Panic crept in slowly, then a bolt of knowing shot through me. She wasn't breathing.

I pulled out my phone and dialed 911 on speakerphone and then desperately tried to recall the one CPR class I had lived through in high school. A, B, Cs was all I could remember. I checked her airway and then started compressions as the calming dispatcher gave me step-by-step instructions on how to perform CPR. Within minutes, I heard the sirens and ran to unlock the door.

"Hurry!" I shouted as I led them back down the hallway. "She's in here and she's not breathing."

A capable bald man burst in with his athletic female partner and a gurney and asked me to step aside.

Relieved help had arrived and she was safe in their skilled hands, I slid down the wall onto the floor. Adrenaline had been surging through me, and now every sense was awake and alive. My hangover dissipated in the wake of terror. I disconnected, watching from a distance as they worked on her. His partner pressed two gloved fingers to her neck and wrist, feeling for a pulse. She shook her head, and her lips pressed together in a straight line. I knew then. It was the curt nod of her head and the pity filling her eyes.

"She's gone. I'm so sorry," she confirmed.

"No! NO! NO!" I popped up from the floor, pushed my way to Ma, and began giving her chest compressions again.

My cheeks were wet when they pulled me away from her. My arms were shaking and my chest was heaving from effort. A gloved hand pulled mine from her chest.

"I'm sorry, but there is nothing more we can do to help

her. She's been gone for a long time, likely passed peacefully in her sleep hours ago."

My resolve crumbled, and I sank to the floor once again.

Was she still alive when I came home last night? Could I have walked into her room one more time and told her I loved her? Why did I run? Why didn't I pick up even one of her calls? I would give anything to hear her voice one more time.

"I'm sorry, Mama. I'm so sorry," I pleaded, fresh tears racing down my face. I sat up on my knees and leaned down to kiss her cold cheek that was already changing. Becoming hardened clay. Ashes to ashes, dust to dust.

"*You're so worthless, even your Ma left you,*" a voice hissed deep inside.

"Shut up!" I said.

"Sorry?" the paramedic asked as the radio cackled in the background.

"Nothing," I muttered and pulled her hand to my cheek, trying to warm it between my own. Studying the face of the only woman I've loved my entire life. Her eyes popped open, and I screamed.

"*Don't listen to them, Freddie. It was my time, I had to go. I didn't want to leave you.*"

"You were all I had left." I gripped her hand more tightly in mine and smoothed the cold skin, not wanting to let her go. I blinked and she was once again immobile on the bed, eyes closed.

The metallic crunch of a gurney being rolled into the house jarred me out of my thoughts. Fresh tears fell like rain.

"Come back," I begged, as I wrapped my arms protectively around her body, shielding her from the crew. "Please, Ma, I need you." I swiped at the tears blurring my vision. "Please," I whimpered. "Please."

A black body bag was rolled out on the gurney and

unzipped, the metal-on-metal zing of the teeth on the zipper a horrifying truth that made me cringe.

"NO!" I laid on top of her, tears coursing down my face. "You can't take her." I pulled her into my arms, willing her to hug me back, her body heavy, leaden, and cold. I bent to kiss her one last time.

"Sir, you have to let us do our job," the attendant said gently.

"Goodbye, Mama. I'll always love you most," I whispered into her hair and gently laid her back down on the bed. I struggled to find my feet, swaying then righting myself. I leaned against the wall, letting the plaster and lath hold me up, and sobbed as they wheeled her away.

"You will need to make arrangements at a funeral home. We're taking her to St. Anne's. We are sorry for your loss."

They quietly left, shutting the door behind them, and drove away with the lights and sirens deathly silent. Emergency over. No reason to rush back to the hospital.

I was alone. Utterly alone. No safety net. Everything and everyone I ever loved had been taken from me. The emptiness choked me. I gasped for air as a full-blown panic attack exploded from my core, making it impossible to breathe. Flushed hot, my skin was on fire, and sweat soaked my shirt instantly.

In and out, in and out. Slowly. Breathe.

Seconds felt like hours as I struggled for air, ravenous for oxygen, my heart pounding in my chest. I closed my eyes and begged it to pass. Finally, my heart slowed down to its normal pace and I exhaled a long sigh.

Why, Ma? Why did you leave me when I needed you most?

The quiet seeped into every nook in my brain as tears coursed down my face. Searching for comfort in the familiar,

I laid down in her bed. The sheets still smelled like the knock-off drug store perfume she favored. I closed my eyes again, pressing the sheet to my face, inhaling the scent, pretending she was close, lying to myself. I pulled her quilts up around me and wailed until I was left hiccupping and shaking, and then fell into a tormented sleep.

THIRTY-ONE

I woke up the next morning disoriented in Ma's bed, for the first few blissful minutes not remembering. Then all at once, the painful reality rushed in and it was like finding her all over again. Gone. Ma was gone. I couldn't bear to stay in the house awake and alone. I fed Alvin and choked down some cereal, standing at the sink, because I couldn't handle sitting at the table without Ma. Fidgety and desperate for distraction, I got dressed, stuffed thick wads of cash into my jacket pockets, put some supplies in a backpack, and left. Finally able to take my first full breath when I was standing in the sun on the sidewalk in the cold December air, I swiped at the tears on my cheeks and started walking.

It was a Sunday, and at ten a.m. when the Sycamore Baptist Church on the corner was in full swing and the choir was belting out "I'll Fly Away," I snuck into the parking lot and slapped dozens of "I Love Porn" bumper stickers on as many vehicles as I could. Snickering as I peeled the backing off, I got a cheap thrill out of pasting them on the bumpers of the official church shuttle vehicles. It was sick and wrong, two of my favorite qualities, and I snorted, wishing with a pang that Cora was there. She would have loved it.

Next, I headed to a local pet store and bought five thousand dollars of dog food and pet toys. I was recognized at the pet store, and the owner begged to take a photo. I relented but didn't post them to my socials.

What was the point anymore?

He helped me load it all into the back of the XL Uber I called to take me to Pawsitive Pet Shelter, where I was kiss-bombed by four slobbering pit bulls up for adoption. Their thick pink tongues left trails of sloppy kisses on my cheeks. I laid on my back while their stubby tails wagged happily as they flopped down on top of me.

"You guys have never heard of personal space, have you?" I asked in the high-pitched silly voice I reserve for dogs. "No one understands you either, but I do. I understand you. Who's a good boy?" Their ears perked up as I scratched their bellies.

Unconditional love. Dogs give unconditional love. I appreciated it so much more now I'd learned the hard way social media was the most conditional love of all.

I scratched the dogs under their necks, then began long tugs on their ears that blissed them out. "You guys get a bad rap. You're a bunch of sweet little babies who wouldn't hurt a fly." Their big sad eyes haunted me; I wanted to adopt them all. "I'll come back and visit," I lied.

I couldn't bring myself to call the funeral home, and I couldn't go home yet. Walking into the empty house filled me with dread. Instead, I stood outside the dollar store and handed out twenty-dollar bills, and if the person walking toward me was with a child, I gave them two. I never had spending money when I was a little kid, and let's face it, if your mom is shopping at the dollar store, you aren't exactly living in the lap of luxury.

The dollar store always held a special place in my heart. When I had a bad day in high school, Ma would bring me here and let me get Hot Tamales candies. In her honor, I went inside and bought a case and gave those away too.

Seeing people's faces light up broke through some of the darkness that enveloped me. A few of them hugged me. One lady burst into tears.

"I can get milk *and* cereal today. I thought I was going to have to choose." The statement broke my heart so much that I pulled five twenties from my stack and discreetly handed them to her when she came out of the store.

Give it away. You have to give it all away.

The thick wad of bills shoved into my rumpled pocket was a heavy weight I couldn't deny. I itched to finish this work. Black moths swarmed me, and I covered my head and ears, knowing that they were trying to get inside my brain. Trying to eat it. They flapped around my head, searching for an orifice to enter, on a mission to destroy me from the inside out. I swatted at them, trying to shoo them away, but they landed and morphed into demons, hellish creatures that enlarged as they walked closer and sent me screaming from the parking lot. I ran as far as my stubby legs would carry me and then collapsed on the corner, gasping for breath. I leaned against the dirty stone retaining wall that was crumbling, scanning wildly for demons. After a few intense minutes, relief washed over me that the demon moths hadn't followed.

My thoughts were racing through a track on my mind, an endless screaming loop whose sound was deafening. Keyed up, I scanned my surroundings, looking for my next project.

Bingo. Home Depot.

I ran across the first two lanes of traffic without looking as cars screeched to a halt and horns honked.

"Nut job!" a man screamed from his passing car, and I bowed at him like he was paying me a compliment. I ran through traffic, playing the ultimate game of frogger. I was untouchable, invincible. No one would hit me. I was the chosen one. Landing in front of the store's sliding glass door, I concentrated, pressing my fingers to my temples to open them with the power of my mind. When they slid open on command, a thrill shot through me.

Inside, the store was jam-packed, filled with uptight women dragging their bored husbands into the appliance section to talk about convection ovens and men testing out power tools. I made a beeline to the paint aisle and scooped fourteen cans of spray paint into my basket then added three impulse Snickers bars at the register.

A fresh-faced cashier in an orange apron handed me a plastic bag full of paints with a menacing smile. Then her face shifted into an elongated crocodile mouth with jagged teeth that began to chomp at the air between us. I dodged my face away and grabbed up the bag before running out of the store.

A masterpiece inspired by Banksy that would make my hero proud was swirling together in my mind. I would paint my piece de resistance, the crowning star of my achievement, and then the world would love me again. Searching for the perfect canvas to make my mark, I walked and walked and finally landed in front of a vast unblemished concrete wall. Light gray and massive, I was inspired. This canvas was made for me. I shook the bottles, humming to myself and dancing to the sound of the marbles rattling at the bottom. Two minutes later, I sprayed the first stroke onto my canvas.

Pshhh. Pshhhhhhh. The air whooshed out of the cans,

delivering stroke after stroke to the concrete canvas. Humming and in the zone, I worked and worked, carefully crafting my larger-than-life-size design. Large swaths of peach-colored paint, then edged in blacks with curly details. It was epic. I painted briskly, swirling like a dervish, egged on by the posse in my head.

"Fucking brilliant you are, mate!"

"Never have I seen anything so striking."

"Bravo!"

"That is quite an impressive feat of anatomy."

"Banksy would be so proud."

I painted at breakneck speed, working faster as the minutes ticked by. Sweating in exhaustion, my hands had a mind of their own as the most beautiful mural emerged in full effect on the concrete wall. Lost in the act, the colors swirled together, and I felt a brotherhood with the masters—Van Gogh, Michelangelo, DaVinci. This installation was my Sistine Chapel. After an hour of focused work, I stepped back, surveying my artwork. It was magnificent.

Hearing a siren approaching, I pulled off my gloves and ran across the street to dump the empty cans into a garbage can. I wanted to see people interact with my piece. Hiding behind a wall on the opposite side of the street, I watched the patrol car pull up with lights flashing.

"You dodged a bullet."

"Perfect timing."

"You're invisible."

"Able to hide in plain sight."

"Unstoppable."

"A God."

The officers looked around, and I ducked out of sight. A small crowd of people began to gather at the mural, animated and pointing at my genius, which made me puff up with pride. People began pulling out their cell phones to take photos. Selfie sticks launched cell phones high in the air to capture their faces and the mural in its technicolor amazingness. I have never been more proud of myself. A news truck pulled up and began filming. A perfectly pressed suit-clad woman with long, straight blonde hair waved her manicured hands at it and then sternly spoke into the camera. Another woman with two small children froze in front of it and then clamped a hand over the eyes of her kids while she ushered them away.

Censorship is wrong, Karen.

There is nothing more natural than the human body.

A group of teenage girls stopped and pointed and began to giggle, deciding to create fish-lipped Tik-Toks in front of my mural.

I should have signed it. Now, no one will know it's mine.

Needing to hear their reactions, I crossed the street and blended into the growing crowd, pulling some gloves on to hide the overspray that painted my fingers. I wanted to be immersed in the experience. Bursts of immature laughter popped up brightly from pockets of teenagers.

"Whoever pulled this off has balls," I overheard.

"No shit, Sherlock. Those are two of the hairiest balls I have ever seen."

"It's an existential narrative on the phallic world we live in."

"Stop reading into it, asshole. It's just a huge cock and balls." One of the teenage boys grabbed his crotch. "I should have asked the artist for royalties because it's identical to mine."

They love me. They really love me.

The police officers scanned the crowd, asking if anyone had seen anything, to no avail. Unable to hold back, I interjected myself into the investigation and offered an opinion to the officer. "It's art. How is this any different than the mural on 42nd street?" It was reckless, and I couldn't stop myself, the truth was a delicious secret that made me smug and self-important. Indulging in my desire to be part of something meaningful, something bigger than myself.

"This isn't art. It's vandalism, and we will find out who did this."

I disappeared into the crowd, offering to photograph groups in front of my installation, happy as a clam that I had pulled it off. After the police left, the crowd began to disperse so I took off walking. An hour later, I found myself in front of a bell ringer at a Salvation Army red kettle. I felt for the wad of cash that remained in my pocket, pulled off two twenties for myself, and dropped the rest of it into the red kettle. It didn't fit, like a post-menopausal woman trying to squeeze into her favorite jeans without Spanx. I had to separate it into four smaller piles in order for it all to sink down into the kettle.

"Wow. Thank you," the bell ringer said after he watched me stuff the kettle full, and then he began to sing "I'll be home for Christmas" with a voice so deep and rich, I settled into the shadows a few steps away and let it wash over me.

I'll be home for Christmas.

Did I have a home anymore? Did it even matter?

THIRTY-TWO

The next day, it took everything in me to get up and make the call to the funeral home. The original cash from the lottery win in my briefcase was getting low; less than twenty thousand remained. I pulled out five grand and tucked it into the money clip that I wedged deep in my pocket, leaving the rest in the case, and then I took a taxi to Poore Brothers Funeral Home. A fully restored Victorian beauty whose cheery yellow façade was incongruent with the business conducted inside its original oak doors.

Soft, soothing music spooled into speakers and discreetly covered the hushed murmurs of people in the two living room-style consultation rooms. I was looking around, desperate to bolt, my neck getting itchy, when a thick, middle-aged woman wearing a gray polyester suit came forward and offered her limp hand. She nearly blended into the greige decor that coated the funeral home in a pale nothingness that left no place for your eyes to focus.

"My deepest condolences for your loss. I'm Ellen Poore, and it's my passion to give your mother's celebration of life the planning and care it deserves," she said with practiced empathy, holding my hand a little too long and giving it a short squeeze at the end. Uncomfortable, I pulled it back and stuck it inside my pocket to discourage any further hand-holding opportunities. I followed behind her and sank too deeply into a gray chenille sofa, setting the briefcase next to me, watching her eyeball it with interest.

Passion? It's no one's passion to plan funerals and talk about embalming. Quickly, I decided Ellen was a liar. "Well, Ellen, no offense, but it's my passion to get in and out of here as quickly as possible. This place gives me the willies."

Ellen's expression soured. Her lips pursed together like she'd just licked a lemon. Ever the professional, she launched into her presentation. "The funeral service is the ultimate act of love. It is the last celebration of a cherished one's life. I am here to help you make critical decisions on how to best honor your mother's last wishes."

She offered me a bottle of water, and I unscrewed the cap and took a long drink to avoid having to speak.

"Did your mother share her final wishes with you?"

"It wasn't something we chitchatted around the dinner table about if that is what you're asking." The words were too harsh for the quiet parlor, and she visibly recoiled. "I think she'd like to be cremated," I offered.

"Let me walk you through our urn options. They are the *most* tasteful way to capture the legacy of your loved one." She pulled out a glossy magazine-style brochure, and I tuned out her businesslike mundane voice. Paging through the offerings, one by one, I noted the investment at the end of each option. She thought using the word *investment* camouflaged what it really was—glorified Glad ware to store the leftovers in. Still, I wanted the best for Ma.

"Poore Funeral Home? That's got to be the biggest oxymoron I've heard in a long time." I laughed at the obvious disconnect, but uptight Ellen didn't even crack a smile. She was unflappable.

She shifted away from me, a hint of barely detectable disgust flashing across her face, but I noticed.

Lose column. Check.

"*She knows the truth*," a man hissed. "*That you're a worthless piece of crap. A mama's boy without a mama. The most pathetic creature in the entire world.*" I dug my fingernails into the palms of my hand, trying to reconnect with my body. Feeling the physical sensation of pain was sometimes the only way to pull me from the voices into the present.

Ellen dove back into her spiel, getting to the final offering. "This might be a little too extravagant for a budget-minded individual like yourself." She stopped herself quickly and began to shut the catalog without even discussing it.

Offended, I blurted out, "Wait. That's the one. She deserves the best."

"It's… it's several thousand dollars," she stammered.

"Perfect, I happen to have several thousand dollars right here to *invest* in her internment vessel." I turned to open the briefcase to flash the remaining cash at her, and her eyes glazed over with greed.

"Well, that is a beautiful choice, the *right* choice, a *loving* choice, Mr?" Now that she had a glimpse of the green stuff, suddenly she was very interested in getting to know me on a deeper level.

"Angel," I answered.

"That name is familiar."

"Everyone tells me that," I dismissed. "What's next?"

"Let's talk about her obituary."

I pulled out a folded piece of paper I'd tucked into my jacket and handed it over. I had written it myself.

Dorothy Marie Angel June 17, 1952- December 12, 2021

Dorothy passed peacefully in her sleep at her home. It is believed that she died laughing at her son's jokes. She was his biggest fan.

Her greatest life accomplishment was the birth of her favorite child, Fredrick Allistair Angel. Her second greatest accomplishment was helping him hide that very offensive middle name from the public.

She left behind a pair of slippers from the 50s, a thousand canisters of Decaf Maxwell House, and a bag of mismatched socks. Her attic is currently packed to the rafters with treasures like original Clark's candy bar wrappers, broken furniture, and moth balls. Arrangements can be made for these items to be picked up after an appropriate amount of grieving time has passed. Later this evening would be fine.

Her regrets were few, but included never setting foot inside a strip club, eating those discount shrimp that had already turned at Frank's Shrimp Shack during a Florida vacation in 2010, and the summer of 2015 when she burned her eyebrows completely off following a propane accident. She had to draw them on for the rest of her life, and she wasn't very good at it.

She married a worthless man who didn't truly appreciate her generous spirit and giving nature. Luckily, he preceded her in death, allowing Dottie to live the rest of her life on her own terms.

She was an exceptional mother, selflessly putting the needs of her family first. Dottie was a true original. God broke the mold when he made this practical, loving, supportive woman. She has left a hole in the lives of those closest to her that can never be filled.

Donations can be made in lieu of flowers to the 777 Club, just in case she hasn't donated enough to those greedy bastards already for the pearly gates to fling open wide upon her arrival. For the record, she has and is going to be incredibly pissed if she has to wait outside.

"I'm not sure we should use the word bastard in an obituary," Ellen mused diplomatically.

"It's what Ma would have wanted," I responded, enjoying her obvious discomfort, pressing my lips together to keep the giggle in.

"Wait… I got it." I saw a flicker of recognition ignite in her eyes as she snapped her chubby fingers together. "You're Freddie Angel, the Funologist! I knew you looked familiar."

I sighed. "Guilty as charged."

"That was quite a performance on *Jimmy Bravo*."

"Oh, you caught that, did you?" I cringed and mumbled, "Regrettably, it was not my finest hour."

Ellen was so silent, I swear I could hear her blink.

"Can we wrap this up?" I finally asked as an uneasiness settled into me.

"Of course." She turned back to the sheath of paperwork on her clipboard.

Over the next hour, I made selections for the service. We hired a harpist and a vocalist and a four-piece string quartet for the service. She recommended a media company to create a memorial video from Ma's old photo albums. We planned a reception following the service for fifty guests. I didn't know how many would show up, but I wanted to be prepared just in case. After a lifetime of letting her down, I wanted to do this one thing absolutely right.

"She loves…" I stopped. It was the first time I had to correct myself to past tense, and the words stuck in my constricted throat. I swallowed hard and continued, "…loved yellow roses. I'd like you to use whatever is left in here after the expenses are paid to completely blanket this place in as many yellow roses as possible."

Sweating and anxious to leave, I sat perched on the edge of the sofa. My left leg bounced up and down. "Are we good?" My mouth watered; I needed something stronger than the bottle of water in my hand.

"Yes, Mr. Angel. We will take care of her from here. You don't have to lift a finger. Rest assured, we will handle everything."

I handed the briefcase over to Ellen, shook her hand, and walked away feeling lighter. Tying up a loose end and giving Ma the send-off she deserved.

THIRTY-THREE

L ater that afternoon, I was wired. Wide awake, unable to slow down or close my eyes. I couldn't stand being alone with my thoughts. There was an entire cast of characters having whole conversations in my head. A virtual cocktail party of shame and condemnation cueing up constantly, giving a running commentary on every thought that entered my mind.

Desperate to escape and my energy levels soaring, I took a bus downtown and got off, walking toward the seedier part of town. Check cashing joints and bail bondsmen popped up, and a huge influx of ladies of the night dressed in faux fur and sky-high stripper platforms emerged on every dirty corner. I stopped at an ATM and withdrew $400 from my Venmo account.

"Do you want a date?" a little waif of a girl asked me from under the streetlight she was leaned against. Her giant blue eyes sunk deep into her face, the purple bruise on her cheek stopping me on a dime. I studied her for a minute. Skinny and too much makeup, she projected a wariness and vulnerability that made me wonder what landed her here on this street in the first place. What series of bad decisions set her on this journey where selling her body to strangers was the most lucrative career path? I was flushed with empathy. I too had made some truly terrible life decisions. Without Ma, I could have just as easily landed out here on the same streets with her.

"What's your name?" I asked.

"Simone." She licked her lip in a gesture that was supposed to be sexy but just felt desperate and sad.

"How old are you?"

"Old enough, mister," she dismissed, and I looked at her hands which had begun to shake. She reached one out to me, and I noticed another fading yellow bruise on the side of her neck. A series of four purple dots that could only have been created from fingers pressed deep into the hollow of her throat.

"Who did that?" I asked, and she looked down. I took a step closer and whispered, "I was sent here to save you." It was a grandiose statement, yet at that moment, I was convinced if I yanked open my coat and shirt, you would see the Superman uniform sprawled across my chest.

Her forehead crinkled in confusion, and then her tough-girl façade broke. "No one can save me," she cried.

"I can." Saying the words out loud made me puff up with pride. I heard trumpets announcing my dramatic arrival in the background.

"Follow me," I ordered, and she looked over her shoulder and hesitated for a moment, then fell in line behind me. She skittered out on heels that were too high for such a tiny girl, awkwardly struggling to keep up with my longer legs. I walked down the sidewalk, tiptoeing to avoid cracks, toward a burger joint and walked inside. Fryer grease, in all its deli-cious state fair glory filled my nostrils. "Order anything you want," I offered, and she looked over at me, hesitating. "What?" I asked.

"It's just…" She struggled to find the words she wanted to say. "If I don't come home with money, Anthony will hurt me."

"I'm guessing Anthony is the one who made your neck so colorful."

She looked down. I ordered for both of us, and we took our number and slid into a sticky booth near the Coke machine. Simone's blue eyes flitted around and out the windows, always scanning, always searching, unable to relax.

"How much for the entire day?" I asked.

"The day?" She was clearly confused.

"You know, *Pretty Woman* style." I smiled. "How much to be my companion for the day?"

"Five hundred?" she asked tentatively, her voice turning up at the end.

I pulled the wad of cash out of my pocket under the table, pulled ten bills from it, and slid the money over to her.

"Here's enough for two days," I said. "If things go well, there might be more."

"Well?" she questioned and gulped hard, stuck on what the word might mean, but eyeing the cash on the table harder than the burgers that were just set in front of us.

"I have some shit to do. It will work out better if I have help."

"You look so familiar," she said. "I feel like I have seen you somewhere."

I closed my eyes as a sea of shame washed over me, feeling the guilt collecting in my soul as a tight smile stretched and stretched across my face.

She snapped her fingers. "Are you that guy everyone was talking about? The Funologist?"

"I was, but all that is over now."

"Wow," she mused. "I've never met anyone famous before."

"Consider this the first of many of your dreams I will make come true. And you won't even have to rub my bottle."

A quick smile turned up the corners of her mouth.

Win column. Check.

She sipped on her Coke and wrapped the paper from the straw around her skinny fingers with stiletto fingernails so sharp, I wondered if they would cut me to ribbons.

We gobbled down our food and then walked to a used car lot. An old red Camaro with T-tops caught my eye.

"God! This was *the* car when I was in high school. I would have given my left nut for it. Not the right one, but definitely the left." I bent down to study it and ran my fingers down its sexy curves as reverently as caressing a lover.

I opened the door as a seedy salesman with a beer belly practically tripped on himself running over to us.

"How much?" I asked.

"Four G's?"

"I got three in cash on me right now."

"Deal!" he said and promptly handed me the keys in exchange for the cash. I didn't even test drive it.

"Get in!" I said to Simone as I turned over the ignition. It roared to life, and I squealed the tires as I ripped out of the parking lot while Simone leaned forward to turn on the radio.

We flew down the streets in my bitchin' Camaro. Wanting to continue my retail high, I pulled into a parking space at a Walmart.

"Come on, I'll buy you anything you want."

Simone perked up and followed behind while I skipped into the store. I yanked a cart free from the tangle at the door and pushed it down the aisles, filling it with electronics and small kitchen appliances. "I was supposed to go to college," she said while looking longingly at the row of tethered laptops. "But then my mom got sick and I had to take care of her." She pressed the home button on one and tested out the mouse.

Mom. The word bolted through me like a sharp dagger to my heart.

"Get the computer," I said and pressed the button to make a robotic voice page out, "Customer needs assistance at the electronics counter."

A middle-aged woman opened the cabinet with her little key and handed it to Simone, who hugged it tightly to her chest. "Are you sure? It's so expensive."

"I'm sure, my dear. You can't take it with you." I pushed the cart faster through the store, running away from her questions and over to the liquor aisle. There, I loaded the cart with two fifths of vodka and a bottle of Rumplemints.

"Pick your poison," I told her, and she added a bottle of dark rum and a two-liter of Coke to the cart. "If you really want to have a good time, I can get us some Molly," she offered.

"Molly?" I asked. "Never met the girl, but she sounds like a good time."

Simone giggled. "We are going to need some water and some snacks. I get so thirsty when I'm rolling." She proceeded to push the cart to the snack cake aisle and added a box of Oatmeal Creme Pies and Zebra cakes to it.

"I love these!" I said and added two more boxes. Then we ran down the aisles and added chips and salsa, crackers, and some grapes. I took over pushing the cart, and Simone threw more random items in. It was like we were married and shopping for weekly groceries for our family of five. In this fantasy, my beautiful wife had kept off the baby weight after nursing our three sons, and I was a proud dad.

"*Never in a million years*," Dad hissed in my ears. "*No woman would ever spread her legs for a loser like you.*"

"Shut up," I said.

"What?" Simone asked. "Did I say something wrong?"

"I wasn't talking to you," I told her and then pushed off with my feet and rode the overflowing cart to the checkout line.

"One thousand, eight hundred, three dollars, and four cents," the cashier said.

A shiver of guilt shot through me, but I pushed it away. Technically, I was using the donations to help Simone. Technically. It was a fine line that I wasn't proud to have butted up against.

I swiped the credit card, packed everything into the trunk of the car, and peeled out of the parking lot as Simone gave me directions to her hook-up. Stopped at a red light, I glanced over to the car idling next to us, and the driver there gave me a sneer of contempt.

"*He knows.*"

"*He knows what a loser you are.*"

"*He knows you don't deserve to be with a beautiful woman like Simone.*"

"*Show him.*"

"*Grow some balls, Freddie, and put him in his place.*"

The light shifted to green, and I slammed on the gas, pressing the pedal to the floor, and we shot out like a champion at the gate. I smoked that pretentious prick and then cut him off and whipped in front of him at the next stoplight. Simone jerked forward and then back, giggling.

"Gonna need a hundie," Simone said.

"Of course, my darling." I pressed the gas pedal with my

foot and shimmied to get my money clip out of my pants and tossed it to her. She peeled one off and handed it back, and I shoved it back into my pocket. She folded the bill and directed me into a darkened corner to park the car.

A few minutes later, a lanky teenager came to Simone's side of the car and offered his hand. She shook it with the concealed bill tucked into her fingers and came away with a little baggie filled with yellow pills.

"Let's party." She grinned, shaking the baggie.

I slammed the car into drive. "I'm immortal," I said as a crazed smile widened across my face, and I pressed my foot deeper on the gas pedal. The Camaro tore through the side streets as I sped toward home. "Wanna see?" I grinned wickedly at her and hit the gas even harder. The force pushed her back into the seat, and her face whitened, which only egged me on to go faster. The rush as the world streamed by in my peripheral vision fired all my brain synapses.

"Freddie?' she squeaked out.

"Yes, dear?" I grinned and slammed the pedal to the metal as we whipped down the street, careening toward a parked car only a few blocks away. I shot through two yield signs, laughing hysterically as Simone reached up and pressed her hand to the door frame and her feet into the floorboards, bracing for impact.

"Slow down," she begged, but I kept going, speeding toward the parked car. She screamed at the last second when I whipped the wheel away and missed the car by only inches.

"See, baby? Nothing to worry about. I'm invincible." Two spine-tingling turns later, I slammed on the brakes in front of the house.

Simone was shaking and white but didn't say anything. I whooped and hollered, popping the trunk and dragging our Wal-Mart haul into the house as she followed behind me.

Alvin squawked from his cage that smelled like piss. I dumped some pellets into his food dish and refilled the water, then quickly put away the groceries.

Simone was mesmerized by the big bird. She pressed her nose to the cage, and Alvin squealed and screeched, flapping his wings to perch closer to her.

"Watch this!" I pulled out my phone and pulled up a playlist, and Alvin began to dance, bobbing and ducking in time to the music. This enthralled Simone, who copied his movements and danced in sync with him in front of the cage.

"You're an asshole!" he screeched.

"Did he just call me….?"

"An asshole? Yes, he did," I admitted.

"That is something you don't see every day." She laughed and then shifted her focus to the pills. She plucked two yellow pills from the baggie and handed me one. I studied it closely, a tiny yellow butterfly imprinted on one side of it. I had never taken pharmaceuticals recreationally, and I was intrigued. Fearless, she placed one on her tongue and swallowed. I hesitated for only a second before tossing it into my mouth.

"How long will it take before I feel something?"

"Fifteen minutes until liftoff," she said and settled herself on the sofa, removing her shoes and tucking her legs underneath her.

I pulled one of the bottles of vodka out and poured a stiff screwdriver, just tinging the liquid the palest orange from the juice. I poured a rum and Coke for Simone and settled in next to her. Minutes later, the first change was the intense need to feel her skin on mine. I shifted closer to her, and she giggled and laid back on the sofa. She pulled her coat off, getting overheated, and I focused on her exposed navel. My fingers walked toward hers until I had her palm in my hand. Her skin was smooth and supple with the tautness of youth. I closed my eyes, savoring the sensation more fully. She kissed the top of my hand and then laid her head in my lap. Her hair was soft as it brushed across my palms, and I began to trace her with my fingers. Following the curlicue of her ear lobe, I then trailed down the long planes of her neck, behind her head to lace my fingers in her hair as I rolled. I don't ever recall feeling hair and skin as soft as hers. I traced over and over, marveling at the richness of the sensation of skin-on-skin contact, not wanting to take it any further than that. I stroked her hair and her skin, my fingers reveling in their satiny softness. I twirled a piece of her auburn hair around my index finger, fascinated with the curly trail that led to her pink scalp.

The flush of heat welled up next, warm and enveloping, and my forehead broke out in a ring of sweat. Then the euphoria rushed in, and a smile broke out across my face as the sweet, yummy, feel-good chemicals surged through me. I felt love. Love for the spider weaving its web in the windowsill. Love for Simone, who was curled into a ball on the sofa with her head still in my lap. Love for the chenille throw that smelled like Ma when I brought it to my face and breathed it in. Love. Love. Love. Pure and unadulterated. Colors surged in my brain—yellows and teals, flashes of bright red, and purple. I wanted to listen to music and cued some up on my phone.

Dancing in front of people was always an embarrassing debacle I shied away from. I would literally rather you dip me in tar and set my hair on fire than to physically move my body in time to any tune, but the Molly made my inhibitions vanish. I stood and began to pulse in time to the music. I jumped and jumped. I cranked it up and pumped it through my new Bluetooth speakers acquired from the Walmart binge.

In my current state, it took several long minutes to connect the technology, but it was worth it. The bass ripped through the living room, encouraging me to jump. I could see the notes reverberating and jamming tighter together and farther apart. I could almost reach out and touch the treble clefs and staccato notes that had smiley faces as they floated by me through the air. I physically felt the notes as they coursed through me.

My skin was throbbing as endless amounts of energy stormed through my limbs. I danced and jumped until I was sweaty. Simone eventually found her feet and jumped next to me, her delicate fist flailing in the air. She laughed and laughed in distorted slow motion, begging me to spin her in circles and dip her. We collapsed on the floor in a sweaty, breathless jumble, and then I crawled to the pile of Walmart bags on the floor and pulled two bottles of water from their plastic netting. I sucked mine down so hard it became concave and squealed in protest. I held one out to her and leaned back onto the sofa, catching my breath.

"My mom died a few days ago," I blurted out, unable to stop myself. The words scrolled out of my lips and into the music that came to a screeching halt immediately as the record in my head scratched in protest to the confession.

Simone's eyes swung over to meet mine. "Oh, Freddie, I'm so sorry."

"Me too," I admitted. "Now, I'm all alone." A tear trickled down my cheek and mingled with the sweat.

"Everyone is," Simone said sadly. "Even in a world filled with billions of people, we are all alone."

THIRTY-FOUR

The next three days passed in a technicolor dreamlike state where I only surfaced from insanity to take another dose. Simone called her dealer again, and he hooked me up with an impressive array of all things chemical. Molly, dabs, benzos, oxy, he had it all and I bought him out. The three guilt-fueled trips to the ATM with Simone dissolved immediately into a chemical haze. Slivers of time that used to be painful were now easy to fill with music and color. The anxiety and tension that had found a permanent home in me for decades now dissipated into the numbness of pharmaceutical bliss.

Luckily, in a moment of clarity, I set multiple alarms and reminders on my phone for Ma's funeral. That morning, a blaring alarm shot me straight up in bed. I woke up alone, shaking and puking. Wanting to take the edge off with another dose of oxy, but knowing it was too risky, I settled for a breakfast screwdriver. I couldn't bliss out at Ma's funeral and become a slobbering, staggering pile. As much as it was going to hurt, I owed it to her to at least attempt some form of sobriety today.

After dressing in my only pair of dress pants and a wrinkled button-down shirt I had stuffed into the back of the closet, I walked down the front steps. It took a second to register the Camaro in the driveway was mine. It took another thirty minutes to find the keys.

I stopped to feed Alvin and then, feeling guilty, cut up an apple and the broccoli that was in the fridge from Ma's last grocery run. Seeing the little trees and knowing they were the last ones she touched made me teary-eyed. Shaking it off, I opened the cage. With a flap of his wings, he landed on my arm, picking up a piece of broccoli from his dish with his beak. He edged his head toward me, ducking it, and I reached out to trace my hand down his soft feathers, smoothing them as he pressed his head more firmly into my finger.

"Who's a good boy?"

He stopped eating and rewarded me with a whistle.

"I can't do this alone, buddy. I think you should come."

He bobbed up and down on my forearm, squeezing it with his talons in agreement. I walked us out to the car, and he crawled up my arm, squawking and bobbing. Shifting the car into drive, a wave of paranoia flooded me, and I scanned and scanned the roads for police cars. When I finally pulled into the funeral home, it was a blessed relief. To soften the knot in my belly, I took half of a Molly, tucking the rest into my pocket. Alvin and I walked into the funeral home, and immediately, the string quartet cued up. He began rocking and bobbing up my arm, landing firmly on my shoulder and dancing to the music.

Ellen raced toward me, a pinched look on her face.

"Mr. Angel, you can't bring a parrot in here. This is a place of mourning."

"Ellen, he's my emotional support animal," I argued.

"You're an asshole," Alvin shouted out at her, and I burst

into loud peals of laughter, a joyous sound completely inappropriate and out of place at a funeral home. I didn't care. If I could have high-fived Alvin's little birdy claws, I would have.

"Nailed it," I said and stroked his head, ignoring the obvious displeasure blooming on Ellen's face. I walked into the viewing room where circles of murmuring people stood stiffly in their darkest formal dress clothes. All eyes swung to me in one perfectly choreographed moment.

I caught glimpses of people that I recognized. Paulie and a few of the regulars at The Punch Line. My eyes darted and connected with Darlene's, and the pity I saw there gutted me. A cluster of the women from the shelter stood in a circle, not as bright and shiny as they were the day of the makeovers now that they had to style their own hair.

I scanned and scanned the room for the only pair of eyes I wanted to see. Walking to the center of it like some kind of pathetic pirate with Alvin on my shoulder, I searched for her, and then the crowd parted. In my mind, it was more dramatic, like Moses parting the Red Sea, a biblical story we had dissected at youth group that I always found fascinating.

In my fertile and dramatic imagination, a spotlight kicked on and illuminated Cora. I blinked and blinked again, afraid she was a mirage. A thrill of hope sprung deep in my belly as a cascade of rainbows and prisms wavered down from floor to ceiling. I could see colors shifting and playing and briefly wondered if these were the auras weirdos at the metaphysical stores couldn't stop yammering about. Tangoing with Cora was the most beautiful pale pink wash of light, concentrating into magenta. It swirled and danced, wrapping around her body that was clad in a black dress and long black boots with a heel. I stumbled toward her with both my arms open, tripping on the carpet as Alvin flapped away to safety. The first tears of relief moistened my cheeks.

"Freddie?" she said as she caught me when I pitched forward. "What have you done to yourself?" The concern twinged her words softly. "Are you high?"

I pulled her thin frame to me, clinging to her. My face nuzzled into her neck, and she was so soft and smelled like peaches and clean laundry. "I missed you so much. I'm so sorry, Cora."

"Oh, Freddie," she whispered into my ear as her hand rubbed my back. The soothing gesture was faintly reminiscent of the way Ma used to comfort me when I was a little child, which just made more tears rush to the surface.

"Do you forgive me?" I pulled back and beseeched her with my eyes while my forearms clung to hers, refusing to let go. "I need you to forgive me," I pleaded. "Please, Cora."

She studied me for a long moment, taking in my panicked and darting eyes, the sadness that had taken up residence in my body, weighing me down with such force I felt like I was drowning.

"I forgive you," she finally said, and her words broke me. Like a dam with a crack, the guttural wails broke free, and I fell to my knees. Clinging to her calves, the scent of leather tingled my nostrils. I didn't dare let go. I didn't care that I was a mess. I didn't give a shit I was making a scene. Everyone else in the room disappeared in that one moment, and Cora forgave me. She struggled to pull me to my feet again as her cheeks pinked.

I wiped at my nose with the corner of my sleeve, and the funeral director appeared at my elbow with a box of tissues. "We need you to take your seat so we can start the service." Ellen pulled me gently away from Cora and led me between the chairs and to the front row. There was an urn in the front of the room set on a white decorative column next to several easels, and there were so many floral displays it looked like a flower shop had exploded. A sea of yellow roses covered every flat surface, and I sobbed, shaking and trembling.

Ma. I miss you, Ma, so much I can barely breathe.

A somber white-haired priest appeared in front of the solid oak podium and began the service. I sat stiffly in a cushioned chair, feeling alone in the crowd of people. With Cora sitting in the seat beside me, it was surreal. The funeral became a scene played out for my entertainment like a Broadway show. Twenty minutes into the service, the priest asked for people to come to the podium to share memories. I walked up, shaky and unsteady.

I pulled the microphone off the stand and held it to my face.

"Cremation. It's weird. Am I right?" I blurted into the microphone. "I mean, you are condensed into nearly nothing. Your entire body can fit into that." I waved at the urn as the audience shifted uncomfortably in their seats. "Talk about downsizing." Alvin punctuated it with a whistle from his perch at the top of the bookcase.

"It's pretty ironic that most people, Ma included, fear going to Hell, but then sign up to be cremated. Actually planning to be burned at the stake, if you really think about it. It's kind of like a trial run of Hell." I chuckled at my own joke. "It's like trying Prime for seven days. No, thank you, I do *not* want to renew my membership."

I tapped the microphone. "Is this thing on?" I looked down at my feet. "Tough crowd." Murmurs began to rise. "My whole life, I wanted to make my mom proud of me. When everything exploded with the Funologist, Ma was so happy for me. I finally figured things out. I finally was going to be somebody—someone she could be proud of. It felt good. Better than good, it was amazing." I paused and looked over at the urn. "As I am sure you all know, it didn't last. Good things never seem to stick around for me. You can call it self-sabotage or failure to thrive or just bad decision making, and on some level, I guess all of those assessments are true." I stopped suddenly, the words I needed to say choking me. "I'm sorry, Mama. I'm so sorry for disappointing you again." A stray tear slid down my cheek, and I brushed it away with a tight smile. "She's the only woman who ever truly loved me, and now she's gone." More tears coursed down my cheeks. I surveyed the audience. I was losing them.

"Enough of that," I dismissed, stuffing down my despair and shame. "Who's ready to put the FUN back in this funeral?!" I shouted into the microphone. The words jolted the mourners, and they jumped in their chairs. My heartbeat pulsed in my ears, and I plunged back into my impromptu set.

"Make them laugh, asshole. This is your final performance. Go out on top."

"People do some weird things with ashes nowadays. Have you heard about this? I could shoot her into the sky by preloading Ma into some memorial fireworks. I could have a tattoo artist add some of her ashes to the ink and give me a tattoo, or I could take pieces of her and compress her into a diamond." I paused to let that sink in.

"Show of hands, ladies, who would be happy with an engagement ring made from your grandmother?" I paced to the other side of the room. "C'mon. No takers? What if Mee-Maw was a big woman, and we could squeeze a four-carat stone out of her? I have a feeling a few of you would be interested then."

I looked into the crowd of widened eyes and heard a few groans, which only added fuel to the fire. "Seems to me like you have two choices, and they both suck. You can either take the fire and brimstone free trial, or you can opt for claustrophobia in a casket and be buried in the ground. Not sure which is worse. Seems like we could have a better recycling program than that. There are almost eight billion people on earth. I mean, eventually, we're gonna run out of room."

I paced to the other side of the room. I was getting heated, so I pulled off my shirt, and the room gasped. I had forgotten the stupid temporary tattoos Simone and I had scored at the gas station on one of our drug runs. They were fading and peeling away, giant ugly cartoons sprawled across my torso and arms. "Don't act so offended. It's the human body, a beautiful thing." I paced back across to the other side of the room, spreading my attention out. You couldn't let one side of the crowd feel more love. "This isn't a striptease, Paulie. Don't get aroused." I picked up the shirt and swung it in circles above my head. "Or *is it*?" I leered into the microphone and savored the one weird laugh coming from the back of the room. Continuing to swing the shirt in a circle, I launched it into the first aisle, where it landed on an elderly woman who yanked it off and threw it on the floor with disgust.

"Mr. Angel." Ellen, the controlling funeral director, appeared at my side, her hand outstretched, her fingers pinching for the microphone. "I think you should take your seat."

"I'm not done."

"I think you've done quite enough," she scolded, and two larger men appeared at my sides as she pulled the microphone from my hand. Alvin squeaked in solidarity, becoming louder and more agitated as the men dragged me down the aisle.

"Alvin, my man. You're the only one who understands

me." He flapped his wings faster and louder, whistling into the tension-filled air.

"Getting thrown out of your own mother's funeral!" I shouted into the crowd. "Gotta be pretty messed up to pull that one off." They shoved me down the aisle. "You have been amazing. I'm Freddie Angel, and remember to give your servers…" I paused then bellowed, "Just… the… tip!" Laughing hysterically, they yanked me toward the door and promptly handed me my shirt.

"Just the tip," Alvin parroted back, making me laugh hysterically. "Just the tip," he repeated.

"Do we need to call someone for you?" Ellen asked with what looked like genuine concern in her eyes. "You don't seem stable."

"Sweetheart, I ain't ever been stable, and I'm not about to start now." I pulled on the shirt and then the coat I was handed and walked out to the parking lot, sucking in the cold air while laughing hysterically, then I doubled over in pain. I ran to the car and slammed the door shut and sobbed, beating my head on the steering wheel. Gripping the rubber between my hands, I wailed in the car. Steaming up the windows, keening that sounded like a wounded animal came from my gut. Ugly tears mixed with snot and slobber mingled and descended down my face. I swiped at them with the sleeve of my coat.

"Go home. Finish it."

"It's over."

"You're washed up."

"You're done."

I turned the key in the ignition, shifted into gear, and slammed down the gas pedal. Driving home as fast as possible, I had things to do.

THIRTY-FIVE

I swept the garbage and clutter off the dining room table with my forearm and then took stock of what I had left. Dumping the pills from the baggies into a pile on the table, I sorted them by color, then created a smiley face design with them. I took a photo and posted it to social media, hashtagged #thefinalshow, #thefunologist, #goodnightkc.

Pulling up the Funologist Venmo account for the final time, I scrolled through the activity. I smiled when I saw a transfer I didn't remember making two nights ago to Simone for ten thousand dollars with the note "Freedom."

At least I saved one.

I was shocked to see there was still almost a hundred grand in there. I made a series of donations, ten thousand to the Animal Rescue League. Twenty grand to Habitat for Humanity. I ordered two thousand dollars worth of Girl Scout cookies to be delivered to a food bank, and another fifteen grand I donated to an LGBTQ foundation that fosters abused teenagers and fights to close conversion camps. The final forty thousand dollars I donated to NAMI, to help poor fuckers like me have a chance at a normal life.

There, that should do it. Should be enough good deeds to open the pearly gates for me so I can spend eternity with Ma.

Then I poured myself a vodka on the rocks and swiped a handful of the smiley face, downing them in one swallow.

"Normal life? People like you don't get to have a normal life."

The fact that I would be exiting mine filled me with a sense of peace. Ma would be waiting for me, and I missed her so much. The two farting rescue dogs we'd taken in after Dad died would be waiting with her at the rainbow bridge. There was nothing left for me here, just pain and misunderstanding. I flopped back down on the sofa, my eyelids becoming weighted and heavier. The panic and mania subsided for a moment until there was only tranquility. There was finally stillness inside my busy brain where so many personalities had waged a battle for control for as long as I could remember. The silence and the stillness washed over me, and for the first time in my entire life, I felt peace. I closed my eyes and smiled. Flashes of memory lit up in my mind and played like grainy home movies from the early eighties. Ma smiling on the front steps of the house. The roaring laughter that night I killed at The Punch Line. Cora skating at Rockefeller Center, enormous fluffy snowflakes drifting down and kissing her hair. Ma's nose buried in yellow roses the day of the makeovers. Her eyes filling with tears when she said, "I'm so proud of you."

I had lived a life. I wouldn't say it was particularly well-lived, but it was mine. I'd made so many mistakes, but I tried to help as many people as I could along the way. I drifted away with a small smile, looking forward to the next place. Hoping it was warm and safe and quiet, three things that had been so elusive in this life.

A gray fog enveloped me, then blessed black.

Thank you, Kansas City, and goodnight. I'm coming, Ma.

THIRTY-SIX

Beep. Beep. Beep. A band tightened on my arm, and I heard the strain of Velcro as a machine chugged mechanically. Tighter, tighter, tighter. My eyes flickered open and then shut against the agony of the obnoxious fluorescent light shining down.

So, *this* is the bright light they were talking about.

The beeping continued. Disoriented, I opened my eyes again and scanned the room for clues, trying to get my bearings.

This version of heaven is messed up! This is not what they promised on the 777 Club.

An IV stood guard next to my head. Wires and tubes snaked from my hand to monitors and pumps. I blinked to clear my crusty eyes that were blurry and sleep-filled. Morning light filtered in through the window, and the antiseptic smell of the hospital singed my nostrils.

Seated on an uncomfortable, industrial love seat across the room was Cora. Her coat was balled up and being used to cushion the hard metal lines. Her mouth was wide open and she was snoring gently. My heart leapt as tears prickled at my eyes.

She shifted and her eyes fluttered open. Seeing mine on hers, she jolted upright. "You're awake," she murmured.

"Guess you better contact TMZ and tell them the rumors of my death were just clickbait." I forced a smile, but my face felt stiff. My mouth was dry and I could *taste* my breath—a filmy, metallic halitosis that made my nose wrinkle. I smacked my lips together, and Cora popped up.

"Thirsty?" she asked, looking for the pitcher. She put a straw in a cupful of water and held it to my lips, and I gulped it eagerly. Her face was so close, I focused on a freckle by her nose.

When the cup was empty, I laid back against the pillows and tried to pull more than two thoughts together to explain. The words I wanted floated above my head, just out of reach, and it was frustrating me. I sighed.

"Why?" she finally asked.

I burst into tears. "I'm so confused. I can't…"

"Shhh," she whispered. "It's okay." Her cool fingers felt like heaven on my forehead as they brushed across and down the stubble on my cheek.

I bit the side of my lip, weighing what I wanted to say, and finally settled on the truth. "It was getting so loud. I figured I'd just put everyone out of their misery."

Dr. McGivern strode in flanked by two nurses. Dark hair graying at the temples, his eyes framed by square rimmed glasses, he spent several silent minutes reading my chart. He offered me a perfunctory smile and then continued. "You're very lucky. If Ms. Butler had found you even five minutes later, you wouldn't be here."

Cora gulped and squeezed my hand.

"How long have you been off your meds?" he asked.

I sighed, knowing it was futile to lie at this point. "A while," I admitted. "I just wanted to feel things again. When I am on them, I feel dull and empty."

"We can try other options," he offered. "But you have to understand that without medication, you will continue to have cycles of mania and depression. Your brain chemistry is atypical, so without regulation, you'll continue to swing from extreme to extreme. The right medication can lessen the curve on both ends and give you some semblance of a normal life."

"I'm not exactly cut out for normal life, Doc. You know that."

He smiled and nodded. "You *are* one of a kind, Freddie. I have been following your Funologist high jinks on the internet. You've done a lot of good. Your mom must be so proud."

"Ma died," I admitted, looking away from his perceptive eyes.

"I see." He scrawled something on the chart. "My deepest condolences. That must have been very hard for you."

"It was."

"Major stressors like the death of a close relative can exacerbate the symptoms. It can trigger a mania response."

I tuned him out. My thoughts were heavy and thick, and stringing together sentences of more than two words was proving to be difficult. Raindrops gathered on the window next to my bed. Drops surged together to combine into one, then swollen with water, they slid down the glossy surface to gather at the sill. A raven sat outside the window, unflinchingly staring me down with its little birdie eyes. A staring contest ensued and there was no way I was going to lose.

"Freddie?" the doc said from the other side of the bed. The bird flew away, and I watched him retreat. Flying. Free. He transformed into a black dot on the horizon and then completely disappeared. I turned back to the doctor and sighed.

"What is your pain level?"

"One," I answered. "No pain, just confusion. Like I can't find the right word I want to use."

"That's normal and a typical reaction from the sedation you've been under. It will get better with time."

"Will it, Doc?" I asked, exasperated. "You've been selling me that load of bullshit for years now. And so far, you've been wrong. It never gets any better."

"Well, Freddie, I can't help you if you won't take your meds." He scolded and then continued, "Medicine is not a magic bullet, but it's a tool to help you that, combined with behavioral therapy, can transform your life."

"Magic bullet, huh?" I smiled. "I'd like to take one of those to the brain."

His eyes squinted as he studied me with a frown. "Careful, that could be considered a plan. Are you having suicidal thoughts?"

"Jesus," I huffed. "It's a joke. I'm a comedian, remember?"

"I remember, but we have to take statements like that very seriously. This isn't a joking matter." He flipped through the chart then shut the folder and looked at me. "I'm recommending a three-day hold. Let's get your meds stabilized and see what the next few days bring."

"Come on, Doc," I begged.

"It's for your own safety," he answered and strode out of the room, and then I realized Cora was still standing there.

"Sorry," I mumbled. "Seems like that is the only word I get to say to you anymore."

A chair screeched as she dragged it across the linoleum. "So," she said softly.

"So," I repeated for lack of anything more brilliant to say.

"I care about you, Freddie," she continued, and the first burble of hope welled up inside me. She tentatively reached out to stroke my hand, and the physical contact felt so sweet and tender, tears instantly welled up at the bottom of my eyelashes. "I have watched you deteriorate, and I think you need help. I think you need to check into a treatment program. I've done some research and think you need a center that works with dual diagnoses. All the self-medicating… it has to stop."

Initially, I tensed at her words. The idea of checking into a treatment facility for any length of time sucked all the air out of the room, and I felt the walls closing in on me. "I don't know."

"If you don't decide to go to treatment, I will cut you out of my life. You need help, Freddie."

"Well, there it is, the boundaries and the tough love," I said sarcastically. "Looks like someone's done her research." I sighed again, considering her request, and after a long pause continued. "But what if I return and I'm not the charismatic ball of fun that you believe me to be? What then?"

"Then I get to know the new you," she said. "The *sober* Freddie Angel."

"I don't even know who that useless fuck is," I responded self-depreciatingly with a crooked smile. Relieved, she rolled her eyes and shook her head.

"Then we'll get to know him together." She offered a small smile, and a smattering of hope shone in her eyes. "So, you'll go?'

"I don't really have another choice. The only person in the entire world who can still stand me is threatening to leave."

"It's not a threat, Freddie. It's self-preservation. I can't bear to sit in the audience of another showing of *The Freddie Angel Titanic* and watch it go down again." She wiped away a tear. "I can't. I won't."

"Okay, okay," I answered. "Fine, I'll go."

She leaned in and kissed my cheek, and I felt Cora's sun warm me again from within.

THIRTY-SEVEN

Three Months Later

Sitting on the perfectly made twin bed, I closed my eyes and slowed my breath, trying to find calm. It was a healthy coping mechanism for my anxiety that I had been taught at the center. Unable to stop myself, I glanced at my watch over and over, anxious for her to arrive. My stomach knit into knots, my meager belongings neatly stuffed into a garbage bag and stacked in a plastic tote sitting on the floor.

At last, Cora rushed in and took my breath away. "Hey." She smiled, gazing deeply into my eyes, and for the first time, I didn't break away. The panic didn't set in, the voices that screamed about my unworthiness didn't start performance art in my head. It was quiet, blessedly peaceful.

"Hey." I stood and pulled her into my arms for a hug. My chin rested on her hair, and I closed my eyes and inhaled the peach-scented conditioner she favored. This was the moment I had been longing for during the course of my ninety-day stay. When you are inside and working on yourself, you fixate on certain things. Foods you craved as a child, a hug from someone you love. You appreciate the idea of them more. Once someone I had taken for granted, Cora was now standing here in front of me and had proven her loyalty more than anyone else left in my life.

Ninety days is a lot of time for a serious amount of soul searching. I was court-ordered to complete treatment and put on probation for my Banksy-inspired vandalism spree. At the time, I didn't consider the pervasion of video cameras in modern society. A grainy video of me surfaced buying the supplies, and another one recorded from a street cam captured the full manic throes of my artistic masterpiece. Luckily, I got a judge who understood the growing mental health crisis in our country and was lenient. I was going to have to pay a pretty hefty fine and continue aftercare, but at least he didn't lock me up.

I had an endless amount of time and guidance in therapy to figure out my why. I discovered that I thrived on the adoration of others and used money to buy their approval. I became a bottomless pit of need, and no amount of love from strangers was ever going to fill it. I thought the world adored me, and maybe for a minute it did. But their infatuation is fickle and fleeting, pouring over you infinitely one moment and rushing to the next shiny thing a moment later, leaving you more depleted and emptier than you were before. I thought money and success would make Cora love me. Turns out, she loved me anyway.

Tommy was a fabrication of my sick mind that used its endless creative resources to cook up a villain. It wasn't enough that I loathed myself; I had to concoct a vile foe that my mind could wage a war against. Tommy was just another version of me, hating who I was and shining a light on my deep sense of unworthiness. When Ma told me I didn't have a brother, it rocked me to my core. I vividly remember the ground rushing up to swallow me whole, leaving me reeling and feeling like I was in freefall without a parachute. It was an epiphany of a deeper mental health issue I was too afraid to face. I will never forget the sensation of spiraling out of control, and I never want to feel that again.

Dying seemed like a good enough solution at the time. I was tired of the conflict and the white-knuckling. When I chose the easy way out, it felt like there was no other choice. It seemed like the only logical way to make everything stop, like being forced to ride a dizzying merry-go-round faster and faster that started out fun but ends with you puking in the bushes. You beg to get off, but the mean kids laugh at you and it just keeps spinning. I was tired of being a problem. I was tired of being a burden to everyone, and I just wanted it all to stop. I wanted to just float away.

I now know, the pills I hated so much are crucial to my well-being. Without them, I can be forced back on the merry-go-round for another terrifying ride. They are a necessary evil, one that I will have to count and swallow for the rest of my life if I want to have a chance at a normal life. And now, when I hold this woman in my arms, I think I do. I *know* I do.

Cora pulled back. "Are you ready?"

"I've been waiting for this day for months." I grabbed my bag and she picked up the tote, and we walked out into the warm spring sun. I tipped my head up and closed my eyes as the warmth radiated from my forehead to my cheeks. The tiniest bits of everyday joy were ones that I focused on now. I collected them like little boys collect fistfuls of dandelions for their mothers in April. I had enough therapy to know I had the choice to pick up the bits of joy scattered around my life, and when I did, it allowed more to pop up around me.

She opened the trunk of the Camaro, the only remnant of my time as the Funologist that remained. I shoved the bags in and settled into the passenger seat, and she turned the key in the ignition and pulled onto the highway.

"I brought your mail. It's in the backseat."

I wriggled in the seat behind me and tossed EOBs from the insurance company off to the side, mixed in with bills for the house, and discovered a thick creamy envelope in the middle. I thrust my index finger in the corner and ripped it open, finding very official-looking documents from the legal firm of Sanderson, Willich, and Black.

"What is that?" Cora said, turning to me as I got lost in the documents. A letter fluttered out of the stack in Ma's perfect penmanship, and it gutted me. My vision blurred as tears filled my eyes. I blinked and tried to clear them out.

Beautiful Boy,

If you are reading this, I have gone on to the next place and I know you are scared. Heck, I'm scared just thinking about how you will take care of yourself. Your life hasn't been easy, I know that, but even a life filled with adversity can offer you a few gifts.

You are smart. Too smart for your own good. Bordering on genius, and I told you that all the time, but you never believed me. You are strong and have all the tools you need to live the life you want to live.

I stunted your growth, and for that I am sorry. I should have helped you navigate your independence sooner. But selfishly having you around all the time was the only way I could be certain that you were okay, and I needed you to be okay.

The older you get, the wiser you get, not by accident, but by living through lessons that force you to open your mind to receive them. They can take you to the brink of insanity before giving you a chance to pull back to a healthy place. There is nothing wrong with living a simple life. I know you've yearned for the spotlight since your dad died. I know that he buried a need in you so deep that only the love and adoration of strangers could fill it. I know you chased that high, looking for your self-worth in the hands that clapped for you when your set was on fire. The same hands that clapped until they were chapped and red can also push you off the cliff. That's the danger of giving other people that power. The only real way to be happy is to learn to applaud for yourself. To turn that approval inward and to see the things you have overcome. To stack up your own successes one by one and celebrate them.

The only real thing I can tell you is that love is all there is. If you are lucky enough to find love in this life, hold on. Hold on with both hands and never take it for granted. Sometimes we get it wrong, sometimes we love the wrong way. But if love is the cornerstone of all the decisions you make and all the plans you carry out in this life, then you will be successful. Define your own success, Freddie. Don't put that in the hands of others.

I have loved you since the second I knew you were coming. You have the purest heart, always wanting to help other people. Always looking to make someone laugh and brighten up their day. Never lose that, just remember to turn some of that love and laughter back toward yourself.

I'll be waiting for you in the next place. Don't you dare rush to meet me here! Take your time. Savor your life, laugh until your stomach aches and tears are streaming down your face.

You always said no one loves you like I do, but I hope you're wrong.

You are the best thing that has ever happened to me.

Mom

I swiped at the warm tears that tumbled down my rough cheeks and sniffled sharply. Cora turned quickly to assess me. She reached out a hand and placed it on my thigh and squeezed it.

"Are you okay?"

I nodded as I continued to page through the rest of the papers.

"What is all that?"

"It's about Ma's estate." I scanned the documents more deeply. "What the…?"

Panicked, Cora turned to me. "What?" she asked as the first beads of worry popped her eyes wide open. Her head darted back and forth from the road to my face, trying to navigate both.

"She managed to scrimp and save over a million dollars." I was dumbfounded. This was the woman who only shopped on double coupon day and wore clothing with holes in it. Grateful my sunglasses were covering my eyes, I looked up into the clouds, certain Ma was sitting on one and watching over me like she always did. "She donated some to the *777 Club*, but the bulk of her estate will transfer to me."

Cora's eyes were huge, and I could see the gears turning in her head. "I'm scared, Freddie. You can't go back… You won't go back, right?" She was verbalizing her fears in the new spirit of total honesty we vowed to each other during my treatment and release. Her fingers tapped anxiously on the steering wheel as she darted her eyes from me to the road, looking for confirmation.

"Just a minute, sweetheart," I mumbled, sharing her fears as I continued to read through the thick stack of papers. The first bursts of anxiety cued up in my belly seeing the final sum of one-point-two million dollars.

"She set up a trust in my name, and I'm not allowed to touch the principal until I'm retired." I exhaled as relief washed over me. She knew I couldn't handle another huge payday. History would have likely repeated itself, and I would have found myself slipping into old patterns.

Good job, Ma.

I reached forward and squeezed Cora's hand. "Looks like we have options. She set up a monthly draw for me on the interest. We won't be living large, but we can start over just about anywhere we want as soon as probation is over."

"Really?" she shrieked. "Can it be somewhere warm this time? You know, Alvin is a *tropical* bird. I can't wait for you to hear the new words I've taught him." Cora babbled on about the dry air of Arizona versus the white sugary sand beaches of Florida, getting more and more animated and excited as each mile spooled out behind us. I didn't even hear a word she said. All I could see was the beautiful woman sitting next to me with the most enormous smile on her face, and I was the one that put it there.

I settled back into the leather seat and pulled her hand up to my mouth, kissing the back of it. Finally, this life was going to be one that I could be proud of. Finally, I could learn to love life again. All of it.

Thank you, Ma.

AUTHOR NOTES AND ACKNOWLEDGEMENTS

Freddie is a fictional character, but I would love nothing more than for *The Funologist* to turn into a real tangible movement that helps the unseen people in society like Freddie aspired to do.

I've set up a Venmo account, and whatever money is donated by readers will be distributed to small charities and underdogs fighting through life's struggles in the spirit of the book.

To donate via Venmo @thefunologist
To find out where we're helping,
visit https://blairbryan.com/

It would be a miracle to be able to bless people in real life. To see this book cross from the fictional world into the real one would be magic, and couldn't we all use a little more magic? I know I could.

Will it happen? Who knows? But if donations come in, I promise I will be out there creating outrageous acts of kindness that would make Freddie proud. Stay tuned.

Special thanks to my two trusted early readers, Kristi and Brooke. You both provide such valuable insight when reading the roughest of drafts. Slugging through the ramblings of a wannabe novelist and discovering plot holes with horrific grammar, you are the real MVPs! I trust you to call me out when I misstep and know without a doubt my books are better because of your thoughtful reflections. A million thank yous and it wouldn't be enough.

To my editor, Kendra, when we met a couple of years ago, I never knew what a gem I had found. I do now. You make every word I write better and I couldn't do this without you.

I write under two pen names, Ninya for Non-Fiction and Blair Bryan for Contemporary Fiction.

By Blair Bryan

Back to Before

Better Than Before

The Sweetest Day

The Funologist

Better Than Before

Non-Fiction

Scotland with a Stranger: A Memoir

First You Then Him: A Former Trainwreck's Guide to Becoming and then Finding a Healthy Partner

ABOUT THE AUTHOR

Blair Bryan's character driven novels are spun from rich memories of growing up in the Midwest.

Her books feature average people facing extraordinary circumstances.

Website: https://blairbryan.com/

www.ingramcontent.com/pod-product-compliance
Lightning Source LLC
Chambersburg PA
CBHW061612190726

48288CB00007B/2280